# BEFORE YOU SAY I DO

by Clare Lydon

custard
books

**First Edition March 2020**
**Published by Custard Books**
**Copyright © 2020 Clare Lydon**
**ISBN: 978-1-912019-83-0**

Cover Design: Rachel Lawston
Editor: Cheyenne Blue
Typesetting: Adrian McLaughlin

Find out more at: www.clarelydon.co.uk
Follow me on Twitter: @clarelydon
Follow me on Instagram: @clarefic

# Also by Clare Lydon

## Other Novels
The Long Weekend
Nothing To Lose: A Lesbian Romance
Twice In A Lifetime
Once Upon A Princess
You're My Kind
A Taste Of Love

## London Romance Series
London Calling (Book One)
This London Love (Book Two)
A Girl Called London (Book Three)
The London Of Us (Book Four)
London, Actually (Book Five)
Made In London (Book Six)

## All I Want Series
All I Want For Christmas (Book One)
All I Want For Valentine's (Book Two)
All I Want For Spring (Book Three)
All I Want For Summer (Book Four)
All I Want For Autumn (Book Five)
All I Want Forever (Book Six)

## Boxsets
All I Want Series Boxset, Books 1-3
All I Want Series Boxset, Books 4-6
All I Want Series Boxset, Books 1-6
London Romance Series Boxset, Books 1-3

# Acknowledgements

I first came across the idea of a professional bridesmaid when I heard one interviewed on Radio Five Live. I was fascinated from the outset, and knew it would make a great premise for a lesbian romance. I hope I was right and did the story justice.

Getting a book over the finish line always involves a host of people in my corner. I'm lucky enough to have a fair few. Huge thanks to my trusted first readers, Angela, Sophie, Iris, Hilary and Tammara for your initial feedback that helped make this book the best it could be. Thanks also to the advanced reader team who were brilliant in their cheerleading, but also in catching those last-minute errors. Particular thanks to JP, who points out all the ways I murder the French language. Pardon, et merci!

Oodles of thanks to Rachel Lawson for the ace cover. Don't you just love the colour? I do. Applause galore to Cheyenne Blue for the skilled way she tells me the book's great, but also that I have a lot of work to do. You make my books better, so thanks. A tip of the nib to Adrian McLaughlin for his typesetting prowess and excellent beard. Both shine in all weathers.

To Yvonne, for going through this even though she was

tight for time. You're the best wife, darling. Thanks for always supporting me.

Last but definitely not least, thanks to you for buying this book and supporting this independent author. I write because I love it. If I've entertained you or made you think, then my work here is done.

If you fancy getting in touch, you can do so using one of the methods below. I'm most active on Instagram.

Twitter: @ClareLydon
Facebook: www.facebook.com/clare.lydon
Instagram: @clarefic
Find out more at: www.clarelydon.co.uk
Contact: mail@clarelydon.co.uk

**Thank you so much for reading!**

*For Mum.*
*Who won't remember this is for her.*
*But it is.*

# Chapter One

Jordan Cohen shifted her left shoulder a fraction of an inch. Then another. She couldn't risk moving any more. Dammit, this was *such* an inopportune moment to have an itch between her shoulder blades. Standing at an altar in front of 120 guests, as the professional bridesmaid to her latest client, Emily.

"Do you take Max to be your legally wedded husband?" The vicar ran through his spiel.

Jordan clutched her maid-of-honour flowers that little bit tighter as she waited for the words to fall from Emily's mouth. The itch suddenly left her mind. This was more important. She gazed at the side of Emily's perfectly styled hair, the bride's round diamond earrings glinting in the church's mottled sunlight. Even Emily couldn't fuck this bit up, could she?

A few seconds ticked by.

Then a few more.

Someone in the church let out an ill-timed cough.

*Please, Emily.*

Jordan switched her gaze to Max, the groom. She knew he was thinking exactly the same.

Heat crept up Jordan's back, then her neck. She stroked the back of Emily's arm lightly with her fingertips.

"I do," Jordan muttered, just loud enough for Emily to hear, but quiet enough that Max wouldn't think Jordan wanted to marry him. That couldn't be further from the truth. Emily and Max were perfect for each other. Not so much a love match, more a biological clock match.

Emily flinched, turning her head.

Jordan scrunched her forehead and nodded towards Max, hoping this conveyed to Emily how much she *really* needed to answer this question. It was all part of the getting-married deal. Jordan had presumed Emily understood that. They'd practised walking, smiling, posing, and even breathing, but they'd glossed over the bit where Emily had to say "I do." Now, Jordan could see that might have been an oversight.

Emily held her gaze, before turning back to Max and the vicar.

The vicar gave Emily an unsure smile, tilting his head to offer reassurance.

Jordan gritted her teeth.

Opposite Emily, Max mouthed the words at her.

Finally, after a few more agonising seconds, Emily took a deep breath and opened her shiny pink lips. "I do," she said, her voice ringing out loud and true. Almost like she meant it.

Relief flooded Max's face.

A collective exhalation of breath sounded from the wedding guests.

Jordan's shoulders unclenched.

She'd done it. Got Emily to the altar, allayed her marriage fears, and kept her from drinking too much champagne while she had her make-up done. Emily had committed to Max. Which is what Emily's family had tasked Jordan with doing four weeks earlier. Her fee for being Emily's fake bridesmaid wasn't reliant on getting her to the altar, but it certainly made the final invoice a hell of a lot easier to send.

"I now pronounce you husband and wife. You may kiss your bride!" the vicar said.

Jordan snapped back into the present. She slapped on a radiant smile for the camera, one that told the world this wedding had been a cinch. Then she swished her shoulder-length blond hair, stood up straight, and smoothed down her light-green bridesmaid dress like it was the best thing she'd ever worn.

It wasn't. It was shapeless and made her look like a stick of celery.

Jordan couldn't wait to get it off, change into her jeans and head down to her local for a glass of sauvignon blanc with friends.

However, that was still in the future. At least eight hours away. First, she had to get through the wedding dinner, the speeches, and the dancing. But at least the end was in sight.

As Max leaned forward and took Emily's face in his hands, Jordan allowed herself a proper smile. Sure, she might be cynical when it came to love, but this part always filled her with hope. Marriage was the start of something, a blank page in a relationship. Even for Emily and Max.

The happy couple kissed, and the wedding guests clapped their approval. Jordan glanced across at the best man, Rob, who gave her a dazzling smile. She hadn't met Rob before, which was unusual. Perhaps he was a professional best man, too. Max had told her that Rob was looking forward to escorting her down the aisle and accompanying her on the dance floor later, as was tradition. As Rob's beam turned into a suggestive wink, Jordan kept her smile fixed in place. Inside, her heart rolled its eyes.

Now she had another thing to add to her to-do list.

First, make sure Emily didn't get so drunk she fell on her face.

Second, charm the pants off the bride's dad, who was paying her bill. He might even give her a tip if she played her cards right.

Third, tell the best man he was very much barking up the wrong tree.

\* \* \*

Jordan swung her beat-up Ford Capri into the space in front of her Brighton flat and shut off the engine. She sat for a few long moments, the only sound the roar of a passing quartet of pub-goers, who'd just left The Rusty Bucket, her local. She opened her handbag and fingered the crisp notes the bride's father had pressed into her hand when she'd left. A thousand-pound tip from him. A snotty, drunk hug from the bride that had left a stain on her dress; and a sigh of resignation from the best man as he realised his normally winning smile wasn't going to cash in this time.

A bang on her car roof made Jordan jump. She turned so fast, her neck did that popping thing at the base. An arrow of pain surged to her brain. She winced as her best friend and flatmate Karen grinned at her through the passenger-side window. She was making a winding motion with her hand, almost as if Jordan's car didn't have electric windows. Which it didn't.

Jordan leaned over, her face still furrowed after her neck spasm. She grasped the window winder and gave it a few turns. The sound it made could never be described as healthy.

Karen's mouth turned up at the sides before she spoke. "Hello, flatmate who I haven't seen all week. Question: why are you sitting in your car like a weirdo?"

"Because I am a weirdo?"

"That's a given." Her friend leaned in further, both hands resting on the Capri's half-down window.

Jordan eyed it, hoping she didn't lean too hard. Her car was a piece of living history, and as such, needed handling with care.

"Why are you clutching your neck like that?"

"Because it just did that weird popping thing."

Karen tilted her head. "It's because you work too hard and therefore your body is too tense. You need to relaaaaaaaaax." As she said the last word, Karen moved her head dreamily, as if she'd never had a neck spasm in her life. "So did you marry off another rich schmuck today?"

"My mission was completed without a hiccup." Jordan rolled her neck tentatively. No pain. She thought back to Emily's meltdown just before the service. How she'd mopped it up, and then reassured Emily her marriage would survive.

Jordan had been in the job too long.

Platitudes and lies fell from her lips like confetti.

"If it helps any, you look gorgeous in your dress." Karen's gaze rolled down Jordan's body. "When I say gorgeous, I mean like a weird green streak. What even is that colour? Celery chic? I particularly love the flower in your hair."

Jordan ripped the flower from her head. She'd been in such a hurry to get home, she'd forgotten to take it out.

Karen gave her a cocky grin. "Get changed, and come down the Bucket. I'll buy you a drink. And you never know, the woman of your dreams might be waiting tonight."

That made Jordan smile. "Because there's always such a glut of good-looking lesbians in the Bucket." She checked her watch. 9pm. She'd been working since 7am. No wonder she was tired.

"No looking at your watch and coming up with excuses. I haven't seen you in the past month because you've been getting Emily and Max married. Now it's done, it's time to relax." Karen straightened up, then gave the roof two quick slaps.

"Hey!" Jordan shouted. How many times had she told Karen not to do that?

Karen's face came back into view, her hands resting on the window again.

Jordan leaned over. "Show Carrie the Capri a little more respect, please." She smacked Karen's hands.

Karen stepped back, holding Jordan's gaze. "If only you loved me as much as you love this car." She cocked her head. "Do me a favour and do as you're told. Come and have a drink with me. You need to be reminded of real life and your real friends. Not the weird make-believe world you inhabit when you're hired as a rich person's bridesmaid."

Jordan took a deep breath, then gave her a nod. "Okay. Give me 15 minutes and I'll see you in the bar. Get me a wine. The largest one they sell."

Karen grinned. "That's my girl." She banged the roof again

before she walked off down the road towards the pub, and turned to give Jordan a wave.

Jordan grabbed her phone from her bag on the passenger seat, then pressed the side button. It lit up. She had a new email. She should leave it until tomorrow, go home, then get down the pub. But she never did. Being your own boss meant you were always on. She opened the email.

Jordan stared at the photo pasted into the top of the email. Whoever this was, she was the definition of a beautiful woman.

Jordan's eyes scanned down the email for a name to match to the face. Abby Porter. 36 years old. Engaged to Marcus Montgomery. Jordan tried to sit up straighter, but her bridesmaid dress had too much material and it caught around the seat belt. Stupid bloody dress. The sooner she got out of it, the better.

Jordan clicked on the light above the dashboard and stared at the email again.

Abby Porter had long, lustrous dark hair, and a rich, hazelnut stare. Her cheekbones were striking, as was the way she angled her head. As if to say 'fuck you' to the world. She didn't look like she wanted to sing and dance about getting married to Marcus. But then, this looked like a professional shot, probably done before Marcus proposed. A work shot, perhaps. If Jordan had to guess, she'd say Abby was something in marketing. Probably a brand manager, or department head. Abby Porter looked like she knew what she wanted, and she normally got it.

Did Abby want to marry Marcus? Jordan didn't know, and it wasn't her job to know.

Her job was to make the experience of getting married as smooth as possible for the bride. This email stated that Abby would like her help, and wanted to meet to talk more. Could Jordan give her a call at her convenience?

Jordan took one more look into Abby's cool, alluring stare, before throwing her phone in her bag. Sure, she could do that. But not tonight.

Tonight, she had some soothing adult grape juice to drink, and a best friend to appease.

Tomorrow morning, she'd see what Abby Porter's story was. For now, Abby could wait.

# Chapter Two

Abby Porter gripped her five-iron and looked out over the green of the driving range. The monitor said her last strike had gone further than she'd ever hit it before. She wasn't surprised. Today, Abby had a lot of frustration to whack out of her system. Was that the technical term? It was now.

She steadied her five-foot-eight frame, raised the club behind her, then brought it down, rotating her body as she smashed the ball into the air and down the range. She wouldn't be surprised if that one went even further. She was in that sort of mood tonight after dinner with Marcus's parents. She knew he was watching, assessing her from the small black couch at the back of their driving bay. Sure enough, when she turned, her fiancé was sitting, one foot balanced on top of his opposite knee, a knowing smile on his handsome face.

She'd chosen well, she knew that. Marcus was tall, dark, and handsome. Their children would be gorgeous.

"Something you want to talk about, Abs?"

"Nope." She balanced the club against the side of their driving range bay, then flopped down beside him. Her body edged into Marcus.

He extended an arm and pulled her close to kiss her temple. "Good. I'd hate to be that golf ball. You left it in no doubt who's the boss in your relationship."

She turned, raising a single eyebrow. "Who's the boss in our relationship?"

He grinned. "You are, of course." He pecked her on the lips, before getting up to take a few shots himself. His long legs were encased in his black work trousers, his baby blue shirt still tucked in. She imagined he'd probably been like that at school, too. Neat, precise. It was what she expected when they moved in after they got married. But she had all that to come. She hoped she could cope. She wasn't all that tidy herself, so perhaps the question should be, would Marcus be able to cope with her? They were getting married in a handful of weeks, moving in together right after that. She guessed she was about to find out.

Marcus turned to her, leaning on his club. "So, was the golf ball my mother?" He didn't wait for an answer, just swung, and missed. He connected the second time, hitting the ball into the air. When he turned back, he was still waiting for her answer.

She shook her head. It hadn't been. She would never take a golf club to his mother. "It's just an outlet. Aren't I allowed one?"

"Of course." He grabbed a ball from the box to his right, bending to steady it on the scuffed white tee, before looking back. "But I also know she was a bit much earlier. A little… intense. We can totally do it your way. *Our way*. We don't have to have all those speeches, all that stuff."

Abby splayed her hands, trying to stop her anger bubbling

up. It wasn't Marcus's fault. He was the opposite of his mother. How that wound-up, sanctimonious woman had given birth to such a calm, measured man was a mystery to her. It wasn't even like his father was the role model either. At last count, Gordon had about three separate mistresses.

No, Marcus had turned out the way he had despite his upbringing. Which was why their wedding having to involve his family so much was more than just a rub.

"It's not so simple, is it? According to your mother, there are a lot of family traditions we have to uphold. *Ways of doing things* was the phrase she kept emphasising, I believe?" By the fifth time she'd said it, Abby had wanted to scream that she got it, but that wasn't appropriate behaviour towards her future mother-in-law. Not when this was only the fourth time they'd met. Did Marjorie approve of Abby? Probably not.

Abby was pretty sure most mothers thought the woman their son was about to marry wasn't worthy of them, but Marjorie appeared to take it to a whole new level today. The next few weeks were going to be trying. Especially with all the extra bridal things Abby was expected to do now she was becoming a Montgomery.

She hadn't even decided whether she was going to give up her surname when she got married. It went against every feminist bone in her body. However, bringing that up today might have tipped Marjorie over the edge, so she'd kept quiet. That battle could wait for another day. Marjorie had enough trouble understanding Abby's Scottish accent.

Marcus strolled over to her, leaving his club by the driving mat. When he sat, he took her hand in his.

Abby closed her eyes. She always felt safe with Marcus. It was one of the reasons she'd agreed to marry him. That, and the fact she'd turned 36 four weeks ago, and time was ticking if she wanted a family. Which everyone kept telling her she did. Marcus was so far ahead of any man she'd ever dated, that when he'd proposed, she felt like she'd won the jackpot.

*This* was her life now. Driving golf balls with her future husband. Marcus Montgomery. She'd landed on her feet. Her life from now on was going to be happy.

Neat and precise.

But happy.

When she opened her eyes, Marcus's gaze was focused on her. He squeezed her hand and sighed.

"You see, this is what I don't want. This is the countdown to our wedding, and you're the most important person on that day." He stabbed his chest with his index finger. "Not me. I'm the luckiest person because I'm marrying you." He leaned forward to emphasise his point.

"And yes, I know Mother got a bit carried away, but she was right on one thing. You need an assistant for the run-up to the wedding. Someone who's just focused on you." He paused. "I thought this after the last time you met her, and today only solidified it. Look at you, you're all flushed and stressed." He sat up straight, before fixing her with his I-mean-business stare. "I've been doing a little research, and I have a solution. It might sound a little unorthodox at first, but it could be the answer to our prayers."

Abby could see his mouth moving and words coming out, but she was struggling to make sense of them. "What do you mean by unorthodox?"

"I've found a woman who runs a service called Professional Bridesmaid. She's kind of a bridal PA, exactly what we're after. So I took the liberty of contacting her."

"You did what?" They weren't even married yet and Marcus was already doing things on her behalf? An alarm sounded throughout her body. This was not okay.

"If you're worried about money, don't be. It's my treat."

"It's more the Montgomery takeover I'm worried about." Abby bristled. "You can't just keep doing things behind my back. It keeps happening with this wedding. Sometimes I feel like a bystander."

But Marcus shook his head, putting a hand on her leg. "It's all been done to make things easier for you. I know you're short on time. You're working towards a promotion at work. You're busy. This woman seems very capable. She can even step in to be your bridesmaid if you want her to, which might not be a bad shout seeing as Delta has fallen to pieces since Nora broke up with her." Marcus wasn't finished. "But mainly, her role is to be there for you, right up until the end of the wedding day."

Abby frowned. She still couldn't believe what she was hearing. "My bridesmaid? Are you mad?"

Marcus gave her a tepid smile. "She's your personal assistant/bridesmaid. There just for you. Someone on call 24/7."

Abby was still shaking her head. "I have bridesmaids, Marcus. I don't need a fake one. Delta is my maid of honour, you know that. And it's precisely because she's just been dumped by her useless girlfriend that she needs something to focus on. Being my maid of honour is it. I can't take that off her. She'd crumble completely."

Now it was Marcus's turn to frown. "I'm not saying take the title from Delta. Just the responsibility. You have to admit, she's already causing you stress, asking you loads of questions about the hen weekend which she should have already sorted. Between Delta and my mother, I'd say this woman could be just what you need."

He had a point. Abby had tasked Delta with organising the hen weekend trip, but had ended up doing most of it herself. Delta had promised to take on the details, but then her split had happened. Since then, she'd holed herself up like it was the end of the world, forgetting her best friend was getting married in a few weeks, and her hen weekend was fast approaching.

"I don't know." But Abby's brain was already processing.

"I think you do. Is Delta going to be there for you? Or your cousin Taran? Think about it. Someone to confide in, someone to do whatever you need. You only get one go at this, Abs. I want you to arrive at our wedding stress-free. If that means paying for someone to hold your hand for the next few weeks, so be it."

"I'm a grown-ass woman, Marcus. I can handle this myself." She could just imagine what her Glaswegian mother would say about a professional bridesmaid stepping in.

He gave her a look. "This woman can deal with my mother for the next few weeks. She can take all the flack."

Abby stilled. "Can she deal with her totally? And take over the hen do?"

Marcus nodded. "All that and more." He pulled back, wincing before he continued. "Like I said, I already emailed her, just to see if she was available. And she is." He held up his hands like Abby was about to shoot him. "Just think about it, okay? For me? At least, have a meeting with her, see what she has to say. Her recommendations are off the chart. If you don't get on, no problem. We'll can the idea. But if she can make your life easier, then why not?"

Her insides were still boiling. How dare he do this? But this was Marcus. It came from a place of love, not control. Unlike his mother.

Plus, if this woman could deal with Marjorie, maybe it wasn't such a crazy idea.

"I'm still mad at you for doing this behind my back."

"You'd never have agreed otherwise." He gave her his special smile, the one he reserved for her.

She gave him a long sigh. "You've already contacted her?"

He nodded. "I sent the email yesterday, so she's going to give you a call. Her name is Jordan."

"Jordan." What kind of a name was that?

# Chapter Three

"Why are we doing this again?" Jordan could barely speak she was so out of breath, but she kept her feet moving. She knew from grim experience that if she stopped, it was doubly hard to get moving again. Beside her, Karen was gliding like she was on roller skates. There was clearly something to be said for regular training, as opposed to doing your first run in at least a month.

"Because you've got yet another rich bitch wanting you to pretend to be her long-lost bestie bridesmaid. To fulfil your clients' wish list, you have to be slim. And hot. Nobody wants a fat bridesmaid, do they?"

How could Karen just chat, like they hadn't been running non-stop for the past 20 minutes? "You're being a bit fattist," Jordan gasped. To her left, the sea bobbed and weaved like the largest waterbed on record. Up above, the sky was grey with white clouds streaked across it. It looked like the grey sweatshirt she'd accidentally sprayed bleach on as opposed to stain remover, and now only wore for home decorating. Which basically meant never.

"I'm being a realist. Although, you don't want to get too slim and hot, because no bride wants to be outshone on her wedding day. It's a tricky balance to hit, isn't it?"

Jordan said nothing in reply. Mainly because she didn't have the breath.

Karen glanced at her. "Although you're not looking so hot right now, with your tongue hanging out like a dog. But you generally do." She grinned. "You can be an inspiration to brides everywhere. Remember Kate Moss's words: nothing tastes as good as skinny."

"Maybe I should get a nasty cocaine habit to aid my quest."

"All your clients probably have one."

A sharp blast of wind blew through, almost taking Jordan's breath away. It might be May, but seasons didn't matter on the south coast. On the seafront, every day was gusty. Up ahead, she saw Walton's, the café that always signalled the halfway mark of their run, where they turned and ran home. But today, with the sun battling to come out overhead and the clouds looking ominous, Jordan needed a break. As they drew up alongside the battered, white wooden café, she fluttered her eyes at Karen.

"Can we stop for a coffee?" Jordan clutched her side. "I've got a stitch and I really didn't get all that much sleep last night. Adrenaline from the past month. What do you say? Can I ease back in slowly?"

Karen gave her a look, before nodding. "So long as we run back."

"I swear on my life." She had her fingers crossed, though.

Inside the café, Karen nipped to the loo. Jordan got them both a flat white, then took a seat by the window overlooking the sea. The air was coated with the scent of fried bacon and sausages, making her stomach rumble. But she couldn't give in to her cravings. What Karen had said was true. She had an image to keep up, a story to portray. Being a professional bridesmaid was akin to being an actress who has to be on stage and in the spotlight for weeks at a time. What Jordan didn't know about being a bridesmaid wasn't worth knowing.

Karen slipped back into the seat opposite, her short, dark hair and piercing blue eyes sparkling as always. Karen was one of life's happy people. She sipped her coffee before she spoke. "How was the grand finale of this job, anyway? We didn't really get a chance to talk about the details last night. Any interesting tales to tell while I was making sure the country still had enough knickers to go around?" Karen was a lingerie buyer for Marks & Spencer, a job that always grabbed the attention of anyone who heard it.

Jordan ran through the past week in her head, playing it out like a movie. All things considered, it had gone fairly smoothly. She'd dealt with far worse than Emily.

"It went fine."

"Nobody rumbled you?"

Jordan shook her head. She was still surprised that hadn't happened yet. After all, the people who could afford her services had money, and those people tended to stick together. She was sure she'd seen a few of the same faces around, but Jordan had perfected the art of blending in very well. Plus, nobody was really looking out for a serial bridesmaid, were they?

"On the contrary. I've been invited to two other weddings." She shrugged. "The bride had a wobble when she was getting her make-up done, but I got her to the altar. A minor miracle in itself."

"And they say romance is dead."

Jordan laughed. "Weddings are rarely about romance."

Karen sat back, glancing at the sea through the window. "But you've got a bit of time off now, haven't you?" She turned back to Jordan. "After your cancellation?"

Jordan shook her head, then sipped her coffee. "Not sure. I've already got another lead to call back, so my rest might be put on hold. This is wedding season. From now until September at least, I should be working flat-out."

Karen pouted. "Do I have to start booking in dates to see you? I miss you."

"You know the drill. Plus, you've got Dave."

"Dave? He's just my boyfriend. You're my best friend."

Jordan gave her a grin. "And I'll still be your best friend when September comes. Your slimmer, hotter, richer best friend, with any luck. I intend to make the most of this season, because I only have a few more left now I'm 35. As well as people not wanting a fat bridesmaid, they also don't want an old one."

"The world is a depressing place."

Jordan grinned. "Not while I'm still young and pretty enough it's not. Emily might have been a pain, but she was a lucrative pain. Here's hoping I get a few more of those this summer."

"People with more money than sense?"

"It's a wedding. People are happy to throw money at problems to make them go away. I'm a professional problem solver. Whoever would have thought that when we were at university?"

Karen grinned. "Not me." She leaned forward. "How much did you get paid for this last one, then?"

"Enough to buy you dinner later."

"Excellent."

"And how is the world of lingerie? Any great strides forward in the past week? Have you managed to get the whole of the UK wearing electric blue bras and matching bottoms yet?"

"Not yet, but it's all part of my master plan. They will succumb, it's just a matter of time."

# Chapter Four

Abby's arms ached after the hard gym session earlier. However, it was a good ache. The sort of muscle fatigue that would morph into strength, and leave her feeling confident when she walked down the aisle, as well as on her honeymoon to the Maldives. Marcus had booked that. Without consulting her.

He'd said it was a surprise, but she'd wheedled it out of him. While most brides would be thrilled about sandy beaches, secluded coves, and five-star luxury, Abby just saw the long flight.

She didn't like flying.

Scratch that, she *hated* flying, especially long haul. Plus, she couldn't focus on the honeymoon yet. The wedding was looming too large.

It was another reason she'd gone to the gym this morning, to work out some of her tension. It wasn't her usual haunt, but she'd bought a month's pass to prepare for getting married.

Should she be more excited about two weeks in paradise? Long, lazy mornings in bed, brunch on the deck, afternoons spent languishing in sunshine? Probably.

She focused on the image in her head, concentrating hard as she walked down her street.

Still nothing.

Her phone vibrated in her jacket pocket. She shook her head, fished it out and glanced at the screen. She didn't recognise the number. Was she about to get an idiot on the phone? She'd had loads of those companies trying to see if she'd had an accident at work recently. She clicked the green button, and lifted her head to the sun trying to peak through the clouds above.

"Hello? Is that Abby?" The voice was strong and sure.

"It is. If you're trying to sell me insurance or get me to sign up to anything, I'm not interested."

"I wasn't going to. My name's Jordan. Marcus contacted me about helping you out. I run a service called Professional Bridesmaid."

Abby stopped walking and blinked. Up ahead, a window cleaner was balanced on a tall, terraced house, his ladder wobbling as he made his ascent. Should she walk under the ladder, where there was more space? Or walk around it, but risk getting run over by a delivery rider? She wasn't superstitious. She was an intelligent woman who believed everything happened for a reason. She walked under the ladder and took a deep breath. No bucket of water fell on her. She'd survived so far. Let's see what the conversation with Jordan held.

"Yes. Hello. He did tell me, but I have to be honest with you and say I'm not sure you're going to be needed. Marcus is trying to make things easy for me, but I've already got a wedding planner and a maid of honour. I'm not sure what there is for you to do."

There was a pause before Jordan replied. "It's not an uncommon response, Abby. I totally get your misgivings. But you'd be surprised at what I can help you with, and in doing so smooth the process so you don't feel a single bump in the road. But none of it works unless you want me there."

"I know that, I'm in business. Business is all about relationships." She sighed. This woman sounded reasonable, and assured. Abby was sure she was good at her job. She just couldn't nail down exactly what the job was. "Look, Marcus did this without consulting me. I told him I'd meet you and see what you could offer, and I'll honour that. Further than that, I can't promise anything."

"That's how most of my relationships start out."

Okay. "Where are you based?"

"I'm in Brighton, but I can travel to you. I understand you're in Balham, which I could get to in a bit over an hour. I can come and see you this weekend if that's convenient?"

Abby cast her mind forward to the weekend. She had a barbecue at her friend's house on Sunday, but Saturday could work. "Can you do Saturday morning?"

Jordan didn't hesitate. "I can. I'll connect on WhatsApp. Then I can fill you in on my services, and we can start from there."

It sounded almost plausible. Not like this was a made-up service. "Sounds good." She paused. "Tell me, Jordan, how many brides have you been a fake bridesmaid for?"

"Twenty-seven so far. With another five booked for later in the year. You were lucky I had a cancellation, so I can fit you in. But like I say, only if you want it to happen."

That figure stopped Abby in her tracks. "Twenty-seven? Wow. That's a lot of bridal help. Who knew there was so much need?"

"You'd be surprised," Jordan replied. "Does 10am work? I like to leave plenty of time for an initial consultation, at least two hours. Think of it as having a coffee with a friend. Just chatting, getting to know each other. At the end of that, you'll know whether we can work together. Does that sound okay?"

Abby nodded. "It sounds almost normal."

Jordan laughed. It had a deep timbre to it which made Abby smile.

"I'll see you Saturday," Jordan said. "And I promise to try to be almost normal."

# Chapter Five

Jordan arranged to meet Abby in Pinkies Up, a recent addition to the café culture on Balham High Street. She'd contacted her friend Sean who lived in the area, and he'd told her this was the local hotspot. He wasn't wrong. The place was a sea of white wooden tables with matching chairs. The walls were painted a shimmering pink, adorned with ample plants in holders whose leaves fell casually everywhere her eye could see. Jordan liked the effect. Plants calmed her, made her feel at ease.

She was early, because that's who she was. Jordan sat and let her gaze sweep the room as she sipped her Americano with hot milk. The café was busy, with the usual mix of parents and kids, along with an array of people typing furiously on their laptops. Jordan had never understood that tribe until she started her own business. Now she got it. The chance to work outside the four walls of your own home, with the hum of human interaction. Although after a long job like the one she'd just done, she craved solitude for a few days. Her business dealt with the public, and that was never an easy ride.

At bang on ten, a woman walked in, wringing her hands, her gaze darting around the café. The woman from the email. Abby.

Jordan sat up. Even if she hadn't known what Abby looked like, she would know it was her. Jordan had done this many times before. Although normally, the brides weren't quite as reluctant as Abby had sounded on the phone. Brides usually welcomed extra attention. So perhaps Abby was going to be more of a challenge than normal.

Jordan had told Abby she'd be wearing a yellow shirt. She knew it popped against her tanned skin; she always got comments when she wore it. She'd teamed it with some black trousers and white Grenson trainers for a casual, but put-together look. On first meetings like this, too formal made things stilted.

Jordan stood up and gave Abby a mini-wave, like she was shining a window.

She held out her hand as Abby approached. "Thanks for coming, Abby. It's great to meet you."

Abby gave her a firm handshake and a curt nod, before sitting in the chair opposite. She was dressed in dark blue jeans and a black top. Her hands were manicured, her nails polished red. They told Jordan she took care of herself. Her dark hair just hit her shoulders, flowing out into a wave as it did. Plus, she'd brought her killer cheekbones. No doubt about it, Abby was striking. She clutched her brown Coach handbag as she gave Jordan the once over.

Did Jordan's blond hair, blue eyes, and winning smile pass the test? It seemed they did, as Abby's body visibly relaxed.

"I nearly didn't come." Abby had a soft, lilting Scottish accent. She leaned back in her chair. "But then my etiquette got the better of me. I knew you'd come all the way from Brighton, and it would be a little rude of me to stand you up."

Her shoulders went up, then down. "So, here am I. How long I'm staying... Well, that depends."

"On what? How tasty the coffee is? I can tell you it's pretty good." Jordan flagged down a passing waitress.

Abby gave her coffee order. Then she shifted in her seat again, before turning to hang her bag on the back of her chair.

She was staying. Round one to Jordan.

"I've got to say, you're not what I expected."

"Oh?" Jordan rarely was. "What did you expect?"

"Someone in a bridesmaid dress. Which is stupid, I know. You're not at a wedding, so why would you do that? It's just, you look like you could be one of my friends. Someone I know. I didn't expect that."

Jordan smiled. "That's kind of the point. My job is to blend in to your life, and I can do that by looking however you want." She lifted a few strands of her shoulder-length blond hair. "This is my almost natural colour, with a little help from a bottle. But I've dyed it auburn, red, and even black when I needed to. I can be whoever you want me to be." Jordan let her gaze run down Abby's tall, lithe frame. Abby was still in fight or flight mode. Jordan's job was to keep talking, and make her feel relaxed. It was her speciality. "But I'm getting ahead of myself."

The waitress brought the coffee.

"Do you want anything to eat?" Did Abby normally eat breakfast? Jordan would lay bets she didn't.

Abby shook her head. "I'm good."

"Okay. So I guess I should tell you a little bit about my business. I started it because I saw a need, and it's grown through word of mouth. How did Marcus find out about me?"

"On a website I think." She pursed her lips, screwing up her forehead. "Although it's a bit weird he even knew such a service existed."

"When he emailed, it sounded to me like he just wanted to make your wedding as easy as possible. That's my job, and I do it well. You can speak to any of the brides I've worked with before and they'll tell you that."

"I'll take your word for it." Abby sipped her coffee, giving Jordan a nod. "You're right. This is good. So what do you normally talk about at these first meetings?"

Jordan cleared her throat. "What I can do to help you out. But also, it's just a chance for us to get to know each other and see if we can work together. Because if we do, it's pretty full-on. I don't take on everybody who asks me, and I don't get taken on by everyone, either. No pressure." Jordan paused. Abby was a tricky one to work out. "Let's start off with something easy. Tell me about your life. Your work, your family. And then of course, the most important thing: how you met Marcus."

Abby crossed one leg over the other, before giving Jordan a nod. "Okay, high level stuff. I'm a project manager for Investwell. Fingers crossed, I'm just about to be made team lead on a project implementing a new system in our Asset Management division. My boss is nice, but dull. If I end up like him, I might shoot myself. The job isn't sexy, but it pays well. I get stuff done, and people appreciate that." She stared at Jordan. "If I'm not mistaken, this is what you're doing too, right?"

She was insightful. Jordan nodded. "In part. But think of me also as your cheerleader, right-hand woman, and a shoulder to cry on." She sometimes said 'therapist', but somehow thought that might make Abby bolt. Abby struck her as an independent woman who rarely asked for help. Would she employ Jordan? She had no idea.

"Plus, if you're a project manager by day, that's the last thing you want to be in your spare time." Jordan paused. "Are you neat at home?"

A smile broke through on Abby's face. It suited her. She shook her head. "Nope. Marcus wins that battle. I've been known to leave coffee cups on the side for days, which makes him cringe."

"You can't be on top of things everywhere," Jordan replied. She'd obviously struck a nerve. "What about your family?"

"My family." Abby's smile got wider. "They're a damn sight easier to deal with than Marcus's family. My mum, Gloria, is a university professor from Glasgow, but she lives in St Albans now. My dad mends vacuum cleaners."

That made Jordan pause. "For a living?"

"He gets that a lot. But, yes." She grinned. "He's not my biological dad but he might as well be. He brought me up. His name is Martin. The same first three letters as the man I'm marrying. Perhaps all men beginning with Mar are special?"

Jordan inclined her head. "Maybe they are. My dad's called Bob, so I wouldn't know." She paused. "Tell me how you met Marcus, and how he asked you to marry him."

Abby smoothed out her blue jeans unnecessarily. "What can I tell you about Marcus? He's a sweetheart. I'm very lucky to have him." Her mouth twitched as she spoke. "He asked me to marry him after a romantic meal at his place. He got down on one knee and popped the question." Abby paused.

"It was old-fashioned and lovely. He'd asked my parents for my hand the week before, because he's a gentleman. I'm not so in love with that, because I'm not my parent's property to give away." Abby's foot jigged at speed. "Still, that's Marcus: traditional and sweet. Plus, he makes a mean Thai green curry. My mum thinks I should marry him just on the basis that he knows his way around the kitchen."

"I've heard of worse reasons," Jordan replied.

"I'm sure you have." Abby sipped her coffee before licking her lips, a ghost of a smile crossing her face. "So tell me why I should go ahead and hire you as my fake bridesmaid."

"Because I can take the stress out of the whole affair and make you enjoy getting married is the short answer. The top-level package means I pose as one of your bridesmaids. If you need me to write your speech, run the hen do, or get you the right bra for your big day, I can. I can even make sure you sleep well the night before."

Abby laughed at that. "Are you a magician, too?"

"It's been said." Jordan gave her a full-beam smile. "If you don't want the full package, I can just be hired on a daily basis as your bridal PA. I'm there to make your life easier, and whatever it is you want me to do, I can do it."

Abby nodded as she took it all in.

"But say you went for the VIP treatment, our back story is normally that I'm a long-lost friend from your childhood, who got back in touch and we've rekindled our friendship." Jordan tucked her elbows into her waist, turning her palms to the ceiling. "We always promised each other we'd be the other's maid of honour, and here I am." She sat forward, fixing Abby with her stare. "That story works like a charm.

However, you'd be surprised how little I have to trot it out."
Jordan scratched her cheek. "In the unlikely event I am
quizzed on our story, I'm discreet and a good actor. Plus, I
get on with anybody, which is part of the job. Marcus tells
me the thorn in your side is your mother-in-law. I'm the
expert on those, too."

Abby's foot began to jig again. "Have you got a mother-
in-law?"

Jordan shuddered. "Nope. If I did, I'm sure I'd find her
tricky to deal with, too." She smiled. "But I come at this with
experience and knowledge on my side. I've got a degree in
psychology and I know how to handle people. I also dress the
part, and I can be there to head off tricky encounters before
they even happen. If it's her who's giving you the most grief,
you can brief me, and you won't have another conversation
before the wedding. My job is to make problems disappear,
and I'm good at it."

Abby took that in for a few moments. "That does sound
tempting. However, I already have two bridesmaids. My
maid of honour is sorting the hen do. So I'm not sure of the
need on that score."

Jordan shrugged. "No problem. I can just be an additional
bridesmaid who takes the pressure off everyone. I can be your
maid of honour in everything but name." She held up a hand.
"Although, I don't want to tread on any toes. If your current
choice has everything in hand, that's all good. But..." Jordan
hesitated. This was always tricky to say. "To put it bluntly,
does she? Is she making your life better or worse?"

Abby tensed her mouth one way, then another. Then, she
let out a long sigh. "She's a fucking nightmare, to tell you

the truth." Then she slapped a hand over her mouth. "Never tell her I said that, she'd kill me. Shit, that was meant to be my inside voice."

Jordan bit down a grin. Two swear words in as many sentences. Abby was starting to loosen up. "It's a common tale." She leaned forward and placed a hand on Abby's arm.

Abby flinched, staring at Jordan's fingers, then at her.

Something shifted inside Jordan. She held Abby's gaze for a moment, before shaking her head. "What was I saying?"

What had she been saying? Jordan wracked her brain, before she remembered.

"Oh yes. Client confidentiality. If you hire me, whatever you say is in the strictest confidence. Anything at all. So never apologise. I can help you best if I know exactly what I'm dealing with. Okay?"

Abby nodded, her cheeks flushed, her eyes not quite settling on Jordan's face. "The truth is, my maid of honour is my best friend, Delta. Who is a very capable, very lovely woman. Only, she's just been dumped by her girlfriend, and is currently only concerned with that. Let's just say she's dropped the ball somewhat since it happened, and I am freaking out a little about the hen weekend that's coming up in Cannes."

Jordan sat back. Abby needed her help with her mother-in-law and her maid of honour. This job was in the bag, surely?

She liked Abby. She liked her forthrightness, and she could listen to her soft, Scottish accent all day. Jordan was sure Abby would have her fair share of meltdowns — every bride did — but she got the impression she'd be reasonable, too. Plus, she had a queer maid of honour. Another tick in Abby's column.

"If we work together, I could sort out your hen weekend, too. Take the pressure off. Deal with Delta, deal with Marcus's mum. What's her name?"

"Marjorie." The name came out of Abby's mouth with a hiss. "Marjorie starts with 'mar' too, doesn't it? That blows my theory out of the water."

"Maybe it only works with men."

Abby's face relaxed into a smile. Again, it transformed her. She should smile more often.

"People really have you in their wedding photos? A complete stranger?"

Jordan nodded. "They do. One woman employed me because all of her bridesmaids were squabbling, so she sacked the lot. I organised the hen, and did everything for her, including walking ahead of her down the aisle."

"I get where she's coming from. I didn't really want bridesmaids either, but Delta convinced me. And now she's crying off. My cousin Taran lives in Scotland still, so she's no use."

"Sounds like Marcus was right. You need help."

"But Marjorie *and* Delta? Are you sure you're prepared? Neither of them is a pushover. Delta played rugby at university."

Jordan laughed. "I'll watch out for any high tackles."

"She's from Scotland, like me. Even though we met at college in St Albans." Abby's face softened as she spoke. "I still can't get over people having a stranger as their bridesmaid, though."

It was nothing Jordan hadn't heard before. "I'm only a stranger now. If I work with you, I won't be a stranger for long, will I? Plus, some brides have relatives as their bridesmaids who they've only ever met once or twice. By the time we get to their wedding, I often know more about them than their best friends do. Weddings bring it out in people."

"A professional bridesmaid." Abby shook her head. "How did you even get into this as a job?"

"It's a long story. I'll tell you all about it if you hire me."

"You could really become a human barrier between Marcus's mother and me?"

"If I remember correctly, it's just over five weeks until your wedding?"

Abby nodded.

"I could ensure that for the next five weeks, you have minimal contact. Apart from the wedding day and anything personal, obviously."

"I'd say in that case, it might be worth a shot." Abby paused, stared at Jordan, and then flopped her head backwards, letting out a long breath. "Decision made." She sat up and held out a hand. "Let's see if this works. You're going to be my bridesmaid. I didn't want any and I've now got three." She raised a single styled eyebrow. "Shall we get another coffee to celebrate?"

"My treat." Jordan signalled to the waitress, before reaching over to shake Abby's hand.

As they connected, a warmth travelled up Jordan's arm. Her eyes automatically turned to focus on Abby. When they did, she found Abby's gaze locked on her, too.

"You're an intriguing woman, Jordan. What's your surname?"

"Cohen." Jordan's heartbeat picked up again.

"Jordan Cohen." Abby tilted her head. "You're definitely

my prettiest bridesmaid. Welcome to Team Abby. I know Marcus contacted you, but it's Team Abby, now. Does that work for you?"

For a moment, Jordan forgot where she was. But then her environment snapped back into focus, and she remembered.

She was in a meeting with a client. One who was getting married. This was business. No matter how pretty her eyes.

"It works perfectly. I look forward to seeing you happily married in the very near future."

# Chapter Six

Delta greeted Abby with a sad smile and a limp hug. She was normally a bear hug kinda woman, but her break-up had hit her hard. Only last month, Delta had been hinting she and Nora might move in together. But then, Nora had changed her plans abruptly. Abby was sad for Delta, but not that upset the relationship had collapsed. Nora had been an unbearable know-it-all who'd struck Abby as cold on their few encounters. Whereas Delta was larger than life and wore her heart on her sleeve. Abby had told her many times to take better care of her heart. Also, to raise her taste in women, because Delta's choices were usually atrocious.

Abby took Delta's hand as they walked along London's main shopping road. Oxford Street's usual bustle rippled past her ears. Black cabs and red buses slid by, and delivery riders wove in and out of the traffic with some skill. Up above, May was still pretending to be April, white clouds covering the pale-blue sky and blocking the sunshine. Abby hoped the weather bucked up for her June wedding. That sentiment went for her best friend, too.

She steered Delta into John Lewis, one of London's

most famous department stores. As usual, their senses were assaulted as they strolled into the beauty department, all glaring lights and floral scents. Abby took a breath as they strolled past the make-up counters, the impossibly shiny sales assistants on high alert. The smell of make-up always felt like home to Abby. She used to be fascinated watching her mum put it on as a child.

They got on the escalator, their destination the second-floor swimwear department. Delta had agreed to help Abby choose a bikini for her honeymoon, as long as Abby agreed to drink alcohol with her afterwards. The rooftop bar was their final destination.

Abby brushed her friend's arm. "How are you?"

"How am I?" Delta clutched the side of the escalator. "Heartbroken. Miserable. Sober, which is a surprise."

"I don't think your work would take kindly to you coming in drunk."

"I know, it's so unfair."

They got off the escalator and walked to the next before resuming their conversation.

"Have you heard from her?"

"Nora?" Delta swept her brown hair behind her left ear.

"No, Santa Claus. Of course, Nora."

Delta shook her head as they reached their chosen floor. "I haven't. But then, I didn't expect to. She made it pretty clear when she left this wasn't a decision she was going to reverse. 'You and I have run our course', I believe were her exact words."

Abby winced. "Ouch. She's read too many self-help books, clearly."

That raised a smile from Delta. "It did kinda feel like I was being assessed when she did it. I failed the assessment, by the way."

Abby gave Delta's arm a squeeze as they walked between over-priced blouses and cripplingly expensive jackets. She stopped, and held up a glittery gold blazer, checking the price tag and making a face. "Would it make you feel any better if I bought you this?"

Delta laughed. "I'm not planning a new career as a magician."

"You could rock this anyway," Abby told her. She whirled around and pointed at a pink chiffon blouse opposite. "With that pink blouse, we could get you another date in no time. That outfit screams ladykiller."

The sad smile was back. "It's a little too soon for jokes."

Abby put the jacket back on the rack, before threading her arm through Delta's. "Never lose your sense of humour, D. That's when the bastards win." She paused, glancing Delta's way. "Anyhow, I've got news. Something to take your mind off you-know-who."

Delta turned her head. "I'm all ears."

"Marcus has hired a professional bridesmaid for me. And she's... well, she's actually quite nice. Sane. Normal. Not society at all." Attractive, too. But Abby wasn't going to focus on that part. "Marcus says she handles Marjorie like a dream. The upshot is, he's thrown money at my biggest headache and the headache has gone away. There are plus points to having money, it turns out."

Delta stopped as they approached the swimwear, and scratched her head. "What exactly is a professional bridesmaid?

You've already got actual bridesmaids who know you, plus a wedding planner."

"We have, but she works for Marjorie, so she's not on my side." Abby sucked on the inside of her cheek. "Meanwhile, Jordan is going to be my right-hand woman, helping me out with whatever I need. Including the hen weekend."

Delta's frown deepened. "Isn't that my job?"

Abby had to be delicate. "Yes, but you've been a bit preoccupied of late. Marcus has hired this woman to help, so I say let her. Then we can both relax and just enjoy my hen. What do you think?" If she'd asked this a month ago, Delta wouldn't have been amenable. Now though, her face told a different story.

"I can't help but feel I'm letting you down."

Abby hugged her best friend. "You're not. Think of it as doing me a favour. I need to give this woman something to do. You've already got the ball rolling, so it's been a team effort. Let her take over from here."

Delta pursed her lips. "I'm still your maid of honour?"

Abby nodded emphatically. "Of course. You're my best friend. Jordan can't replace that, can she?"

Delta approached a nearby swimwear display, before turning back to Abby, her face nearly back to normal. "So, this Jordan." Delta paused. "Who the hell's called Jordan apart from people in American sitcoms, by the way?"

"It was good enough for Katie Price." Abby grinned at her own joke.

"She doesn't look like Katie Price, does she?"

Abby conjured an image of Jordan in her mind. Her laughter that crackled in the air long after she'd stopped.

Her easy smile. The way she looked directly at Abby as if she knew far more about her already.

"Far from it." Abby picked up an orange bikini bottom, but threw it back down just as quickly when she spied a pink glittery flower on it. "Plus, as you know, the Montgomerys and their friends are all from a certain background. Jordan isn't. She could be one of our friends. It's early days, but it's nice to have someone on my side who's in the middle of it all. Someone who gets me."

"I get you."

"You know what I mean. On staff. You're not staff."

"Oh my god. You've got staff for your wedding. Slippery slope. Have you told your mum yet?"

Abby shook her head. She wasn't looking forward to telling Gloria. "Not yet." She paused. "Are we good? I'll tell Jordan she can take over the hen?"

Delta eyed her for a few moments, before nodding. "So long as she's not ordering a second stripper."

Abby nudged her. "You better be joking." She held up a bikini that had more holes in it than material. "Do you think Marcus would appreciate this?"

Delta's mouth curved into a smile. "If he doesn't, he's gay. Have I mentioned I've still got money on that, by the way?"

Abby rolled her eyes. "He's not gay, believe me. He's just sensitive."

"Gay is not an insult. I'm just saying, I think there's more to your husband-to-be than meets the eye. A little like his future wife, might I add. Does Marcus know you dabbled in college?"

Abby's head whipped around to her best friend. "Enough." There was a warning tone in her voice, and Delta heeded it.

"Okay, no going there today." Delta picked up a baby-blue bikini with white orchids printed on it. "How about this one for our totally straight bride?"

Abby sighed, but couldn't stop the smile spreading across her face. "I slept with one woman 15 years ago. You'd think you'd have let it lie by now."

"Maybe you don't know me that well." Delta gave her a wide grin. It was good to see. "Tell me more about Jordan, aka Wonder Woman."

"Let's see. She's about our age. Pretty, too. You'd like her." Abby already did. "Blond hair, blue eyes, stylish. But the main thing is, she's dealing with Marjorie, so I love her."

"How much does she charge?"

"I don't ask questions like that, because I'd probably baulk at the answer."

"If I was the more sensitive type, I'd say I was being edged out."

Abby raised an eyebrow. "Good job you're so stoic, then, isn't it?" She paused. "I still expect you to be there for me, by the way. Jordan is just a help. But there are some things I want your opinion on. Like the final wedding dress choice that's happening soon. You're definitely going to be there for that, right?" Abby and her mum had narrowed it down to the final two options and had them fitted.

Delta made the sign of the cross on her chest. "Cross my heart and hope to die."

Abby wagged a finger in her direction. "No dying on bridesmaid watch."

Delta gave her a look. "Just so long as Jordan knows I've been your friend for 20 years. I know you and what you like.

41

Maybe we could meet up before the hen, and I can fill her in on a few things."

Abby nodded. "Totally. I'd already thought that."

"Good." Delta eyed her. "Is she going to be there on the wedding night when you're consummating the marriage?"

Abby punched her in the arm. "At least we'd be having sex." She sucked in a breath. She hadn't meant to say that out loud.

"You still not doing that?"

Abby shook her head. She held up a navy-blue polka dot bikini from the rack. "What about this one?" She'd heard not having sex in the run-up to the marriage was common. But their slump was more than that. It had been months in the making.

But Marcus was kind.

She had to focus on that.

# Chapter Seven

"Which of these do I pick?" Jordan backed away from the golf clubs Abby set down at the side of their driving bay as if they were radioactive.

Up ahead, the driving range was a luscious pea green, scattered with flags and bunkers, the width of 30 bays. Each side was flanked with 100-feet-high nets to keep the balls inside. They were needed, too. As Jordan stood there, balls flew out from above and either side, the rhythmic thwack of them being hit a constant background noise.

Abby gave her a throaty laugh. "They're called clubs. Do you really know so little about golf?"

"This isn't golf, right?"

Abby shook her head. "This is the driving range, where you come to practise your driving and your swing. Or just to whack some balls."

"Got it. Me and sport aren't friends. I was the person who always had my period during PE at school. My flatmate Karen makes me go running, because I have to stay in shape. But if I didn't have to, I wouldn't go."

Abby looked her up and down. "Really? You look like the sort of person who goes to the gym all the time."

Jordan shook her head. "Nope. Nervous energy. Pure and

simple. Probably learned from childhood. I was a forces kid, always moving around. You learn to be on your toes, and be able to pack up and move in an instant. It's why this job works for me. I'm organised and unflappable."

Abby nodded. "From my professional bridesmaid, that's great to hear." She paused. "Plus, if you hate sport, golf might be the perfect one for you. It's gentle, and involves nothing more than a walk and a swing. The driving range cuts down the walking to zero. All you have to do is focus, and hit."

That didn't sound so scary. "I can do that," Jordan replied.

Abby selected a club with a thick head — had she called it a driver? — then turned to Jordan, fixing her with her conker-brown eyes. "I'll show you how to grip the club and swing in a minute. First up, sit on that sofa, then watch and learn. Okay?"

Jordan nodded, and sat on the black wicker sofa at the back of the bay.

Satisfied, Abby licked her lips, flexed her back, then placed her feet wide apart. She rocked her hips from side to side as she settled her hands on the club, eyeing first the range, then the ball. The concentration was immense, and Jordan was transfixed. Abby's hips were low and loose, and looked like they could knock out a figure eight and perhaps a samba, no problem. Jordan let that image settle in her brain, before nudging it aside. She was here to work. And impress with a golf swing.

A little more hip wiggling, then Abby raised her club, twisted her body and rotated her torso at speed, smacking the ball down the driving range. It sailed high and long, eventually hitting the right-side netting.

Jordan sat up and let out a low whistle. Damn. Not only did Abby know how to move her hips in a more than dangerous way, she could also put a golf ball in its place.

Next up was Jordan. Bugger.

"You're good at this."

Abby looked up. She gave her a louche grin. "Let's just say, this is where I come to let off steam. If I've had a bad day, I pretend the golf balls are my clients. If I've had a good day, I pretend the golf balls are my mother-in-law. Works well every time."

She put another golf ball onto the scuffed blue tee, steadied herself, then whacked it again. Abby repeated the move twice more, then she turned, letting out a contented sigh as she took off her single golf glove and walked over to Jordan. Abby slumped into the sofa's plump cushions, far more relaxed than when Jordan had first met her ten days ago. This was her safe space. Jordan was impressed she'd let her in so quickly.

"So does Marcus come here with you, too?"

Abby nodded, not turning her head from the vista ahead. "Yes. Although he's humouring me, I know that."

"He doesn't play golf?"

"He does, but only for business reasons. He gets a lot of his business on the golf course, as is the way of the world. But if he didn't have to go out on a golf course again, he wouldn't."

"Do you play golf, too?"

"On occasion. But this is easier to fit into my life. Just coming to a bay, getting a bucket of balls, and hitting them down the course. It's therapeutic. It can be social. But I can also do it on my own. Some people go to the gym, some people meditate. I come here." Abby paused. "Are you going to give it a go?" She raised an eyebrow at Jordan, before standing up and holding out a hand. "Come on, I'll show you how. I promise the clubs don't bite. And neither do I."

Jordan gulped, knowing she couldn't get out of this. She took Abby's hand and jumped up, ignoring the roll of her stomach as their fingers touched.

Abby gave her a seven iron, holding its head in her hand. "See this?" Her fingers traversed the thick iron wedge. "The head is more angled, which means you're more likely to hit the ball and drive it into the air."

Jordan nodded. "Airborne is what I'm after." She took the club in her hands and swung her hips the way she'd seen Abby do.

Even that wasn't easy.

"Interlock your hands together like this." Abby grabbed a nearby club and showed Jordan. "Little finger in between the opposite index and middle finger."

Jordan frowned, then slipped her little finger inside her thumb.

Abby shook her head. "No, your pinkie in between your index and middle." She leaned in and rearranged Jordan's pinkie. A waft of her floral perfume sailed through Jordan's airwaves, before Abby stepped back.

"Now watch the ball, not the club. Swing it up behind your head, and follow through by rotating your top half. Keep your hips still."

Jordan cleared her mind of everything else. She focused on the small white ball, before looking down the driving range.

Above her, balls flew out from the other driving bays. To her right, a man in a cap was muttering under his breath as he swung, and missed.

Jordan took a deep breath, moved the club behind her head, swung, and missed.

Shit.

She turned to smile at Abby.

Somehow, it was important she did this. That she impressed Abby. Jordan was competent in most areas of her life, but golf didn't fall into that category.

Abby was standing with a hand on her hip, staring at her intently. Her hair shone under the lights of the bay, her cheekbones front and centre. "You're gripping it too hard. Relax, loosen up, and you'll find you hit the ball easier." Abby wiggled her hips as if to show Jordan what she meant.

Jordan copied what Abby had just done. She wasn't sure it was going to help. She swung again. And missed again.

Shit the bed.

It didn't look this hard on TV.

In seconds, Abby was beside her, standing with her feet hip width apart, gripping a club. "You've got the grip right, but your placement is off. You're holding it too high. Grip it towards the bottom of the black handle, like this." Abby demonstrated on her club.

Jordan stared at her fingernails, with their French polish. They were perfect. Just like most of her brides to be. However, Abby was the first one who'd ever brought her to a driving range. She normally got taken to spas, or to lunch. Never to a driving range.

Abby was not Jordan's usual client.

Jordan did as she was told, manoeuvring her hands into what she hoped was the proper position.

"Now you've lost your interlocking grip." At least Abby said that with a hint of a smile. This was already proving a challenge, and she hadn't even hit a ball yet.

Abby dropped her club and stepped closer, arranging Jordan's hands with her own. A tingle ran up Jordan's body from her fingertips to her scalp. She turned her head to see if Abby had noticed her slight shudder. If she had, she wasn't showing it. Abby was purely focused on Jordan's grip. Her hand was wrapped right around Jordan's as she stepped up behind her, then she wrapped her other arm around Jordan's waist, the length of her body pressing into Jordan fully.

Okay, they were doing a full body grip. Jordan gulped, and steadied herself as Abby pressed herself up against her.

"Sorry if this is invading your personal space a little, but you were the one who said we should get to know each other more intimately."

Jordan could hear the smile in Abby's voice.

"My first instructor did this to me, and it really helped." She pressed a little harder, and settled herself into Jordan.

Jordan's mind scrambled.

Abby swung Jordan's golf club over her shoulder, her breasts pressing between Jordan's shoulder blades.

Yes, this was intimate alright.

Jordan tried to focus on what Abby was doing.

On her grip.

On her swing.

On being in public.

But it wasn't easy when her libido had woken up, and her heartrate had decided today was the day to practise sprints.

"You see what I mean?" Abby dropped the club slowly, rotating through the swing and over Jordan's shoulder.

Then her expectant face was peering around and into Jordan's.

Could Abby hear how loud her heart was beating? Jordan hoped not.

Abby let Jordan go and stepped back.

Jordan cleared her throat, shaking her body, ignoring her fluster.

Because the fact was, it had made a difference.

She now saw how to hold the club, and also how far she had to swing.

"Focus on the ball, and put your all into it. Try again."

Abby stepped right back, as Jordan wiggled her hips in exaggerated fashion.

Abby let out another healthy chuckle. "You're certainly looking the part. Now it's a short step until you actually hit a ball."

"Stands to reason, right?" Jordan raised her club, holding it correctly. But she only succeeded in smashing it into the fake grass underneath her. The vibrations as she connected with the ground zapped up her arm. She grimaced, taking a step back.

"Try again," Abby told her. "I hit the ground constantly when I started."

"I don't believe that." Jordan took a deep breath, focused, swung and hit the ball, but also the tee. The heavy thud shook her ears, and she watched as her ball trickled off the tee and onto the range. She'd hit it, barely.

Behind her, Abby burst into a round of applause. "First hit ball! It's only up from here."

Jordan turned and raised an eyebrow. She knew sympathy clapping when she heard it.

* * *

An hour later, all the balls had been hit. Jordan was at the bar, getting drinks. She'd insisted as a thank you for Abby's patience. The truth was, Abby had enjoyed it. She was good at golf, particularly the driving part, and she thought more women should do it as a form of exercise and a way of letting off steam. Jordan hadn't been proficient at first, but halfway through, after she got her first decent connection and got a ball airborne, her manner had changed. Then, she'd been eager to hit more balls, and sad when it ended.

Abby had invited Marcus because she thought she had to. She'd never brought Delta, who was golf-averse. Her mum had come once, and loved it, but hadn't had time to return with her crazy work schedule. When Jordan had asked Abby to take her to a place that described who she was, the driving range was what first sprang to mind. It wasn't her job, which was something she did for money. It wasn't her home, which she hadn't taken the time to furnish as she should.

For Abby, this was where she came to think, to be herself. Sometimes, she just came to have a beer on this patio, overlooking the range. Marcus didn't like bars like these, preferring restaurants or cocktail bars. It felt strangely thrilling to be in here with someone else. Someone she felt at home with already. She'd invited Jordan into her inner sanctuary, and it felt okay. That wasn't lost on Abby.

Jordan was walking towards her now, concentration on her face as she tried not to spill their beers, a packet of Walkers Salt & Vinegar crisps dangling from her mouth. The last button on her black shirt was undone, revealing a little of Jordan's flat midriff. Her golden hair was styled just-so, and she was wearing a pair of Nike trainers that Abby had looked at herself a few weeks ago. Marcus had told her they were "unclassy".

They didn't look unclassy on Jordan.

Nothing had so far.

Maybe she should have bought them. Although it would have been embarrassing if they'd both turned up wearing the same style.

"Here you go." Jordan put the drinks on the table, then took the bag of crisps from her mouth. "I wasn't sure if you were a crisp eater or whether you'd banned carbs in the run-up to your wedding. Most brides do. However, you did order an IPA, so I figured it was worth the risk. Plus, if you don't want them, I'm sure I could polish them off."

Abby shook her head as she took a sip of her beer. "I can help, have no fear. This is dinner tonight, so I think I can spare a crisp or two for today's calories. Although no Instagram stories. If Marjorie saw this, she might have a heart attack."

Jordan laughed, opening the pack wide so they could both dip in. "I met Marjorie the other day, and she was very nice to me."

"Because you're skinny. And pretty."

Jordan looked at her like she was mad. "Says you. You're hardly ugly. And I bet the last time you knowingly ate a slice of white bread was at least four years ago."

Abby let out a howl of laughter. "Maybe three." She liked the way she laughed with Jordan.

She'd liked the feel of her in her arms earlier, too, when she was showing her how to swing.

But she wasn't going to think about that.

After all, they were friendly feelings, nothing more.

"In my defence, I ate enough of it during my childhood to last a lifetime. Growing up in Glasgow, white bread was a staple of any diet." Abby sat back in her chair, stroking the rim of her glass. "Now I've taught you how to drive a golf ball, it's your turn to teach me how to pretend we know each other well. I'm still not sure I can pull this off."

Jordan shook her head. "Course you can. Nothing to it. Plus, because I am a long-lost friend from your past, you're not going to know everything about my life in detail, seeing as we're just catching up. So the story is perfect. The key thing is to spend as much time together before the wedding. Not every waking moment, obviously, but times like this. You show me what makes you tick, and it's a two-way street. Ask me anything you like, too. I'm happy to answer."

Abby nodded. It made sense. She wasn't worried about the wedding day itself, because nobody was going to quiz her about their past then. It was more the hen weekend. The lead-up drinks. The rehearsal dinner. Delta knew, along with Marcus's parents. Her parents would know by then. Everybody else, they had to convince.

"So you were whisked away from my school when we were what age?"

Jordan stroked her chin. "Let's say nine. That way, it gives us a few years of being besties. The beauty of this story is that

I'm not really lying. Like I said, my childhood was studded with moves, and leaving behind new friends. In the end, I didn't try so hard to make friends. It was easier that way. Saved the heartache."

"My childhood was the opposite to you. I had a very settled time. My mum worked full-time, my dad worked from home and did the school run most days."

"I could only dream of that," Jordan said. "Do you still see friends from your childhood?"

Abby shook her head. "Not so much now I live down here. But some of them will be coming to the wedding. But I'm not worried about our cover being blown. Give them enough wine and they won't ask any questions."

"Works every time." Jordan paused. "When little Abby was running around her Scottish playground, dreaming of white bread sandwiches, did you want to work in finance then?"

Abby scoffed. "Does anyone dream of that?"

"My cousin did. But he is a little odd."

"You'll be surprised to hear the answer is no. In fact, I'm currently going for a promotion which will mean longer hours at a job I hate." When she put it like that, she made herself question her life. "I wanted to be a golfer in my teens, but I left it a little late to start. Tiger Woods started playing aged one. So my second choice was to work for a charity, achieve big things, and save the world."

Jordan nodded. "Start small."

"That's what I thought. I went to Oxford University because I read that's where all the big decision-makers in life went. I wanted to be on their team. However, I didn't really like many of them. The only one I did like was Marcus. He was kind and considerate."

"Wow, you've been together for a while."

Abby shook her head. "No, we never got together at uni. Our paths crossed, we had mutual friends, but we never got romantically involved. That didn't happen until just over 18 months ago, when I met him again at a work function. We had a drink to chat about old times, then he asked me to dinner. The rest is history."

Jordan smiled. "A classic second-chance romance."

Clouds formed on Abby's brain, but she nodded anyway. She and Marcus were no love's young dream, she knew that. Perhaps that was truer for Marcus than for her. But she did love him. And she knew that Marcus would always be there for her, no matter what.

"Something like that," she replied.

"And when you're married, do you think you're going to take up those childhood dreams of saving the world?"

Was she? Abby hadn't really thought about it. Marrying Marcus and moving in with him had been consuming all her thoughts of late. She hadn't thought much about anything past the wedding.

Not even the honeymoon.

Getting married, changing her name, moving house.

One step at a time.

"I live on Charity Street. I thought that was a good start."

Jordan tilted her head. "But you always said you wanted to save the world when we were eight. You wanted to be a name on everyone's lips. Someone who really made a difference, and did it for reasons known only to herself. You also wanted to be the sixth member of the Spice Girls, and I applauded such lofty ambition."

For a moment, Abby thought she was telling the truth. "You're good." She stared at Jordan. A good actress. Silver-screen smile to match. Firm arms which she'd held earlier.

She shook herself.

"Now you're making me believe we really did know each other when we were little, because I *did* have such grandiose thoughts back then. I was a little girl who wanted to stretch myself beyond my limits even from a young age. I also wanted to be a cross between Baby and Sporty Spice."

"You could have been Golfy Spice."

"The member they never knew they were missing."

The corners of Jordan's mouth turned upwards. "You could still do it."

"Be a Spice Girl? I think that ship has sailed."

"Not for your other ambitions. You're young. Your business skills would still work in a new environment. Maybe it's something you should think about when the wedding is done."

Abby nodded. Maybe it was. Maybe she'd been cruising for far too long.

Including into this engagement?

*Not now, Abby.*

"Plus, this bodes well for our working relationship, right? If I can read you this well, we don't need to have too many of these sessions."

"Oh no, we definitely do," Abby said. "I don't know you and I don't trust my reading of situations as much as you do. Plus, your golf swing needs work. Serious work." Abby gave

Jordan a grin, then looked away for a moment, as the blood rushed to her cheeks. She wasn't quite sure why, but she was embarrassed about her life in front of Jordan, who was so clearly put together.

Whereas Abby was doing a job she'd accepted because it afforded her the lifestyle she'd become accustomed to. Meeting someone new like Jordan shone a light on that fact. Abby had drifted very far from her childhood goals. Very far from even where she wanted to be in the previous decade when she graduated from university. Then, armed with the most prestigious degree certificate, the world was her oyster. She could have gone into charity work as she'd intended, but her head was turned by what all her friends were doing. She wanted the inflated pay cheque they were all getting. Now, she'd forgotten she ever wanted anything different.

Until Jordan turned up. With her bad golf swing. Her easy smile. Somehow, Jordan had made Abby start to question her life.

Just by asking one simple question, Jordan had pulled at a loose thread in Abby's life she'd been ignoring for years.

Another tug, and Abby might begin to slowly unravel.

# Chapter Eight

"Have you sorted the bagpiper, or do you need Dad to ring his uncle?"

Abby's mum, Gloria, sat on her red velvet sofa, eating fish and chips out of the paper they arrived in. She said they tasted much better that way.

Abby had to agree. Although, her life these days didn't often feature things like eating chips out of paper. She could just imagine Marjorie's face. Come to think of it, she wasn't sure neat-freak Marcus would cope, either. He'd have a fit about this amount of grease near velvet.

"No, Jordan's sorted it."

"Who?"

Abby blushed. "Just someone who's helping out with the wedding." She had to tell her mum that Jordan was working for her, but she'd been putting it off. She wasn't sure how to say it without it sounding like she truly had turned into the sort of people they used to ridicule when she was growing up.

Posh people.

Abby wasn't posh. She hadn't forgotten her roots. She was getting a bagpiper. She still enjoyed eating chips out of paper. She was still very much grounded.

"The wedding planner? I thought her name was Lauren?"

Abby ate another chip. Then she put them down. She couldn't afford to eat too many chips, could she? The wedding was only three weeks away, and she had a dress to get into. Society people to impress. Marcus had told her that morning their wedding was going to feature in the pages of a society magazine.

It was a very different world from where she sat with grease-stained fingers.

"No, that's right. Lauren is still the wedding planner, and she's sorting the bigger stuff. But she's still on Marjorie's staff. Jordan is someone new that Marcus hired."

"More staff at the Montgomery household?" Gloria held up her pinkie as she ate another chip. In her smart M&S trousers and shirt, she didn't look that dissimilar to Marjorie. However, as soon as she opened her mouth, the differences were immense. That, plus Gloria's proud mop of Scottish red hair.

Abby took a deep breath and looked Mum direct in the eye. "Not quite. Jordan's come in to be my professional bridesmaid. She's there to help me out before the wedding, and on the wedding day. Right up to the altar."

"What do you mean, professional bridesmaid?" Gloria's furrows deepened.

Abby knew it sounded mad at first. "She's posing as my bridesmaid so she can be there for all the key events and truly help me out. And she is, believe me. She's lovely."

She'd chatted with Jordan that very morning and had come off the call uplifted. Jordan had a certain way about her, something Abby couldn't quite pin down. "The thing is, because she is my bridesmaid, we're telling everyone she's a long-lost friend from my childhood. One who moved away when I was nine, and we've just got back in touch via social media. So if you could play along if that comes up in conversation, that would be great." She knew it was a lot to take in, but she hoped her mum would agree.

Mum paused, a chip close to her mouth. "A wedding planner and a professional bridesmaid with a whole fake back story? Things really have changed since my day." She patted Abby's knee. "But you seem more relaxed. If that's Jordan's doing, well done her. I'll go along with whatever you want."

Relief flowed through Abby. "Thanks."

"Of course. I'm your mum. What else am I going to do?" She paused. "So she's taking over the hen weekend now Delta's having a meltdown?"

Abby nodded. "She is. Delta was resistant at first, but she soon got over it. She's still my maid of honour. Nothing's changed on that score."

"We're still going to Cannes? Where it costs an arm and a leg for a gin and tonic? Did I tell you Janet went there last year, and came back with a second mortgage?"

They'd been through this. "Yes, we're still going there. Plus, it's not going to cost that much, seeing as the accommodation is free, as is the in-house chef."

Mum clicked her tongue on the roof of her mouth. "Do I need to remind you where I went on my hen weekend?"

She didn't. It was etched in Abby's memory. "Blackpool. I know, I've been told once or twice."

"Rained the whole bloody time, but we still had a ball. You don't need to fly to fancy places to have a good time."

"I know. But it's a short flight and there's a free house. Rude not to." Abby gave her mum a look that she hoped told her to shut up.

Gloria heeded it.

# Chapter Nine

"I've told you before, Marcus. You're having a top table, and that's the end of it." Marjorie bristled. From what Jordan had seen, bristling was her favourite pastime. "And you've got to have more flowers than Abby wants. At least two bouquets per table. Otherwise, what will people think?"

Jordan sat forward, tapping her pen on her pad. "On the contrary, Marjorie, less is more these days. I've been reading all the latest bridal magazines, and they all say that minimal is the new look. It's all about browns and greens, nothing too ostentatious. Makes it more environmentally conscious."

Marjorie sat up at that. "Is it really?"

Did her bobbed dark hair ever move? Jordan didn't think so.

"It is. I was thinking, we could go with what Abby wanted — one bouquet per table — and then we could have some foliage on the tables, too. Something a little different." She sat forward. "Apparently, it's what all the young royals have at their weddings. Including Princess Olivia and Rosie."

Marjorie raised both eyebrows. "If it's good enough for them, it's good enough for us." She paused, looked down at her list, then back up at Jordan. "Anything else you can advise us on, seeing as you're in the know?"

Marcus gave Jordan a look that told her he didn't quite believe what he was hearing, but Marjorie had said it. This was the third meeting she'd had with Jordan, and Jordan was acing it. The thing was, having been in this game for the past three years, she'd met Marjorie before in many different forms. Sometimes she was called Cressida. Sometimes she was called Sophia. Many times she'd been called Arabella. But they were always the same. They wanted the wedding to go off seamlessly. They wanted the best for their offspring. But mainly, they wanted to look good in front of their friends and family, and for people to think back to their child's wedding for years to come and say it was the best they'd ever been to.

Jordan couldn't guarantee that. However, she could guarantee that her suggestions would make the wedding the best it could possibly be.

"Let me see," Jordan said, staring skywards in contemplation. "I'd say wood is definitely in this year. Earthy elements, and simplicity over anything too busy. It's all clean lines, subtle colours, and traditional flavours with a twist for the food and drink. Which is why going overboard on the flowers isn't the thing to do. Think less is more." She leaned towards Marjorie. "I had lunch with the editor of *Perfect Bride* magazine last week. I got it direct from her mouth."

A slight lie. Jordan had eaten lunch in the restaurant underneath where the magazine was produced. Her friend, Donald, worked for *Vogue* and had told her words to similar effect. That was good enough, surely?

Judging by Marjorie's face, it was. She was eating it up. Every word.

"If *Perfect Bride* says so, we'll follow suit." Marjorie shuffled her notes, before nodding towards Jordan. "Lauren's got all the details for the table arrangements and decorations, but perhaps you might be able to add a little something to them with your insider knowledge. You said you could take over the wedding planning too, now that Lauren's mother is ill?"

"Absolutely. Consider it done," Jordan replied.

"And Marcus?"

Marcus turned to his mother. "Yes?"

"I know Abby doesn't want to deal with me, but could you both decide on a cake choice and topper? I know I'm not meant to know about these things, but I do. It's Valerie's daughter who runs the shop, and word gets around. And please, nothing too gaudy or modern. A traditional cake with a traditional bride and groom on the top should do the trick. Don't you agree, Jordan?"

Jordan gave Marjorie a slow nod. "Traditional, or traditional with a twist works well. But let me have a word with Abby and see what she thinks. Having done many weddings, I tend to think it's the bride who cares more about these things than the groom." Jordan glanced up at Marcus. "Of course, if you have strong feelings one way or the other, just say."

Marcus shook his head. "So long as you get Abby to the altar happy and relaxed, we could be eating plain old carrot cake with no topper for all I care."

"I'm sure Abby wouldn't sanction that," Jordan replied, before turning back to Marjorie, giving her a curt nod. "Leave it with me. Remember, my job is to alleviate your stress. Let me do that."

Marjorie gazed at Jordan, wonder in her eyes. "In all my years of organising events, I've never met anyone who does that quite as well as you."

* * *

Marcus waited until his mum and her Chanel red dress had disappeared around the corner before he turned to Jordan. His mouth hung open.

"My mother may never have met anyone as slick as you, but I guarantee, neither have I. I've watched a million staff try to tame her over the years, but you just breezed in and did it."

Jordan grinned at him, shielding her eyes from the sun as they walked around the side of Marcus's parents' house. Her sunglasses were in the car, so she'd have to squint for now. "Let's just say, I wasn't as good when I first started, but I've learned a few tricks along the way."

Marcus came to a stop when they reached Jordan's Capri. "Is this your car?"

Jordan nodded. "Guilty. I have a thing for 70s bangers. Blame all the repeats of *Minder* on Gold."

Marcus grinned. "I have no idea what that means, but your car's cool." He paused. "One thing, did you really have lunch with the editor of *Perfect Bride*?"

"Absolutely. No word of a lie." Marcus needed to believe in her credentials just as much as his mother. Maybe more. He was the one paying her wages, after all.

"Well, you're worth every penny whether you did or you didn't. Abby loves you. My mother loves you. All of which means, I love you, too."

"Wow, that's a lot of love from all of you. I hope I can live up to it."

"You already are. Apart from Abby saying yes to me in the first place, you're the best thing that's happened during this wedding preparation. I mean it."

Jordan gulped, thinking back to Abby's hands around her waist, her breasts pressed into her back. The way an arc of pleasure had gripped her tight throughout.

She chewed the inside of her cheek, before giving Marcus a confident smile. "Glad you think so," she replied.

# Chapter Ten

"There's my gorgeous almost-daughter!" Gloria bowled up to Delta and they embraced. A full, squidgy, Scottish hug. None of those southern air kisses, as Mum always said.

Warmth rolled through Abby. Mum had always loved Delta, and vice versa.

When they finally let go, Delta stepped back, giving Mum her full smile. "Great to see you, Gloria. Ready for your daughter to marry into almost-royalty?"

"I've been waiting since she was a tiny tot." Gloria put an arm around Abby's shoulder, squeezing tight. "Seeing my little girl married to a posh boy? That bit I hadn't quite imagined. Mainly because I'm from Glasgow. Have I told you that before, hen?"

Mum's accent was suddenly as Scottish as could be. Abby rolled her eyes. That was another thing Delta and her mother had in common. Putting on thick Scottish accents for comic effect.

"You did, Gloria, aye!" Delta responded.

They fell about laughing, before they all sat at the table Abby had commandeered when she'd arrived. They were in Bart's Bar in Canary Wharf, where both Abby and Delta worked, in the heart of the financial district. It was 6pm on a Thursday, and the bar was packed with workers out for a drink, jackets discarded, ties loosened. This was Abby and Delta's world, but it wasn't Jordan's. What was Jordan's world? Abby had no idea.

All she knew was that Jordan was a problem solver supreme. Someone who threw herself into her job. But who she really was? Abby was clueless. She wanted to rectify that soon. Jordan had quickly become someone she relied on. Jordan had said she could ask her anything, but they always seemed to end up talking about Abby, and not her. She'd moved around a lot as a kid. She lived with her best friend in Brighton. She had good taste in clothes. That was about as far as Abby had got.

"Can you refrain from doing your Scottish comedy act when Jordan turns up? I'd like for her not to think we're all crazy the minute she arrives."

Gloria reached over the table, patting Abby's hand. "If the shoe fits, hen." She hadn't dialled down her accent an inch.

"Anyway, Marcus is not royalty. His family have just done well in the property business. Plus, his money isn't why I'm marrying him, so can we not make jokes about that when Jordan's here, either?"

Mum sat back with a sigh. "I never said Marcus wasn't lovely. I know he is because of the time you came to stay. He ate your dad's square sausage for breakfast and never once asked what the hell he was eating. That's love, right there."

Abby laughed. That was Marcus all over, fitting into his surroundings.

"I just want to make a good impression on Jordan, that's all."

Delta raised an eyebrow in her direction. "Jesus, Abby.

It sounds like you're marrying Jordan, not Marcus. She's staff, as I believe you pointed out to me when we met last."

Abby's cheeks burned. She hated that term, it was one Marjorie used. But yes, she did recall saying it. Maybe the Montgomerys had rubbed off on her too much already.

"I just want it all to go well." Abby checked her watch. "She's due any moment. So just remember, play nicely." She pointed at Delta. "No baring your teeth, okay?"

Delta nodded, a butter-wouldn't-melt smile gracing her lips. "You're the bride, and we're both here to make your life easier. Yar-di-yar-di-yar. I get it. Jordan is my new best friend, okay?"

Abby gave her a nod. "Perfect."

Jordan swept in ten minutes later, and Abby gulped. She looked stunning. She was wearing a blue jump suit and tan heels, her slim waist accentuated with a matching tan belt. When she saw Abby, she gave her a wide grin and waved. Marcus had told Abby that Jordan turned up to see his mother in a stunning gold dress. Jordan was a fashion chameleon, fitting into whatever the occasion.

Jordan pulled out the spare chair from the table, then held out a hand in greeting to Mum. "You must be Gloria." Jordan pumped her mum's hand like she was the most important person in the world. "And you must be Delta." More hand-shaking, as Delta nodded.

Jordan sat, smoothing her clothes as she spoke. "I've heard so much about both of you. I'm Jordan, and I'm looking forward to getting to know you better over the next few weeks in the run-up to Abby's big day."

"We've heard a lot about you, too." Gloria paused, tilting

her head to the side. "But Abby never told us you were so stunning. You could be a model!"

Abby closed her eyes. Oh god, Mum was babbling like she was starstruck. Perhaps this was what had happened to Marjorie. Maybe Jordan really did have some kind of magic juice when it came to mothers.

Jordan took it all in her stride. "I was briefly, in my youth, but modelling wasn't for me. Too much standing about and posing. Plus, far too many lecherous men everywhere you turned." She stowed her handbag at her feet. "I prefer my current line of work any day. As a professional bridesmaid, my job is to deliver happiness. That's something nobody offers you as a career in school, is it?"

Delta snorted. "That's quite a ticket you have on yourself."

Abby kicked her under the table. So much for playing nice.

Delta flinched, but said nothing, scowling at Abby.

Abby glanced at Jordan. If that comment had irked her, she was giving nothing away.

The waiter brought over the bottle of sauvignon blanc Abby had ordered earlier, along with four glasses.

Abby gave the bottle to Delta with a pointed stare.

Delta poured with a flourish.

"A professional bridesmaid." Gloria was still transfixed. "How did you go about getting that job, if you don't mind me asking."

Jordan shook her head. "It's a valid question. I kinda fell into it when a friend of mine, Catherine, asked me to be her maid of honour. We were friends, but not particularly close, so it felt odd. If my flatmate Karen asked, that would be normal. We're best mates.

"When I asked Catherine why she chose me, she admitted it was because I'm organised and unflappable, and she wanted someone who would take charge of the hen do and help her out. So when I was made redundant from my job as an events planner months later, I put up an ad on Gumtree offering my services doing just that for other brides, and woke up to 20-plus emails. That's when I knew it was a viable business."

"Wow." Gloria took a sip of her wine that Delta had just finished pouring. "And you've done how many other weddings?"

"This is number 28. Lucky number 28, of course."

There was a lull in conversation as everyone took that in. Abby was keeping a close watch on her mum and Delta. Mum seemed smitten. Abby knew Delta would be harder to win over. She might say she was fine with the situation, but Abby knew she'd get jealous. She'd already proved that with her snark. Abby hoped these drinks would put Delta's misgivings to bed.

Abby glanced Jordan's way, taking in her perfect make-up, her styled hair. When she took a deep breath in, she could smell her perfume. It reminded her of summer days.

"Have you been asked to do anything weird in your role?"

"Delta!" Abby hadn't expected that question this early on.

"No, that's fair enough," Jordan replied. "I've stepped in for dads who couldn't handle the father-of-the-bride speech. I've dyed my hair brown to fit in with the rest of the bridesmaids. I've held brides while they've thrown up all the tequila they had on their hen do. No day is the same. I feel very privileged to be able to contribute to such an important time in people's lives, and help them to the goal of a happily married life." She paused. "I have high hopes for the run-up to this wedding. No vomiting at least."

Abby glanced at Delta, whose face was still drawn into a straight line, giving nothing away.

Jordan leaned forward, flashing her audience a killer smile. "At the end of the day, I'm a mix of on-call therapist, virtual assistant, social director, and peacekeeper." She glanced at Abby. "Now Lauren's stepped back, I've taken over the wedding planning, too. However, my key role is being the bride's right-hand woman, but also being there for all the bridesmaids, too. Think of me as at your beck and call. All of you, particularly the three at this table. The bride, her mum, and her maid of honour. Three of the most important people at the wedding. I'm totally Team Abby, and I'm full-time working in Cannes. I promise you, I'll make it a weekend to remember." She paused, looking directly at Delta. "But I also promise to defer to the maid of honour and the bride in what they want to do. I don't want to tread on any toes. If I do my job right, I should be invisibly making things seem easy."

Gloria held up her glass. "Well I'll cheers to that. You sound like Wonder Woman and Superman combined."

"Will you be wearing a cape all weekend?" Delta asked.

Abby held her breath. This would get easier. She hoped. This was the first meeting. Teething trouble, that's all.

"I'll wear anything the bride wants. If that means sporting a Wonder Woman costume all weekend, I'm in." Jordan paused, eyeing Delta with interest. "Although I think I rock a Cat Woman PVC jumpsuit better. More edge."

Abby conjured that image in her mind. Then let it go

as quickly as it had arrived. She had to focus on getting her bridal party on the same page and on-board with Jordan.

Not how Jordan might look in PVC.

The answer, obviously, was stunning.

Definitely better than Marcus.

However, Abby brought her mind back to the present. She cleared her throat, gaining everyone's attention.

Delta's wary blue eyes; Gloria's bright green stare; and Jordan's baby blues.

So capable, so strong.

*What the actual fuck, Abby?*

She slapped that thought away as quickly as it had arisen. "Just to reiterate the back story, because it might come up at the hen. We met at primary school. Then she was whisked away by her military parents to Germany. We got back in touch via Facebook in the last six months and I always promised Jordan she'd be my bridesmaid, so here she is."

"Shame we never met before, Jordan," Delta said. "I've known Abby since we were 17. So not quite as long as you." The snark in her voice was audible.

"We all know the truth, that's the main thing," Jordan replied, skilfully side-stepping the tension seeping from Delta. "I'm relying on your input as you know Abby best. She tells me you came up with a good few of the grand plans for the weekend."

Delta dipped her head, at least having the good grace to look embarrassed.

"Thanks to everyone's efforts, the weekend is now in tiptop shape." Jordan swept her gaze around the table. "Transport, food, entertainment, surprises. It's going to be great."

"It will be, because we're all going to be there," Delta said.

Abby eyed her. Was that the sound of her thawing a little? She really hoped so, otherwise the hen weekend was going to be long. "Just like you're going to be at my final dress decision, dearest maid of honour?" Her tone was pointed.

Gloria glanced at her daughter. "I told you I can't make that, right? I've got a conference."

Abby nodded. "You did. But you were at the first one, so that's fine. I've had both dresses fitted already. I held up the final decision on which one to choose so Delta could be there. Plus, now Jordan's coming, too."

Delta gave a salute. "I'm there. Jordan might have taken over some things, but not *everything*."

"Good." Abby sat back, smiling at her wedding crew.

This was it.

It looked like she was getting married.

# Chapter Eleven

Abby sat on the bridal shop sofa, flicking through *Perfect Bride* magazine. It'd been six days since Abby had seen Jordan at the drinks with her mum and Delta, and she had to admit she'd been impressed. Jordan had won Abby around with her charm, but she'd also won over her mum and Delta, which was no mean feat. Whatever bomb Delta had thrown at her, Jordan had defused. Had she said she studied psychology at uni? If so, she clearly remembered everything she'd been taught.

Unlike Abby, who'd done an economics degree, and never used any of the theory she'd learned. Still, she looked back on college as fun years, albeit ones she wished she'd paid more attention to. But college, like youth, was wasted on the young. Then she smiled. She was still only 36. She was hardly ancient. Some days, she just felt like it.

Delta had texted the following day to say that she was *okay with Jordan*, which was tantamount to a blessing from her best friend. Delta had promised to give Jordan a far easier time on the hen weekend, which had made Abby sigh. Weren't all the hens meant to make an effort to play super-nice and do everything Abby wanted? Or perhaps that was just a facade, too. Just like her relationship with Marcus's parents. She was grateful to Jordan for coming in and taking over, but she couldn't help but think it wasn't going to fix anything in the long run, was it? She was still going to be Marcus's wife. His parents were going to have to pretend to like her for years to come.

*Marcus's wife.*

Abby shivered. Was that the reaction she was meant to be having, fewer than two weeks away from the big day? Perhaps these were the wedding jitters everybody spoke about.

That was probably it.

She wished she could share her reservations with someone, but she didn't know who.

She'd kept herself occupied with work. Her mum was taken up being the head of her department. Delta was too wrapped up in herself. And Marcus? He was too busy running around trying to keep everyone happy.

No, this was something Abby had to deal with herself.

What would Jordan say if she knew? Maybe she should talk to her. She must have seen it before. She'd probably have the right thing to tell Abby.

She took a deep breath, pushing the thoughts from her mind. As she did, the scents of the bridal shop wafted into her nostrils. She glanced around, trying to find where it was coming from. Some kind of diffuser? One of those plug-in types? Whatever, it smelled a little chemical-laden. Like the relaxation it was trying to promote was too contrived.

A little like most things wedding-related, as Abby had come to realise ever since she'd said yes to Marcus six months ago.

Was it weird that since that time, they'd had sex twice? Not at all in the past three months? They didn't live together, so it wasn't something they could do before work, or have a quickie on the sofa after a chicken-and-mushroom stir-fry.

Since he'd proposed, it was like her body had gone into shutdown. She hadn't even pleasured herself much. She'd gone into survival mode, only doing the basics. Eat. Sleep. Drink. Work. Survive.

In fact, the only time her body had sprung to life was when she'd met Jordan.

But she was trying to ignore that.

Jordan's presence made her feel wonky. Skittish. Off-kilter. Which was ridiculous.

She wasn't attracted to women.

Most of the time.

Abby stared at a candle sat on a side table opposite. That was probably the source of the smell. Geranium and some kind of flower if she had to guess. Maybe rose? She didn't like it, whatever it was.

Guessing wasn't her strong point. She was second-guessing herself all the time when it came to Jordan.

Abby hadn't been attracted to many women since university. What had happened there had been one night. She'd experimented. She'd slept with a woman. She'd enjoyed it. Ticked it off her list. But that was that. One and done.

Since then, she'd only slept with men. Did that make her bisexual? Pansexual? Did you need a relationship with a woman to earn that label? She wasn't sure three orgasms counted.

Jordan was the first woman who'd snagged her interest in 15 years. She was trying not to focus on that. These weren't the thoughts a bride was meant to be having about... her staff.

Perhaps, by not thinking of Jordan like that, Abby had crossed a line.

Funny thing. She didn't care. From the moment they'd met in that café a few weeks ago, Jordan had intrigued her. Made Abby sit up. Stirred something inside her she thought was long dead.

Jordan was simply someone on Abby's wavelength. Someone she clicked with. That she had breasts and a vagina was incidental.

However, Abby would be lying if she said she hadn't wondered what those breasts looked like. Or what it would be like to kiss them.

*Stop it!*

She sucked in such a deep breath that her rib cage felt like it was riding up her body and about to strangle her.

She let it out.

Jordan had done her job and lessened Abby's stress on one level. But she was also proving a distraction. Together or apart. Jordan had started messaging Abby on a regular basis, and her messages always made Abby laugh. They were personal and witty. Did she do that for every bride she worked with? Abby hoped not. Somehow, it was important. Jordan had told her she was different. Not so spoilt. A normal person. Abby enjoyed Jordan's company. They worked well together. They made a good team.

Just like her and Marcus, obviously.

Abby closed her eyes, choking again as she breathed in the aromas. She was surrounded by calming colours and satin fabrics. It wasn't Abby's natural habitat.

Moments later, the shop manager, Lisa, came back with

Abby's latte, along with a tray of shortbread. Did any bride this close to the wedding ever take a biscuit? Abby doubted it.

Lisa was one of those women who believed there was no such thing as too much make-up. Her eyelashes were so thick, it was a miracle she ever managed to pry them open. Abby had nothing but respect for her attention to detail.

Abby took the coffee, just as her phone lit up by her side.

It was a message from Delta.

Abby stiffened. She better not be bailing.

Abby clicked the message. Delta was sorry, but she was working from home today, and also waiting for Nora to collect some things. Nora was late. Delta couldn't leave until she arrived. She wasn't going to make it.

Delta was putting Nora over Abby. She wasn't coming.

Heat rose up through her. Hadn't they already had this discussion and Delta had sworn she'd fulfil her maid-of-honour duties? She was turning out to be more of a maid of dishonour. After the other night, Abby had thought things would change. Apparently not.

The trouble was, she wasn't all that surprised. Delta was still hung up on her ex. Hopefully this would at least mean the end of Nora, so Delta would be present for her hen weekend. Get closure.

But that still left today. No Mum. No Delta.

At least she had Jordan.

She just had to put all those inappropriate and frankly irrelevant Jordan-type thoughts out of her head and focus on the job at hand.

Picking a wedding dress.

For her marriage to Marcus.

"Everything okay, madam?" Lisa had clocked her frowny face.

Abby gave her best fake smile. "My maid of honour can't make today."

"Oh dear. That is bad news. Is anyone else coming for a second opinion?"

Something dropped into the pit of Abby's stomach. Fear? Excitement? She wasn't sure.

Abby chewed the inside of her cheek and glanced at Lisa. "Yes, my other bridesmaid."

Lisa gave her a relieved smile, and rubbed her hands together. "No problem, then. Between the three of us, we'll make sure you look beautiful on your big day."

Abby nodded, uncertainty prickling her skin.

Yes, it wasn't just Jordan. It was Lisa, too. Much better.

Lisa could act as a buffer between them.

However, one thing Lisa couldn't do was control Abby's heart, which was suddenly beating so fast, she'd swear people could hear it on the street outside. Were people running up and down the pavement, wondering where the heavy bassline was coming from? In Abby's head, it sounded like she was one of those annoying cars who pull up at traffic lights, bassline thumping, shaking the entire road.

Lisa's face was blank. Lisa was a pro. Even if she was wondering what the hell Abby was thinking, she wasn't going to say anything. Abby was a customer who was spending a lot of money on the most important dress of her life. Lisa was going to do everything to make Abby feel like the most important person in her shop.

Abby picked up her phone again.

That is, if Jordan turned up. She was normally early.

Oh my god, what if Jordan didn't even turn up?

Worry goose bumps broke out across her skin.

But then, just like that, her worries were vanquished as Jordan appeared. A vision in black, her cheeks flushed, her hair not quite as styled as usual. Artfully messed up? Jordan's hair looked like Abby imagined it might do right after sex. Tussled. Hot. Ravishing.

"Hey!" Jordan put her bag on the sofa, her sparkle filling the room. "Ready for this?"

Lisa took Jordan's coffee order and disappeared.

Abby gulped. Then opened her mouth to speak. When no words came out, she closed it again. Okay, she hadn't been expecting this. She blew out a small breath, her heart still kicking in her chest. She took another deep breath. Calm.

In front of her, Jordan was scouring the room, an odd look on her face. "What's that smell?" she whispered. "It's like some flowers farted."

That broke the tension. Abby's heart burst. "I think it's that candle." She pointed.

Jordan eyed it. "Is it okay to blow it out?" Jordan didn't wait for permission. She blew the candle out.

What had Abby done in her life before Jordan?

"No Delta yet?"

Abby shook her head. "She's bailed, so it's just me, you, and Lisa."

Jordan gave her a concerned look. "That's a shame, but we'll cope. I'm looking forward to it already." She eyed Abby. "You look gorgeous today, by the way. Excited. Ready."

Abby blushed, casting her gaze to the floor. Her excitement

had nothing to do with the dress. "You look more excited than me."

"I'm just happy today. Spotify played one of my very favourite tracks, and it's made me feel energised." She jigged from foot to foot. "Do you remember the song, *Drops of Jupiter*?"

Abby nodded. "I love that song."

Jordan grinned wider. "Me, too. Whenever I hear it, it takes me back, you know? To when I had my first girlfriend and I was in love for the first time." A look crossed her face as she regarded Abby. "You of all people must know that feeling. You're just about to get married. That feeling of love when it gets so caught in your chest that you can hardly breathe. When you just want to bottle it up and save it, because you know that first flush doesn't last forever. But it's so precious while it does. That song sums it up for me."

When Jordan's gaze settled back on her, Abby had to grind her teeth together to stop herself fidgeting too much.

Jordan was gay. Or at least bisexual. Queer. Whatever label she wanted to use. She was also blushing furiously all of a sudden. Which only made Abby's mind jump to what Jordan might look like after she'd orgasmed.

*She had to get a grip.*

Jordan cleared her throat, rubbing her hands together.

"Are you ready to say yes to the dress?"

Abby nodded. "I'm ready."

\* \* \*

Abby drew the curtain across quickly, and disappeared behind it.

The clatter of the curtain track sounded like Jordan's mind, about to fly off the rail. Jordan's hands went to her face to rub up and down. She couldn't do that, as it would mess up her make-up.

She dropped her hands, and shook her head.

She'd just come out to Abby. She hoped Abby was cool with it. Yes, she had a gay maid of honour, but you just never knew. Maybe her quota for gay bridesmaids stopped at one. Jordan hoped Abby realised not all lesbians were as flaky as her best friend, who was proving to be a terrible maid of honour. Of course, Jordan had seen it before. But even she was mad at Delta today. Jordan could really have done with Delta's presence to stop her fixating on Abby's hourglass figure.

The good news? Abby was about to get into a bridal gown. If there was anything that would cool Jordan's feelings it was a big, fluffy white dress. She'd never found wedding dresses sexy in the least, and had no idea why anyone else did, either. White suited just about nobody. Match it with a tiara and satin shoes, and Jordan was out.

"Shit." That was Abby's voice from behind the cream curtain.

Jordan got up and hovered outside, flexing her toes in her shoes. "Everything okay?"

Abby poked her head out. Her shoulders were naked.

Jordan kept her gaze at eye level.

"It's just, I'm wearing the wrong bra for one of these dresses. One of them is an off-the-shoulder number, and I forgot to bring my strapless bra." Abby's fingers tightened around the curtain.

Something inside Jordan clenched. She ignored it.

"You think they have one here?"

Jordan sucked on her top lip. "They might, but I'm not sure I'd want to put on a second-hand bra. You want me to get you one? I know the M&S lingerie department like the back of my hand." There were perks to her flatmate, and the shop was just around the corner. "Nude and strapless, right?"

Abby nodded. "Would you? That would be a lifesaver. I really want to see it as it'll be on the day."

"That's my job, right?" Jordan gave her a grin. "What are you? A 32D?" She felt the blush hit her cheeks almost instantaneously. Did that sound like she'd been checking out Abby's tits? Because she hadn't, she'd just taken a normal interest. Okay, perhaps a greater interest than the average person on the street. But that was her job.

Abby held her gaze, an emotion flitting across her face Jordan couldn't quite pin down.

"Spot on. If you ever stop doing this job, you could always get a job as a bra consultant. Isn't that what they call them these days? Consultant rather than fitter?"

Guessing people's bra size was Jordan's super-power. If this business went tits-up, she could always fall back on tits. She twisted on one foot, tapping her pockets as was her habit to make sure she had her wallet. She did.

"Back in five. Don't go anywhere."

Abby smiled, still clutching the curtain in front of her. "I'm naked. I'm staying put."

Jordan didn't reply, trying to put that image out of her brain as she jogged out of the shop.

True to her word, she was back in ten minutes with a 32D nude, strapless bra. When she drew up outside Abby's changing room again, she hesitated. How was she meant to do this?

"Knock, knock," she said, even though there was nothing to knock her hand on. Sometimes her Britishness exasperated her.

Abby poked her head out, gratefully accepting the bra. "You really are the best," she said. "I don't think Delta would have jumped to my aid like you just did. She couldn't even make it here in the first place."

Jordan gave a gentle shrug. "That's why I'm here." She sat on the biscuit-coloured sofa outside the changing rooms, trying to regulate her breathing.

Nerves jangled throughout her body.

This wasn't like her. Jordan was calm and collected around brides. It was her job.

It didn't work around Abby.

*Jordan* didn't work as she should around Abby.

She wanted Abby to like her.

Because Jordan liked Abby.

*She was attracted to Abby.*

She shook her head.

She had no time to be attracted to Abby.

The curtain being drawn back interrupted her thoughts. Jordan looked up.

Her right leg started jigging up and down. A bubble of warmth swelled in her chest, then burst, dripping down her body.

Yep, she was totally in control.

But godammit, Abby looked hot.

A hot bride.

This was new and unwelcome territory.

Abby's dress came in at the waist, and puffed out from there, with layers of frills. Jordan should not be finding this attractive. But it had nothing to do with the dress, did it?

Jordan cleared her throat and jumped to her feet.

When her gaze connected with Abby's, she saw doubt. It was her job to fix that.

She swatted aside her inappropriate feelings, and flipped into professional mode.

"You're not looking sure about this one." Not a gamble to say, as Abby's face was currently twisted into a frown. "What don't you like?"

Abby stared at Jordan, then stepped back in front of her changing room mirror. "It's just a bit... busy? I mean, I still like it, but something is off." She ran her hands up and down her front.

Jordan tried not to follow them.

Abby's hands settled on her flat stomach as she turned one way, then the other, looking at the dress from all angles in the 360-degree mirrors set up in the spacious changing rooms.

"If you're not feeling it, try on the other one. You had two choices, right?"

Abby nodded. "Marcus told me to buy them both and hang the expense. But now I'm worried. What if I don't like either of them? What then?"

Jordan walked over and stood next to her, trying not to breathe her in, and failing. Abby was quickly turning into one of her most favourite smells in the world.

"You chose these two out of many options. You'll love one of them, trust me. Try the other one, but if that doesn't do it, I think this one looks amazing on you." For once in her professional life, Jordan wasn't lying.

Abby turned, her gaze settling on Jordan. "You do?"

"I do. You look incredible."

Abby blushed. "Thanks." She waited until Jordan stepped back, then pulled the curtain.

Jordan sat back down, recovering her poise, hoping she'd been as professional as possible. A few minutes later, her right leg started jigging up and down again.

"Jordan?" Abby pulled the curtain back on dress number two.

"Yes?" But the words stuck in her throat when she saw Abby. Because if dress number one had been a solid choice, dress number two was a knock-out. Fitted, with minimal beading on the front, and exquisite lace scattered across it. This dress had Hollywood glamour stamped through it. It helped that it had a Hollywood-style bride inside it, too.

Abby raised her arm, showing off her toned bicep. Was that from all the golf? Jordan made a mental note to do some extra press-ups this week.

"I'm having trouble getting the zip done all the way up. Could you give me a hand?"

Jordan walked up behind her, trying to ignore her racing heartbeat. Despite everything, her hands were steady as she grasped the zip on Abby's dress and tugged it upwards. The dress fitted perfectly. As Jordan finished, her hand grazed Abby's bare back.

Jordan stilled. She flicked her eyes upwards, and caught

Abby's gaze in the mirror. Had she gasped slightly when Jordan touched her?

Whether she had or not, Jordan was still standing motionless, expression trained on Abby. The moment sat between them, pulsing.

Abby was giving her a weird look.

It was one Jordan had seen before.

A mix of want, but also frustration. She'd glimpsed it before in her life. But never with a bride.

Jordan didn't look away for a few more moments, trying to work it out.

She must be mistaken.

Abby was getting married.

To a man.

She was simply getting carried away.

Eventually, Jordan moved her hands and stepped back, giving Abby a wide smile, hoping it smothered all the feelings rampaging around her body.

She shook her head. There was nothing there. It was all in her head. Jordan had to sort her head out and do her job.

"Marcus is going to go berserk when he sees you in this." The words came out of her mouth sounding sure, measured. Professional Jordan was back. Besides, she knew it was true, because it was exactly what had gone through her head when Abby had stepped out in her dress. Now, seeing her close-up, looking into her brown eyes, being near enough to reach out and trace Abby's smile with the tips of her fingers... Well, she could only imagine how Marcus would feel.

Because Abby was marrying Marcus, not Jordan.

Abby cleared her throat, giving Jordan an unsteady grin.

She walked out into the changing area, twirling once, twice, then back again. In this dress, she twirled with confidence. Jordan already knew this was the one.

"It looks pretty good, doesn't it? I'm not quick to give myself compliments, but this dress…" she trailed off. "It makes me think of long, hot summers, of being barefoot on the beach." She glanced up at Jordan, but then quickly away. "It makes me happy."

Jordan nodded. She could see that. "Just like Marcus will," she replied.

At her words, Abby stilled and glanced up at her. Something in her eyes made Jordan shudder.

Abby nodded. "Yes, just like that."

# Chapter Twelve

It was the night before they were due to fly, and Jordan was doing press-ups in the lounge. She'd been to the gym that morning, too. And the day before. Seeing Abby's toned physique up close had spurred her into action. If the bride was that cut, the very least her bridesmaid could do was support that. Although, admittedly, it might be a little late for Jordan to gain ultimate definition in ten days. But she could try her best.

Karen walked in carrying two crumpets on a plate. Jordan didn't even have to look to know they'd be slathered with butter. They were Karen's favourite. Or, as she liked to say, her downfall. She sat on the sofa, curling one leg underneath her, assessing Jordan silently. The only sound was Jordan's faint grunts as she lowered herself down, then up. When Karen finished, she put her plate on the wooden coffee table. She waited until Jordan collapsed on their wooden floor after her final set before she spoke.

"So tell me again you don't like this woman."

"Shut up." The floorboards weren't very comfortable. She sat up and dusted off her hands, before swivelling onto her feet and then standing. Jordan stretched her arms above her head, in a bid to put an end to this conversation.

"I feel like I should come on this hen weekend, to protect you from yourself."

"I can handle it, I'm a pro."

"You're doing press-ups without me nagging. You're going to the gym of your own accord. This is not the Jordan I know and love. You've even started buying kale. That's when I know things are bad."

Jordan bent forward, touching her toes with her fingertips. "I'm just trying to be healthy, that's all. You've been telling me to do this for years. I thought you'd be happy." She eyed Karen as she came back upright.

"I am. I'm all for it. I'm just questioning the reason, that's all." She paused, pushing her fringe out of her eyes. "How long are you away for?"

"Four days. Friday to Monday. The itinerary is packed, too. I get to flex my French in Cannes, plus the whole party will fall in love with my supreme organisation skills."

Karen paused before she spoke. "Four days is a long time to be in a confined space with someone you're developing feelings for."

Jordan flopped down on the sofa beside Karen, covering her face with her forearm as she blew out. "I am not developing feelings for Abby. Plus, I'm not an animal. I don't act on my feelings. I've liked plenty of women before and not acted on it. I mean, that's basically the story of my life. You remember. You've been there for most of it."

That brought a smile to Karen's face. "You're not wrong there."

"So I don't know why you're stressing. I am the world's worst at telling someone how I feel. At doing anything to move romance forward. Everything that's ever happened in my life romantically has been the result of an accident, or someone else taking the lead. And that's not going to happen this weekend, is it? Not on Abby's hen weekend."

"You have a point." Karen nudged Jordan with her elbow.

"If anything, I'm still puzzled why she's marrying Marcus. I mean, he seems absolutely lovely, but I wouldn't put the two of them together, you know?"

"He's loaded."

Jordan nodded. "He is. But his money also brings issues. Plus, I wouldn't put Abby into the gold-digger bracket. She's got a good enough job herself."

Karen shrugged. "Biological clock ticking?"

"More likely." Jordan blew out a breath. "It just seems a shame for her to get married if she's not totally into him."

Karen gave her a look. "How many brides have truly been into the guy they were marrying? From what you've told me, not many. Maybe you think Abby is different to the others, but in this instance, she's not. She's looking for status, financial security, and a father for her child. Even in this day and age, women have to think about these things."

Jordan shook her head. "True enough. Depressing, isn't it?"

"No argument here." Karen yawned, putting a hand to her mouth. "But anyway, let's steer the subject away from off-limits Abby and back to you. When was the last time you had a shag? Was it that woman you met on Tinder?"

Jordan frowned. "Not that it makes any difference, but yes. However, I'm not planning on sleeping with anyone in Cannes. I'm working."

"I know you are. But maybe when you get back, you could open yourself up a little more." She held up her hands. "Before you go off on one with me, I know you don't do relationships. You've been hurt before. One-night stands are easier in your line of work. I get it. But you're getting older. Time ticks on. Take it from me, it's kinda nice to have a relationship. I'm sure you had some good moments in ones in your past, didn't you?"

Jordan slumped. "A couple. But they all worked out the same in the end, didn't they? Heartbreak. Me losing my home and some of my possessions. They take up too much time and bring too much pain. I'll stick to one-night stands. But not until this job is over." The thought of having a one-night stand with Abby made all the hairs on the back of her neck stand on end.

She could never imagine that. Abby was not your one-night stand kind of girl.

Neither was Jordan when she was around her. She buried that thought.

Karen got up, then reappeared a few moments later, throwing a Marks & Spencer bag at her.

"What's this?" Jordan opened the bag and pulled out a red bikini. As she unfurled it, her eyes widened. "Who's this for?"

"You. I knew you wouldn't buy it for yourself, but you were eyeing it up the other day in the shop, and so I got it for you. You want to look the part in your fancy Cannes villa, don't you?"

Jordan gulped. She hadn't stopped to think too much about the poolside activity, but now she was realising she was going to be seeing Abby in a bikini too, most likely.

That thought sent her pulse into overdrive. "Good job I'm doing those sit-ups, because this bikini leaves little to the imagination."

"It's a bikini. It's kinda the point."

Jordan peered into the bag, and brought out some black lacy knickers, along with a matching bra. "Are these for me too?" She held them up like they were part of a police forensics operation.

Karen nodded. "They are. Free samples from work, so I got us both some." She leaned into Jordan. "Put these on and you'll feel invincible. Nobody else has to see them. But if anyone does, they'll be jealous. Or about to rip them off. Just make sure it's not the bride, and you're golden. Didn't you say the maid of honour was gay?"

"She is. And recently heartbroken. I know where your brain's going, but stop right there."

"You say recently heartbroken. I say single." Karen put air quotes around 'recently heartbroken' and 'single'.

"That's why you should never be a matchmaker." Jordan raised a single eyebrow in her direction.

"A gay best friend. They should do a movie about that. Is she fit?"

"Not my type."

"You have a type?"

Jordan gave her a look. "My type is available. Delta is not that. She's still snivelling over her last girlfriend. Plus, I'm not exactly her favourite person."

Karen tapped her nose with her index finger. "But isn't that how all the best romances start off? You hate each other, but then grow to love each other over time. I see promise in this one. She could be your French Fancy." Karen chuckled at her own joke.

"Do you lie in bed thinking of these jokes?" But Jordan was smiling. She couldn't help it.

"Focus on the maid of honour, not the bride. Got it?"

Jordan stood up, stretching out her arms as she did. "This weekend is business. Abby is getting married in less than two weeks. *Pas de problème*, as the French say. This is Abby's last hurrah, and I'm going to be there to make sure it's one she never forgets."

Karen stood, walked up to Jordan, and pressed the lingerie bag to her chest. "That, my gorgeous friend, is my worry."

# Chapter Thirteen

Abby climbed the steps up to the plane door. A private, smaller plane than she was used to travelling on, the door was located at the back. They were greeted by the steward, Gavin, and their pilot, Michelle. Both were around her age, impeccably suited and booted. Michelle even had a peaked cap. Gavin, meanwhile, had perfectly styled eyebrows.

"I hope you enjoy the flight," Michelle told her with a wide smile as she shook her hand.

Abby was pretty sure she wouldn't. Her stomach was already tight as she boarded, nausea a constant friend. She was feeling woozy, too. She hadn't let her hatred of flying stop her from getting on a plane, but it was never a happy occasion. Her ideal holiday would be somewhere in the UK. Or somewhere she could get to by boat or train. She loved the Eurostar. She'd tried to persuade Marcus to honeymoon in Paris. To no avail. He wanted to go to the Maldives. He thought everyone wanted to do that for their honeymoon.

On the handful of flights they'd been on together, Marcus was far too full-on when they boarded. He smothered Abby, asking if she was okay every two seconds. He didn't understand she just needed space, along with gentle reassurance.

He didn't understand how to make take-off and landing

as easy as it could be, just by holding her hand and being there.

*He didn't understand Abby.*

She pushed that thought down the back of her mental sofa, then turned her focus to Michelle. Long, dark hair, matched with long, dark lashes. Abby's stomach rolled again as she shook Michelle's hand.

"Thanks, Michelle," she said. "And it seems fitting we've got a female pilot for a hen weekend." She'd never seen one before and it was kind of a thrill. But whatever the gender, Abby's rules still stood: please get us there in one piece and don't let us die.

However, when she glanced back to Delta, it was all Abby could do not to burst out laughing. Delta's mouth might as well have been hanging open. From the look on her face, she was trying so hard not to punch the air and whoop out loud.

Abby didn't blame her. Who didn't find pilots sexy?

As they walked up the aisle of the plane with its two neat rows of seats, Abby spotted what was on them. A Tunnock's Tea Cake and a can of Irn Bru. Happiness burst inside her. She glanced back at Jordan, who was busy checking her phone. Abby was picking up a weird vibe from her. She was cooler than normal. Aloof. She shouldn't read anything into it. Jordan might have slept badly. Or she might just be concerned about the weekend.

That was probably it.

Putting the thought out of her mind, Abby looked to Delta, who gave her a massive grin.

"Is this your doing?" Abby held up a Tea Cake in one hand, a can of Irn Bru in the other.

Delta shook her head. "It's not. This is all down to your other bridesmaid. The one who's known you the longest." She inclined her head towards Jordan, raising an eyebrow.

Jordan walked around Abby, and put her hand luggage in the overhead locker as they were in the front row, before turning.

Abby was still holding up the Scottish items from her childhood.

For the first time that day, Jordan gave her a smile.

Damn, she had impressively straight, white teeth.

"This was you?" Abby couldn't quite believe her fake bridesmaid had gone to such trouble. Scrap that, had even known this about her.

Jordan shrugged. "Of course. Wasn't this what we lived on in school in Glasgow? I thought it might take you back to the playground, sitting in the summer sunshine, making daisychains."

Abby stopped short, staring at her. How did she know that?

"I miss Tunnock's Teacakes," Mum said. "Good call, Jordan!"

"What the hell are these?" asked Marcus's cousin, Arielle.

Mum put a hand to her mouth in response. "These, my dear, are Scottish heritage. An orange fizzy drink made of girders, and a chocolate biscuit. If you haven't had breakfast, this is the perfect pick-me-up. So much sugar, you'll be buzzing."

Arielle didn't look convinced.

Abby glanced around the plane, to the rest of their party holding onto Jordan's thoughtful gift. "You're good at this shit, you know that?" She leaned in as she spoke, breathing in Jordan's scent. She remembered it from the dress fitting the other day.

Their gazes met, and Jordan stilled. "I've done my research. I want our story to be watertight. I thought this would be a good way to begin."

Abby nodded. "It certainly is."

Jordan dropped her gaze, then gestured to the locker. "Need anything putting up?"

Abby handed over her Louis Vuitton carry-on.

Jordan stowed it, before turning to Abby, her face puzzled. "Are you sitting next to me?"

"If that's okay?" She'd decided to put Mum and Delta on the opposite side, so all four key players could be up front and centre.

"Whatever you want, it's your weekend."

And there it was again. Business Jordan. Not happy, smiling Jordan.

She shook herself. She was probably reading far too much into it.

"White leather. Very rock star, isn't it?" Gloria stroked the seats with a grin. "And did you see the loos? They're huge for plane toilets. Three times the size and so plush."

"Whose plane is this?" That was Delta, still giving Jordan a bit of side-eye.

"Family friend of the Montgomerys. They've given us the plane, complete with Captain Michelle and Steward Gavin. There are definitely some plus points to marrying into money." They weren't going to be a full flight today, only taking up 10 of the possible 30 seats. However, Michelle had already told them she was picking up a party of 25 hens from Cannes today and bringing them back. That made Abby feel better about her carbon footprint.

"Are we getting champagne, too?"

Abby smiled. "You can have anything you want. You're the mother of the bride."

Gloria clapped her hands. "I'm so looking forward to this already." She leaned forward, half hanging out of her seat. "Are you going to spend the flight fixing everything on that big spreadsheet of yours, Jordan? I saw it when we were having coffee. I've never seen a hen weekend look like a corporate trip abroad before."

Jordan smiled. It was a little forced, but it was there.

"Abby loves a spreadsheet, too," Mum added. "You're a match made in heaven."

She was never going to stop embarrassing her, was she?

"I'm just trying to make this trip the smoothest ever, Gloria," Jordan replied. "But of course, don't think your help in the run-up — or Delta's — hasn't had a huge impact on the plans."

Abby bit down a smile. When Jordan went into charm offensive, she was one of the best Abby had ever witnessed. What was she like when she was going after a woman? Did she have a spreadsheet then? Or was it purely based on instinct and attraction?

Abby glanced at Jordan, her own attraction tapping her on the shoulder. She jumped up, going down the plane, making sure all the hens were fine.

Her cousin Taran was sat beside Abby's old friend Nikita. They were followed by Marcus's cousins, Arielle and Martha, plus Abby's friends from university, Erin and Frankie. Ten in all. It wasn't a big hen party. She'd been on a couple that had over 20 people, and Abby had vowed never to do that. A night out in London with a nice meal would have done her fine, but it was Marcus and Marjorie who'd insisted on this, coming up with the plane, the villa, the contacts. And, of course, Jordan.

She walked back to her seat and sat down.

"Okay?" Jordan said, as if noticing Abby for the first time that day.

Abby nodded, goose bumps breaking out across her skin. This was really inconvenient. Being around Marcus wasn't this distracting. Being around anyone else wasn't as distracting as Jordan.

"I will be, once we take off. I'm a bit of a nervous flier. It was one of the reasons Marcus arranged this flight, so I wouldn't stress quite as much."

"Is it working?"

"I'll tell you when we take off."

Michelle walked past them, before stopping and turning around. "Would you like to sit up-front with me for any of the journey?" she asked Abby. "You're very welcome to come in after take-off."

Abby's stomach rolled again. "I don't think so," she said. "Just get us there safe."

Michelle gave her a salute. "I'll do my best. And if you change your mind, let me know."

Abby gritted her teeth as she settled back in her chair. Even the thought of going into the cockpit sent her pulse racing. Seeing the entirety of the sky and how the plane defied gravity just by the will of a friendly pilot? She was pretty sure that would only add to her flying issues, not heal them. She gripped the seat arms and closed her eyes. It was going to be fine. The plane wasn't going to crash with her and all the people she loved the most on it.

Although if it did, at least then she wouldn't have to marry Marcus.

Her eyes sprang open and she sat forward, clutching her chest. Where the fuck had that thought come from? She took a deep breath, as Jordan's worried face hovered into view.

"What happened? Are you okay? You jerked forward so swiftly then."

Abby shook her head. "I'm fine. Just nervous, that's all." Not questioning everything about this wedding one little bit.

No siree.

Not her.

Jordan's concerned gaze didn't shift. "I wish you'd told me before. I would have brought something to chill you out."

Abby tilted her head. "Like what?"

Jordan stuck out her bottom lip. "I dunno. Valium?"

"Is that even legal?"

Jordan gave Abby a shrug. "If you wanted Valium, I'd have got some."

"Too late now." She paused, looking down the plane. "Some booze would help."

Jordan unclicked her seatbelt. "I'll get you something." She stowed her laptop overhead.

"Aren't you meant to have your seatbelt on?" Abby asked.

"I'll be fine." Jordan headed down the aisle.

Abby gulped. She closed her eyes.

A hand on her arm made her jolt. Abby opened her eyes, as the plane began to taxi.

There went her stomach again.

"You all right, love? I know this isn't your favourite part." Mum's green eyes were kind, just like always.

Abby nodded. "I will be, once we're airborne. Plus, Jordan's gone to get me a drink. It should help."

Mum twisted, looking down the aisle. "How did you ever cope without Jordan?"

Abby wasn't sure.

Moments later, Jordan slid back into her seat, clipping her seatbelt into place. In the aisle, Gavin greeted them, then began going through the safety drills.

Abby glanced her way.

Another grin from Jordan as she slipped something into Abby's hand. She leaned in, her lips stopping just shy of Abby's ear. "I wasn't sure what to get you, so I went for mini bottles of vodka and whisky. Both will give you a relaxing jolt that should settle your nerves. But you're going to have to swig it secretly, as you're not meant to be drinking right now."

Abby's brain processed the words, and she nodded. She tried to ignore the whirl of her senses after Jordan's hot breath had piped into her ears, but she didn't quite manage it. She waited for Gavin to demonstrate blowing into the top-up tube for the life jacket, and how to locate your light.

When he was finished, Abby gulped back the vodka, wincing as the neat alcohol hit her taste buds. Jeez, alcohol tasted bad on its own. She tried not to imagine the vodka stripping her insides like dried paint from her fingertips, and instead focused on the dull buzz that slowly began to seep through her. She pocketed the whisky in her handbag, and tried to recall how to wrap the life jacket ties around her waist. Who was she kidding? If the plane crashed, she was a goner.

"Gavin, take your seat," said Michelle over the PA. Gavin promptly disappeared.

This was it, they were about to take off. Abby's least favourite part of flying. She tugged on her seatbelt to make sure it was secure, then glanced Jordan's way.

Jordan gave her a smile, then took Abby's hand in hers and settled their joined limbs on their shared armrest.

Abby almost stopped breathing, fixing her eyes on their hands, before deciding it was too much. She snapped her eyes shut.

"I hope everyone's ready to fly, because the runway is within sight. Have a great flight everyone." That was Michelle again, before the PA snapped off.

There were whoops from behind.

Abby couldn't work out who they were from, and she didn't much care. All she could hear was the roar of her heartbeat in her ears. The wobble of her body as every muscle she possessed clamped shut. She was on a plane and she was holding Jordan's hand. The strangest part about it? It was having the desired effect.

Jordan was a calming influence.

As the plane gathered speed and lifted off the tarmac, Jordan squeezed her hand tighter still, and Abby put all of her focus on that, and not on the fact they were now airborne in a metal tube. Abby glanced across at Jordan, catching a glimpse of the outside world getting smaller as the plane climbed.

Big mistake.

She took a deep breath, pulling her eyes to the front. But all the while, Jordan didn't let go of her hand, and didn't say a word.

The exact thing she'd always wanted a partner to do, and they never had.

Jordan understood her.

That wasn't lost on Abby.

# Chapter Fourteen

They were staying at Villa Francois, and it was just as high-end as Jordan had imagined. Not that she was surprised. She'd been to Marcus's family home. To Marcus's house on the edge of their estate. Met his mother. Seen how well laundered Marcus's shirts were. There was a precision and order to the Montgomery family. This wasn't their house, but Abby had told her it was the house of some good friends who had a love for modern stylings. Those stylings had been very evident when their minibus rolled into the spacious driveway and the group saw the house.

The villa sat in the hills of Super Cannes, the exclusive neighbourhood where all the rich people played. Close to Cannes and the beach, the property came with staff, along with floor-to-ceiling windows where it counted. Plus, of course, the back of the house, the pool and terraces overlooked the incredible Cote d'Azur, its wide expanse glittering below. The inviting pool was big enough to do laps in. There were multiple jacuzzis. There were enough striped, cushioned loungers underneath crisp white umbrellas for everyone. Jordan had no doubt the towels would be extra-fluffy, too. This was a hen do where no detail had been spared.

The towels had been put away by the staff, and the hen party was now back at the villa after the first night out, which had been deemed a success. Relief slid down Jordan as she walked onto the terrace overlooking the pool, tastefully lit with low lights and candles. Below them, the exclusive neighbourhood glittered, and the French Riveria air wrapped itself around them. The air even smelled French, if that could possibly be a thing.

"I don't know about everyone else, but I'm stuffed." Abby patted her non-existent belly as she approached the large outdoor table, where Jordan held out a chair for her. She was wearing cute culotte trousers, a green top and wispy chiffon scarf, not unlike a 1950s socialite. The effect wasn't lost on Jordan.

Abby gave her a smile as she sat. "Thank you, long-lost bridesmaid."

Jordan performed a curtsy. "Anything for the bride-to-be," she replied. "Can I get you a drink?"

Someone walked up behind her. "Did someone say drink?" Gloria's Scottish accent had got thicker as the evening had worn on. "Have the staff gone home?"

Jordan nodded. "They clock off at nine. Seeing as it's after ten, we're on our own. But as a bridesmaid, I'm at Abby's beck and call."

"You hear that, Delta?" Abby shouted, leaning back in her seat. "Jordan is offering to get me whatever I want because she's my bridesmaid."

A hoot of laughter from Delta as she appeared on the terrace, along with the rest of the hen party. "That's because she's paid…"

Jordan's stomach dropped as the words died on Delta's tongue. She swivelled and eyeballed Delta, but she was pretty sure Delta couldn't see her in the dim light. Was she going to give the game away on day one?

Delta walked towards them, the rest of the hens behind her. "She's paying the price for deserting you for all these years. I've got Abby a million glasses of wine in the intervening couple of decades that Jordan's been absent. She's got a lot of time to make up for."

Nice save, Delta. Jordan clicked a finger and pointed it in her direction. "She's got a point. If I get white wine and some glasses, will everyone drink some?"

Cheers from the group was Jordan's cue to go to the kitchen.

"Where's Taran?" Abby asked. "She could help."

Gloria rolled her eyes. "She's chatting to Ryan." They'd only been away for 12 hours, but it was already apparent that Taran and her husband couldn't go a couple of hours without speaking. "I'll come with you," Gloria added.

They got to the kitchen, its shiny white surfaces cleared of this afternoon's detritus.

"God bless those wonderful staff," Gloria said. "We must tip them well."

"Agreed." Jordan busied herself getting white wine from the fully stocked wine fridge, while Gloria grabbed the glasses. They'd only been together a day, but Jordan and Gloria were already working as a well-oiled machine.

"I just wanted to say, too," Gloria added, as they put their goods on a couple of metallic trays. "Thanks for doing all you've done so far. I know you've really taken a weight from Abby's shoulders and even made her start to enjoy the run-up to her wedding. A few weeks ago, I didn't think that was ever going to happen."

Jordan didn't meet Gloria's gaze. "I'm just doing my job."

Gloria put a hand on her arm. "I know, but you're doing more than that. You're making Abby relax and that's a rare thing. Before meeting Marcus, she was always so focused on her job. If it was one she loved, I'd be happy for her." Gloria frowned, tilting her head to one side. "I was hoping she'd get excited about the wedding with time, but it's only since you've come on board that she's really started to have a sparkle in her eye." She squeezed Jordan's arm. "So thank you. Seriously. I just want to see my only daughter happy."

This time Jordan did meet her gaze. "That's what I want, too."

When they got back out to the terrace, Taran had returned to the group and was talking about her recent wedding. "Abby was such a star on the hen weekend and on the wedding day when I was having a meltdown. I wanted to do the same for her, but it seems like she's covered, with Delta and now Jordan who's just materialised out of thin air!"

There wasn't a hint of disbelief in her voice, which allowed Jordan to breathe easy.

It wasn't everyone else she had to worry about believing their story.

It was Delta blowing their cover.

"I'm just thrilled we reconnected in time." Jordan put her tray on the table. "When we were little girls and talking about getting married, we always promised we'd have each other as our bridesmaids. But after nearly three decades apart, I never thought it would happen." Why did this story seem more real than the others Jordan had taken part in?

Jordan poured the wine, passed the glasses around, then sat beside Gloria.

"I'm thrilled you did, too. You always were a good influence on Abby." Gloria patted Jordan's hand.

Jordan was pretty sure Gloria wouldn't be saying that if she knew the full extent of Jordan's thoughts over the past couple of weeks. When Jordan glanced up at Abby, her cheeks were flushed, and when she caught Jordan's gaze, she looked away. Why was Abby looking shifty, too? She had nothing to look shifty about.

"Mind you, Abby's always been a model daughter, which just goes to prove, the apple does sometimes fall very far from the tree."

The group laughed at that.

"I dunno, Gloria," Delta said. "You should have seen her in her 20s. She was a bit of a hellraiser. Especially at uni."

"That much is true!" shouted Erin, her face split with a grin.

Gloria shook her head, waving a hand in the air. "There are some things a mother should never know, and what their daughter got up to at university is definitely one of them."

When Jordan glanced at Abby again, she was shaking her head, shooting Delta an evil look. Jordan chuckled. She'd like to have seen Abby as a hellraiser.

"As for me, unlike Abby, I didn't get my choice of husband right first time. I was flattered by my first husband's attention, and he was a lovely man. Also, I was pregnant, and it was what you did. I had a miscarriage before we got hitched, but we still went through with it. Then we had Abby. It took me a year to work out that behind his dazzling smile and his money, we didn't have that much in common. Second time around though, there's never been a minute when I doubted him.

"Martin and me just click. When that happens, everything that's gone before is suddenly cast aside. I'd be lying if I said that when I met Marcus, I didn't have my doubts. Because he's got money, and he's got charm. The two things I fell for with my first marriage. But what Marcus has also got is heart. A big one. He's generous, kind, and I know he loves my daughter. As a mother, I couldn't ask for anything more." She held up her glass, waiting for everyone else to follow suit. "A toast to what's going to be a fabulous weekend. To Abby, and to Marcus who is currently wandering the streets of Dublin on his stag do." Her eyes roamed the group with a devilish grin. "We know who won out on location, don't we, ladies?"

Clapping all round.

"But seriously. May your smiles be wide and your worries small. Abby and Marcus!"

A chorus of 'Abby and Marcus!' rang out in the air.

Taran turned to Jordan. "I'm interested, though. Has Abby missed the boat on your wedding, Jordan? Could she still be your bridesmaid, and then both your childhood dreams could really come true?"

Jordan ground her teeth together. She'd been asked this before at previous weddings with previous brides.

"She hasn't missed the boat," Jordan replied. "I'm still

single, so I'd be honoured to have Abby as my bridesmaid when the time is right."

Their gazes met one more time, but this time, Jordan didn't look away.

Abby held up her glass, licking her lips. "I look forward to being at your beck and call sometime in the future."

\* \* \*

Two hours later, and most of the party had gone to their rooms. Abby was clearing glasses, even though Jordan had told her to leave it.

"I honestly can't believe Mum and Delta have both gone to bed this early on night one."

"It's a marathon not a sprint, like they said." Although Jordan was surprised, too. She'd never seen a first night where everyone was in bed at just gone midnight. It was a modern-day hen weekend miracle. She would have to write this one up in her journal. If she had a journal.

When they'd taken everything to the kitchen, Jordan came out to do a final sweep of the terrace. Satisfied it was clear, she walked to the edge, stopping at the glass wall that came up to her hip. She leaned her arms on the top, and admired the view over the water once more. After such a full-on day, it was nice to soak in a few moments of solitude. Seconds later, Jordan's skin prickled with sensation. Her solitude was short-lived. Not that she minded. Not when the one piercing her bubble was Abby.

Jordan breathed her in, her pulse beginning to sprint, even though externally she was calm. She hadn't drunk anything tonight, because this was work. She'd had a glass at all times, and she'd played the part of the tipsy bridesmaid, but the glass had remained full. She was glad she had a clear head.

"Gorgeous, isn't it?" Abby's smoky voice thrummed through her.

"It really is."

Jordan looked to her right.

Abby's dark eyes flashed at her. "What are you thinking about?"

*You. How you make me feel. The excruciating heat of you standing next to me.* That's what Jordan wanted to say. But she didn't.

"Just soaking all this in. It's a gorgeous place to be for the weekend." She glanced at Abby again. She'd taken her scarf off, exposing her neck and cleavage.

"Even if it is work? I'm sure this is nothing out of the ordinary for you."

Jordan gave her a smile, a spark lighting inside her. "You're anything but ordinary." Then she looked away swiftly. She hoped she hadn't overstepped the mark.

"I could say the same about you," Abby replied.

Jordan's muscles clenched, then unclenched as she flicked her eyes to Abby. What did that mean?

"Have you left anyone behind this weekend who's missing you? You don't seem to have anyone special in your life, but then again, you might not have told me." When Jordan looked her way, Abby raised an eyebrow. "You did say I could ask you anything about your life, so this is me playing that card, by the way."

Jordan had said that. She shook her head. "There's nobody,

it's just me. I haven't had a girlfriend for a long time. This job keeps me too busy." Jordan had never discussed this with a bride before. Most brides were too busy thinking about their wedding and themselves.

Abby was not most brides.

"Plus, I'm not sure many girlfriends would be all that happy about me disappearing for weeks on end. Or spending so much time with beautiful women and getting close to them. It's enough to test even the most secure of relationships." She'd never admitted that to anyone before, either. If she wanted a relationship, she might have to give up this job. From March to September, it owned her.

Abby twisted her body around, frowning at Jordan. "Wait, you've been doing this three years, and you haven't had a relationship that whole time?"

Jordan shook her head. "Nope."

"And before that?"

Jordan stilled, flicking through the cards of her life. When it came to relationships, they weren't stacked in her favour. Anna, Queen of Hearts. Yvette, Queen of Pain. Brianna, the Joker. She'd given months, sometimes years to those relationships. None of them had worked. All of them had left her heart on the floor.

"I haven't had the best luck with women." She said it like it meant nothing. "Let's just say that."

"It sounds like we're not so different when it comes to love. Before I met Marcus, I hadn't had a partner in a few years. I hadn't had my heart trampled. In fact, anything but." Abby shrugged. "Every man I got together with, the spark was never truly there. I always finished it in the end. But then

I stayed solo for a few years, and everyone was getting on my back to meet someone."

"So Marcus came along at just the right time?"

Abby gripped the glass wall with both hands, taking a small step back and dropping her head. Her hair fell forward. "He did. When he turned up at my office, I did a double-take. Then after we went out for dinner, it just happened. No drama." She shrugged. "Getting together with him was easy. There were no fireworks, no grand gestures. We just fell into each other. Our wedding felt inevitable."

"That's a good thing, right?"

Abby lifted her head and ran a hand through her hair. She didn't look so sure. "I guess so. But we don't have a relationship like Taran and Ryan. We live apart, and I don't have to speak to him all the time. Sometimes I wonder if I'm settling. That it's just my time of life to get married. If I've taken the easy road."

This conversation was a well-worn theme among her brides. "If Marcus is the easy road, perhaps it's one worth travelling?" She turned and leaned her bum on the glass wall, staring at Abby. *Damn, she was beautiful.* "He loves you, you love him, and you come from a basis of friendship. I'd say that counts for a lot."

Abby sucked in her cheeks. "So everyone tells me."

Jordan tried so hard not to stare at Abby's exposed neck. At the way the moonlight danced on her skin. But she failed. Desire lodged itself in her throat like a fishbone. She swallowed hard.

Abby stared at her, then shook her head. "But back to you. Much more fun." Her smile lit up the night. "Are you gay, bi, or something else?"

That was direct. "Card-carrying gay."

"What does the card say?"

Jordan smiled. "Come back in October when I'm done with weddings, then we can talk."

*Had she really just said that out loud? Like she was some kind of lothario?* She couldn't trust herself to say the right thing anymore.

Abby laughed. But was there hesitation in her tone, too? "I'm intrigued you haven't had a relationship for so long." Her face turned pensive. "Brings a whole new meaning to the term 'married to your job'."

"There's a certain irony." Jordan's heart was hammering in her chest. What she would give to wind the clock back 30 seconds.

"Doesn't it make a difference that the women you're getting close to are getting married?"

She wasn't making this easy, was she? "Of course. But the job involves long hours and lots of weekends. Plus, I have to be on-call 24/7. It doesn't leave much time for me. Or anybody else involved with me."

Abby nodded, processing that. "I apologise."

Jordan gave her a rueful smile. "Don't. Marcus is paying me well."

Abby nodded slowly. "But do you miss having someone?" Her eyes were back on Jordan.

Was there a right answer here? "Sometimes. It would be nice to have someone to crawl into bed with at night, even if I got home at 2am." Jordan imagined crawling into bed with Abby. She blinked. "You're about to get that with Marcus, which you must be looking forward to."

Abby turned her head skyward and didn't reply right away. "Sometimes I worry we won't like it, and perhaps we should have tried it out first. Most couples do."

Jordan knew they lived at separate addresses, which was unusual. "But there's some romance to it, right?"

Abby took a deep breath. "But is it weird? Have we not wanted to move in together for a reason?" She paused, glancing at Jordan, then shook her head. "You know what, ignore me. It's just last-minute nerves. Marcus is wonderful, and I'm a lucky woman to have found him. He's going to make a great husband and father."

Jordan didn't let her gaze linger on Abby. She'd seen these freak-outs before, and she knew the people responsible needed space. That's what she'd give Abby.

A good few moments slid by before she spoke again. "Last-minute nerves are par for the course. It'll all work out in the end."

\* \* \*

Abby nodded, but uncertainty flooded her system so hard, she was surprised she wasn't short-circuiting.

She'd had too much to drink, hadn't she? Why else was she blurting out her doubts to a stranger?

Only, Jordan wasn't a stranger anymore. She was almost a friend. A woman who'd walked into Abby's life and pierced her resolve where it was most vulnerable. Making Abby question not only her relationship with Marcus, but also her sexuality.

This wasn't in the weekend script. She was on her hen do, for goodness sake. This wasn't the time to be having such huge doubts. This was a time to focus on her future and on

Marcus. Not on feelings that had crept up on her, and were now unsettling her completely.

"I slept with a woman once." Abby closed her eyes. Really? After the promise she just made to herself, then that comes out of her mouth? Had any other bride ever told Jordan this? For some weird reason, Abby hoped she was the first.

Jordan licked her lips before replying. "I slept with a man once, too. I guess we're even."

Which made Abby smile. "You haven't done since?"

Jordan shook her head. "Once was enough. Just to see what all the fuss was about." She paused. "What about you?"

Abby nodded. "Same. At university. I went to a gay club with Delta, and I met a woman. We got talking. And I thought, why not? She was cute, and you only live once. There might have been some tequila involved, too."

A grin. "Ah, tequila. Fuelling life's key moments for decades."

"You could say that." Abby still recalled the absolute terror mixed with total elation of waking up the next morning, knowing she'd done something forbidden. Off limits. She'd never had that feeling with Marcus. It had scared her at the time. Now she longed to feel it once more. To be near to daring again.

To cross her carefully placed lines.

Step close to an electric current.

Once she said 'I do', everything was off limits.

Abby stared at Jordan. The crackle of possibility was there.

"Was tequila involved when you got together with Marcus?"

Abby shook her head. "Marcus doesn't like it. He says it usually ends in bad decisions being made. He's probably right."

Jordan's stare was intense, her eyes brooding in the moonlight. "What do you think?"

Abby moved her mouth left to right, then shrugged. Like the next sentence meant nothing. "I think that sometimes, you have to leave things to chance. Chance can lead you down a different path than you intended, but sometimes, it can be a fun one. A right one. I guess I'm worried that once I get married, those paths might be closed off to me."

What the hell was she saying?

Abby strode across to the other side of the terrace, then stopped and clutched the glass wall again. Putting some distance between her and Jordan was the right thing to do. She was too frightened to truly think about what all her thoughts meant. Why, every time she was on her own with Jordan, did her carefully planned life threaten to spin out of control?

The distance didn't last long. Within seconds, Jordan drew up alongside her, and all the desire Abby had been keeping so carefully under wraps began to seep out, trickling down her body like a leaky tap.

Godammit, she was attracted to Jordan. Abby really didn't need this. Not when her life was just about to be sorted.

But all those rational thoughts fled from her head when Jordan put a hand on the top of her arm.

Abby stopped breathing as all the blood in her body rushed south, to her groin.

What the hell did Jordan do to her? She made her forget

who she was. But also, Jordan made her dare to imagine what she could be.

"All these thoughts are perfectly normal. Getting married is a big deal. Making all these promises to one person. But Marcus loves you."

"I know," Abby said. "But what if I'm not meant to be with Marcus? What if I'm meant to be with someone completely different? Maybe even a woman?"

Jordan's hand rubbed up and down her arm, sending an arrow of lust straight to Abby's clit.

Abby closed her eyes for a second. Then she blew out a long breath, before pulling away from Jordan, to untangle them physically.

It was necessary, even though it had only been Jordan's fingers and her arm that had been touching.

That had been enough.

"You're going to be fine. Try to relax and enjoy your hen weekend. And my advice? Steer clear of tequila."

Jordan's accompanying smile cut right to Abby's core. Jordan left her exposed.

She shook her head, before folding her arms over her chest. "You're good at this, you know." There was one thing she still wanted to know. It was important, even though the reason was still foggy in her mind. "Have you had many brides confess they've slept with a woman?"

Jordan shook her head. "You're the first. I'm sure there have been others, because the law of averages states there must have been." She paused, fixing Abby with her gorgeous eyes once again. "But you're the first one to tell me."

A warmth rose up through Abby. She was the first.

Her gaze fell to Jordan's round, pink lips. And for the first time Abby allowed herself to imagine leaning forward and kissing them.

She'd forgotten what the last woman she'd kissed tasted like. It didn't matter anymore.

But she'd love to know how Jordan tasted. How she felt. Abby closed her eyes, thoughts and visions swirling against her eyelids.

Stop.

What was she thinking? Jordan was her professional bridesmaid. She was getting married next week.

She opened her eyes. Jordan was right. She only got one hen weekend, and if she wanted to enjoy it fully, she had to throw herself into it.

And it didn't include kissing Jordan.

"Abby?" She hadn't heard footsteps. She turned, and the light snapped on above the terrace making her squint.

It was her mum, in a silky T-shirt and shorts.

"What are you still doing up? We all went to bed a while ago."

Abby ignored the quake of her heart. She'd done nothing wrong, and yet it felt like her mum had just found her with her hands down Jordan's pants.

That thought caused a small earthquake at her centre.

She gave Gloria a tight smile as she approached. "We were coming to bed." She took her mum's arm and guided her towards the door.

Abby was ignoring the question in her mum's doubting stare. Ignoring the way her mum was glancing back towards Jordan.

None of it was real.

Her wedding was real.

From now on, that was all Abby was going to concentrate on.

# Chapter Fifteen

Abby woke the following morning drenched in sweat. She'd had a sex dream about Jordan.

As she opened her eyelids, heart pounding in her chest, she knew she had to get this under control. Had to work out how to enjoy her hen weekend as any bride should. She had to focus on her friends and family celebrating her upcoming wedding, and not solely on her fake bridesmaid. Her sexy as hell, fake bridesmaid.

Piece of cake, right?

She slipped a finger into her pants and closed her eyes as it connected with her wetness. She cast her mind back to her dream.

Jordan had been dressed in a skimpy red bikini that left little to the imagination. Her long, lean body reclined on a lounger as she baked in the sun. Abby had approached, climbed on top of her and slid her fingers into Jordan's bikini bottoms, a little like she was doing to herself right now. Jordan had been wet like her, too.

No words had been said.

Jordan had simply spread her legs a little more, making room for Abby to slide into her.

*Stop!*

Abby opened her eyes, withdrew her fingers, and wiped them on her thigh. She let out a strangled breath, then jumped up, and walked over to her window to open the blinds. It was a glorious day in Cannes. But as she stood there, she couldn't shake the image of Jordan in her red bikini. It had been so real. Jordan's skin had been so real. The feel of her. She'd smelled like sunshine.

Abby closed her eyes as her heartbeat slowed in her chest. Her clit twitched, but she ignored it.

She had to snap back into being a normal bride.

Whatever that was.

Today was the yacht trip. A boat ride out into the ocean with music, fun, and a free bar. She should take it easy on the free bar, she knew that already. Thankfully, her head was clear for today, as she hadn't gone completely overboard last night. Enough to blurt out some stupid things to Jordan, however.

She shook her head as she remembered telling Jordan about sleeping with a woman. Telling her that perhaps she was meant to be with a woman. *Fucking hell.*

She had to get her head in the right frame of mind for today. Had to focus on why she was here and what she should do. She glanced down to the pool area, right below the terrace. She couldn't hear anybody else. Abby checked her watch. 7.15am.

Would an early morning swim help to work off some of her sexual tension and excess energy? It had to be better than staying in her room and fretting.

She went to her suitcase and got out her black swimsuit. The one that wasn't built to get attention. She'd save her more sexy attire for the yacht, when she had an audience.

Abby walked into the kitchen, its shiny white floor showing some long, dark hair. That's what happened when you had a gaggle of women in a house. She went to the fridge and grabbed a bottle of water, drinking some as she did every morning. She loved this time, when the day was still there to be written. Later on, there were sure to be dramas about hair, make-up, clothing, and itinerary. But for now, the day was unsullied.

She left her bottle of water on the side, then strolled through the sunroom, and drew back the large glass doors. She stepped out onto the ground-floor terrace. The view was magnificent. Terraces and pools stepped down the hill below the villa to the sea. Dazed sunlight caught the water's surface.

"Good morning, Cannes." She couldn't help the grin that split her face as she stretched her arms high up above her head, her muscles waking up one by one. For a perfect moment, she forgot all her doubts. Now, it was just Abby, the sunshine, and the view.

She threw her head back, and shook her dark hair out behind her. She walked over to the pool, the concrete warm under her feet. It was what she always loved about being outside the UK. Heat made her happy. The pool's surface rippled as she dipped her toe, then drew back. It was colder than she'd thought. But she should just dive in, take the plunge.

A little like she should do with this weekend. Decide to be the bride she wanted to be. Self-assured.

She nodded. That's just what she was going to do. Starting right this second, by jumping in the pool. Project-Manager Abby was coming out. Only, for this weekend, the project was her.

The shock of the cold water woke her system, and it was all she could do to hold in her scream. She just about managed it. As her head broke the surface she flailed a little. But then, after a few deep breaths, she spread her body long and began to swim. She'd made the right call. The water was cleansing, and as she began to pump her muscles, her worries started to melt, too.

Abby swam ten lengths, loving the dimmed morning sun on her face. She reached out and clutched the edge of the pool, and stroked the baby-blue tiles.

When she and Marcus were married, would they come back here? Marcus had said the family who'd lent them the villa were close friends. The thought of returning regularly filled her with calm and happiness. They could do couples yoga, like he'd been trying to get her to do. She glanced up at the cloudless sky.

She and Marcus were going to be exactly the same. Cloudless.

Someone clearing their throat nearby made her look. She squinted.

Then she did a double-take.

Because there at the side of the pool, wearing a red bikini that left little to the imagination, was Jordan. Just as she had been in her dream.

So much for working it out of her system.

Now, instead of that, her dreams were coming true. In the worst and best possible way.

"Nice stroke work." Jordan walked around the pool to where Abby was still clutching the wall, frozen in time.

Stroke work? Seriously? Jordan had no idea. "Thanks. I didn't realise I had an audience."

"Great minds think alike. I thought I'd get down here before there was too much of an audience and wake myself up. How is it?" She dipped a toe in the water, then recoiled. She hunched her shoulders and made a face. "Yikes. Colder than I thought."

Abby took a deep breath and regained her composure. She could totally do this. "It is at first, but it's gorgeous when you get in. Just go for it. It certainly woke me up."

Jordan raised an eyebrow that told Abby she didn't believe her.

Abby tried not to stare at Jordan's flat, tanned stomach. Exactly as it had been in her dream.

Nope.

The bride-to-be should definitely not be doing that.

Jordan climbed in via the metal step ladder on the side of the pool, gave a little scream as she submerged herself, then swam over to Abby. When she drew level with her, she ducked her head under water, then came back up, sweeping her blond hair off her face. She wiped the water out of her eyes, before giving Abby a wide smile.

Scrap what she'd just thought. Maybe she couldn't do this. If anything, seeing Jordan up close and all wet was making things worse.

Abby tensed, then tried to think of horrible things. Things that were not a semi-naked Jordan.

Jellied eels. Bone marrow on toast. Parsley. Martin Keown. It didn't work.

Her eyes could still see Jordan's gorgeous face in front of her, and her whole body was processing that with some joy.

"How did you sleep?"

"Really well." She was blushing, she could feel it.

Jordan didn't need to know about her dreams.

But Abby knew.

Her body knew.

When she'd woken up, she'd been inside Jordan.

Desire slid down her, landing right in her core.

"Me too, I slept like a log. Didn't wake up until I heard you out here." She paused. "Ready for today's yacht trip?"

Abby nodded. "Totally. Yesterday was a gentle introduction to my hen weekend. I feel like today, it's going to explode into life."

Jordan flashed her a killer smile.

She really wasn't helping. Abby was still hanging onto the side of the pool. Also hanging onto her sanity for dear life.

Jordan studied her like she was a work of art.

"I just wanted to say, too, that whatever you tell me this weekend stays with me. Total confidence. Just in case you were feeling a little exposed after our chat last night."

"I can't even blame it on tequila." Abby paused. "The only other person who knows I slept with a woman is Delta, and I'd like it to stay that way. If Marcus's cousins found out, it might get back to him. Or worse, to Marjorie. She already has a low enough opinion of me as it is."

Jordan gave her a rueful smile. "If sleeping with a woman is the worst thing you can do, Marjorie definitely needs to broaden her horizons. But of course, your secret's safe with me. I told you that from day one. I tell all my brides that."

All her brides.

Because this was a job to Jordan.

Nothing more.

Abby had to remember that.

"Anyway, how about a race? Last one to the end of the pool and back makes the coffee."

Abby grinned. "You're on."

# Chapter Sixteen

The yacht wasn't just a yacht; it was a superyacht. A slice of heaven on the water.

"Fuck me," were Jordan's first words as she boarded, admiring the polished wooden decks under her feet. Jordan had seen this level of opulence before, but experiencing such a boat was still a treat.

Taran came dashing up from the lower deck, and grabbed Delta's arm. "You have to come and see the bedrooms down here," she said, giving Delta no choice. "It's absolutely unreal. The lush fabrics! The amount of cushions! And there are mirrors *everywhere*."

Jordan followed Marcus's cousins, Arielle and Martha, up some steps to the middle deck. The sun was already hot on her back, and now she saw where the wall-to-wall Beyoncé was coming from. Beyond an outdoor round table that could seat ten, was an indoor lounge and bar, accessed via double glass doors. They were wide open, with a blond bartender hard at work within.

"There better be at least a plunge pool onboard." Arielle turned to Martha. "We don't want this trip to turn out like Cassandra's disaster, do we?"

Martha shuddered. She pointed through the double doors.

"At least the barman is good looking. Cassandra's yacht had no pool and female bar staff. Hen party suicide."

Jordan already felt sorry for Cassandra.

Up some more stairs was the top deck. Gloria stood there, mouth open. She beckoned to Jordan and Nikita. "Come and see this!" Had she become more Scottish since she boarded? "There's a pool! On a boat!"

Jordan and Nikita did as they were told. The aqua blue of the plunge pool shimmered in the middle of the top deck, surrounded by loungers and sofas. Perhaps Arielle and Martha wouldn't be giving this weekend such a bad write-up after all.

Jordan had expected a bloke called Pierre behind the bar, or perhaps Thierry, with a cool, French accent dripping from his lips. Instead, they'd got an Aussie named Travis. Not that any of the hen do were disappointed with Travis's easy charm and rippling muscles.

The sun beat down as Jordan reclined on one of the sun loungers. It was a lot of boat for ten of them to fill, but they were going to try their best.

Next to Jordan, Gloria had her pale Scottish skin out. She sat beside her daughter who'd inherited the same. If Abby matured like Gloria, Marcus had struck some deal. Gloria was wearing a black bikini, and it was showing off toned legs and hard abs that had already drawn amazed stares from the rest of the hen party.

"I want to know now, Gloria. Tell me the secret of looking as good as you do in your late 50s." Jordan held up her phone. "Tell me now, and I'm going to broadcast it live on Instagram so the rest of the world can watch and learn."

Gloria threw her head back and let out a cackle of laughter.

"Square sausage and brown sauce, of course." She grinned at Jordan. "Do you know what that is, hen?"

Jordan shook her head. She had absolutely zero idea what the hell Gloria was talking about.

Gloria tapped Abby on the thigh. "You need to get this one around to yours for a bit of square sausage. Although it's usually eaten for breakfast, so you might have to turn up very early in the morning. Or else stay the night before. You girls have got years to catch up on, so that wouldn't be a problem, would it?" She gave them both an extravagant wink.

Jordan glanced at Abby, who was giving her mum the universal "please don't embarrass me" face.

She smiled.

She was also busy imagining staying the night at Abby's place, but instead of breakfast, she was imagining all-night sex, and waking up naked and sated, their skin sticking to each other in a deliciously new way.

Jordan blinked hard to get rid of that particular image. Square sausage couldn't compete with that.

*Not safe for work.* Jordan was very much at work.

"I think Jordan can live without that particular breakfast." Abby sat forward, moving her sunglasses up her face.

Was it Jordan's imagination, or was Abby's gaze sliding down her body?

She blinked again.

Something rushed in her chest.

It must be her imagination.

"The world always needs square sausage, young lady," Gloria said. "Don't shy away from your roots. I know we had eggs, avocado, and smoked salmon this morning and it was

131

delicious. But sometimes, a square sausage is the only thing that'll cut it." She pointed at her chest. "At least for this proud Scot."

Abby laughed, her gaze still on Jordan. "When we get home, I'll cook you some, okay? Mum's right. You need to experience it once in your life."

Desire pooled in her stomach as she focused on Abby in her blue polka dot bikini. Damn, her legs were fine.

"I'm always up for new and exciting experiences, so count me in." Had she managed to make that reply light and throwaway?

Gloria looked from one to the other, as if she might say something, then didn't. "Anyway, we've been on this boat for 20 minutes and nobody's brought the bride a drink!"

Jordan jumped up. Shit, she was forgetting her duties.

However, Gloria shook her head. "Let's get her other bridesmaids on the case, shall we? Delta! Taran! We need drinks!"

Abby bent down and rummaged in her bag.

Jordan stared at the piercing blue sky. Cloudless. Unlike her mind.

"Can you do my back?" Abby held up a bottle of sunscreen to Gloria.

Gloria jumped up. "I have to go to the loo, I've been dying to for a while now but I keep putting it off. Why do we do that?" She glanced Jordan's way. "Jordan can do it for you, can't you?"

Jordan nodded, her mouth a desert. "It's what I'm here for."

Abby moved in front of Jordan, giving her the bottle.

"Thanks." She didn't look sure about this turn of events, either.

Jordan cleared her throat, glancing around the boat. Everyone was elsewhere. It was a big yacht. None of them were taking any notice of Jordan and Abby.

After all, it was just applying sunscreen. To Abby's firm, pale shoulders.

The same ones Jordan may or may not have imagined kissing earlier.

She gave the bottle three pumps before applying it to Abby's back, trying not to overthink this. Her fingertips tingled as she swept them across Abby's satin skin.

"Make sure you get a good coverage," Abby said. "A burnt or peeling bride is never a good look."

"Gotcha." Jordan sprayed some more, applying it to the back of Abby's arms, the side of her back. Jordan's fingertips strayed near to the edge of Abby's breast, but she made sure there was no contact.

Abby turned her head, snagging Jordan's gaze for a moment. "You need me to unhook my top?"

So many answers swirled around Jordan's head, but she shook her head. "I'll work around it. Don't worry, this is not my first rodeo."

And yet, in many ways, it felt like it was.

\* \* \*

A few hours later, after a spot of jet-skiing, they had lunch around the back table, before retiring to the front of the boat. Travis was pumping tunes across the deck, and the hen party volume had gone up considerably. Nikita and Erin kept freaking everyone out with their Jaws impressions. Gloria had missed a spot with her sunscreen and had burned the back of her neck.

Meanwhile, Delta had her phone out, and was getting the hens to pose two by two at the front of the yacht, "just like Leo and Kate in Titanic."

"I'm going to edit it and put it in a video, with Celine singing in the background." Delta seemed to have put aside her heartbreak like a hero, and was taking her lead bridesmaid role seriously.

Abby was impressed. Delta had stepped up today, making sure the group were constantly entertained.

So far, Taran had tried to be Kate Winslet, with Gloria her willing Leonardo di Caprio. However, it hadn't been a silver screen moment. Taran had looked down and wobbled, thinking she was going to fall into the ocean and get eaten by sharks. She'd shrieked and fallen backwards, sending Gloria toppling to the floor. Gloria's bikini bottom had ridden up her arse, giving the whole group far more than they'd bargained for.

Everyone was still getting over it. And still laughing.

"Okay, who's next for the Leo and Kate treatment." Delta scanned the group. "What about you two?" She pointed a finger at Abby, then at Jordan.

Abby cleared her throat, shaking her head. "Someone else can go first."

Beside her, Jordan nodded. "I'm still full from lunch."

Delta looked at them like they'd gone mad. "I'm not asking you to perform a dance routine. You just have to stand at the front, clutch the metal rod and give me your best Hollywood impression. Abby, pretend Jordan is Leo. Or Marcus. Whichever one makes you most weak at the knees."

Jordan glanced at Abby, giving her a shrug. "I'm game if you are."

Abby stalled. More close contact, after she'd nearly collapsed when Jordan had applied sun lotion earlier? She'd made sure she sat away from her at lunch, but they just kept getting drawn back together. Mainly because whatever she wanted, Jordan was always on hand to get it. She was impossibly good at her job.

"Remember Abby. Give the camera those come-to-bed eyes!"

From being impressed with Delta, she wished she was just a little sadder and heartbroken right now.

Jordan climbed up onto the sofa, holding out a hand to Abby.

She took it, taking in Jordan's sun-kissed hair, and her dazzling smile. In that moment, Abby knew just who was making her weak at the knees.

Their eyes met, and Jordan gave her a beaming smile, her hand wrapped around one of the boat's white poles, her pose relaxed.

Desire hit Abby square in the gut, almost winding her. She styled it out, giving Delta what she wanted, with much whooping from the group as she slotted herself in front of Jordan. Abby could hear them, but they weren't as loud as her heart, that was beating like a drum in her ears as Jordan's arm encircled her, their bodies melding.

Abby stared out at the ocean, just as the boat hit a wave. She wobbled to one side. Jordan saved her. She righted herself.

"You okay?" Jordan's concerned eyes were on her.

Abby nodded. "More than okay."

"Okay, now let's have the money shot! Arms up in three, two, one!"

Jordan stepped closer behind her, both arms now holding her in place.

Abby almost forgot to breathe. She leaned back into her, relishing the moment. "I'm the king of the world!" she shouted.

Right then, at that moment, she believed it.

More whooping from behind, just as the boat hit another wave.

Both Abby and Jordan were knocked off balance. Jordan fell sideways, bringing Abby down on top of her. They landed on the sofa with a cushioned thud.

When Abby opened her eyes, her lips were inches from Jordan's.

Electricity crackled between them as Jordan opened her eyes.

Was she feeling this, too? This connection? Abby would love to ask.

But now wasn't really the right time.

Delta appeared at their side. "I didn't ask for that extra bit at the end, but it's going to make a cracking video for my bridesmaid speech. I thank you!"

Abby had forgotten she was being recorded. "Fantastic."

Jordan was still staring at her.

* * *

Even though the sun was high in the sky at 4pm, the water was cooler than they'd imagined. Abby climbed down the aluminium ladder on the side of the boat, then flung herself backwards, floating in the sea. For a moment, she was at peace. Just her, the sea and her thoughts.

Until Delta jumped in with a yelp, breaking the moment.

The salt water stung Abby's eyes and she spat some out of her mouth as her perfect moment was ruined. "You're a real pearl, you know that?"

Delta grinned. "It's been said before." She took Abby's face in her hands and kissed her lips. "Cheer up sweet cheeks. You're on your hen weekend, on a gorgeous boat ride, and you've got a hot woman at your beck and call." She paused. "That's me, just in case you were wondering." She gave Abby a wink, kissed her cheek, then swam towards the others.

Abby shook her head, her eyes still stinging. When she turned left, Jordan was there.

"Race you," she said, for the second time that day. The first time, Abby had lost. She was determined not to do so again.

They were in front of everyone else. Abby kicked her feet, clear water ahead as they entered the cave. Up above were incredible rock formations carved from the teeth of nature. Without the sun overhead, the temperature dropped considerably, and they were plunged into semi-darkness as they raced for the far side of the cave.

Abby touched first, just ahead of Jordan. She took a deep breath, but ducked under the water at the same time. Bad mistake. She swallowed a ton of salt water. She broke the surface, choking. She bet she looked a sight.

Before she knew it, Jordan was behind her, her arms wrapped around Abby's waist.

Jordan pressed down on her stomach.

Abby coughed. A small fountain of water spurted out of her mouth.

Jordan gave another press.

Abby duly coughed up more water. But that was the end of it, and then she was just coughing, trying to regain her equilibrium.

Jordan swam around to Abby's front, hooking Abby's arm around her neck to steady her. "You okay?"

Abby nodded. "I just want to say, even though I nearly swallowed the sea and am currently hanging off you like a straggly piece of seaweed, I won the race. Granted, not many style points, but I definitely won."

Jordan gave her a grin. "You absolutely did." She dropped her gaze to Abby's cleavage, before moving it upwards.

Abby wasn't sure which was worse. Jordan staring at her tits, her mouth, or into her eyes. Every part of her body and every inch of the air between them was loaded. It was delicious, but it was also purgatory.

She had to move, but she seemed frozen to the spot.

Besides, her arm was crooked in such a comfortable position around Jordan's neck. She was almost sitting in her lap.

*Think about something else.* "Good move with the Heimlich," Abby said. She could hear everyone else, but there was nobody else in her eyeline.

Jordan smiled. "I learned first aid at my old job, and it's come in handy on hen weekends I've been on. You'd be surprised at the amount of mishaps that occur."

Abby's heartbeat thudded in her chest as Jordan's voice dropped lower as she spoke, her tongue brushing her lips.

It would be so easy to lean forward now. To kiss her full

lips in the semi-light of the cave. Instead, she pushed herself off the wall, rolled onto her back and stared up at the cave's roof. It was far more calming than staring at Jordan's lips.

Moments later, the silence was broken as the rest of the hen party entered the cave, splashing and chattering about how cold and dark it was.

"Was that a bat?" Taran shouted.

There were screams and splashes from the rest of the group. Within seconds, most of them had turned and swum out. Everyone apart from Delta, who was nearing the two of them. As she swam up to them, she gave them a grin.

"Fancy meeting you here." Delta raised a single eyebrow. "You know, every time I turn around, you two seem to be together." She turned her gaze on Abby, then Jordan. "Are you up to something? Plotting a surprise for the rest of us?"

Abby wouldn't be surprised if Delta's gaze had burned a hole in her skull, it was that intense. "We swam in here, then I swallowed half the sea." Was guilt stamped on her forehead? She hoped not. "Jordan came to my rescue. So if she's plotting anything, it's not my untimely death." She laughed, but it sounded hollow even to her ears. Or maybe that was the cave.

Jordan shivered. "But now I've saved the day, shall we get back to the yacht before we're eaten by bats or die of hypothermia?" She swam a few metres, before turning back to them.

"That's not on your spreadsheet, is it, Wonder Woman?" Delta gave Jordan a grin.

# Chapter Seventeen

Jordan led the group out of the cocktail bar. Their volume had crept up as the alcohol consumption rose. It was now at jet-engine level. Delta and Erin were the ringleaders, with Gloria making a valiant effort to keep up.

The superyacht had been a success. Abby hadn't drowned, and Jordan had resisted pressing her up against the walls of the cave and kissing her into oblivion. Probably for the best. Since then, she'd got the group home, changed, out for dinner, and then to a swanky cocktail bar with shimmering gold walls and a gold-embossed menu, which Gloria had declared "fit for a princess!" So now, the whole group had renamed the bride-to-be, Princess Abby.

"What's next on the agenda for Princess Abby?" That was Delta shouting at Jordan.

Jordan checked her phone. Their next stop was Club Orange, which was the only stop she wasn't sure Abby truly wanted. She texted their driver to let him know they were ready to be picked up, and led the group to a lay-by a few metres away.

Their minibus appeared within minutes, and Jordan slid open the door, telling the driver where they wanted to go in smooth French. She'd always loved the French language, and was thrilled to put her skill to good use. That it never failed to impress women was a happy side effect. Tonight was no exception.

"You're not my usual type, Jordan, but I could honestly listen to you chatting to that driver all night. Even if you are just telling him the quickest way to the club and to stop for a loo break on the way."

Jordan smiled at Frankie as she took her seat. "I can ask him where the nearest McDonald's is later, too."

"I couldn't eat another thing. Apart from perhaps a stunning French man named Jacques." That was Gloria, grinning from ear to ear at her joke.

It earned a slap from Abby. "Mother! What did I tell you earlier? Stop showing me up. Plus, less of the desire to chew up French men. If you're not careful, I'm going to record you and send it to Dad."

Gloria whooped at that. "Martin would be fine. You youngsters are so uptight! Loosen up, live a little! I snogged four men on my hen do and nobody died. It's a rite of passage." She tapped her index finger on Abby's shoulder. "You haven't even snogged one yet." Gloria raised an eyebrow as Jordan got in, sliding the van's door shut. "What do you think, Jordan?"

Jordan turned in her seat so she could see Gloria. "About what?"

"Abby snogging some men tonight. Is it on your agenda?"

Jordan smiled, eyeing Delta, then Abby. "It's not on the spreadsheet, but then, life can't always be run by spreadsheets, can it?"

Cheers all around.

Gloria nudged her daughter with her elbow. "Shall we say one ginger, one blond, and one dark-haired man in Club Oraaaaaaange?" She sounded out the orange in a very French way, making Jordan smile.

More cheers, as Abby gave a rueful smile.

"Do I have a choice in this?"

"Noooooo!" came the reply.

"Although, do they even have ginger men in France?" That was Martha. "I've never seen one."

"Of course they do. Although they call them *roux*."

"I love it!" Gloria said. "Ready team?"

"Ready!" came the rousing reply.

* * *

Club Orange was a favourite destination of the Cannes elite. Belgian royalty partied here, as did French high society. And now, Abby Porter and her hen party. The lights were low, they had a private booth, and a bottle of Grey Goose had just arrived, sat atop a satin cushion with sparklers.

"Is this what clubbing is now? It's a bit different to the Blackpool Ritzy, isn't it? That's where I went on my hen do. Not a 'Kiss-Me-Quick' hat in sight." Gloria's eyes were almost popping out of her head at such a display of decadence. Waiters buzzed around, pouring drinks for the group, and when everyone had one, Delta proposed a toast as the music boomed in their ears.

"To a successful night two," she shouted, as the beat kicked in and the dancefloor pulsed beside them. "And of course, to Princess Abby marrying her Prince Charming, but also to getting a frenchie from a Frenchie along the way."

Abby burst out laughing, before taking a swig of her drink, then fixing the group with a narrowed stare. "Shall we dance?"

Delta turned out to be a dancer who needed plenty of floorspace, her flailing arms clearing a path all around them. Nikita and Erin had taken it upon themselves to scope the dancefloor for possible snogging targets, which left the rest of the group spinning in Delta's orbit, occasionally ducking to avoid being hit by her arm or her leg. Jordan stayed put in their booth, checking her phone, making sure their posh breakfast was on schedule for the morning. Sunday was the staff's day off, so Jordan had ordered a service that delivered breakfast on silver trays to arrive at 10am.

Her eyes moved to the dancefloor, as Delta produced another power move.

Taran ducked just in time.

Delta hit Gloria on her cheek, which led Gloria to cuff Delta around the head.

Jordan suppressed a laugh. Everybody needed a Gloria on their hen weekend.

A man with blond hair was being ushered at speed towards Abby by Nikita and Erin. When he stopped in front of Abby, they shook hands, and the man leaned in and said something to Abby.

Jordan's stomach tightened.

This was a hen weekend ritual. And yet, it felt different. She didn't want to watch, but she knew she would.

Jordan ground her teeth together as Abby nodded, then flicked her gaze towards Jordan.

Seeking her out.

Their stares met in mid-air, and Jordan froze.

She wanted to shout at Abby, tell her to not be railroaded into kissing the man. Even though it meant nothing. Even though it was just a bit of fun.

"Loosen up!" Gloria had said.

Jordan wanted to leap over the white leather low-slung couch in front of her, push the man aside and shield Abby from what was about to happen.

But she couldn't. Instead, she gave Abby a tepid smile, and then a thumbs-up.

A thumbs-up? Really? Was she 12?

Seconds later, Abby leaned in and kissed the man on the cheek.

Delta shook her head, and held onto both Abby's and the man's arms. Erin and Nikita leaned in too. More discussion.

Then Abby shook her head, pulled her arm away, and almost ran up the four steps to their booth, not looking back. Just as she was about to make it to the top, she wobbled and fell sideways.

Jordan dropped to her knees as Abby righted herself, a frown creasing her face. One hand grasped her ankle as she sat up.

"You okay? What happened?"

Abby winced, shaking her head. "I think my heel broke." She took off her cream heel and held it up. Sure enough, the heel was barely connected, flapping as she waggled it from side to side. She rubbed her side where she'd fallen. "Plus, that really fucking hurt."

"Can you move your arm?"

Abby did so, wincing again. "It's fine. It's more my ankle. I don't want it to be buggered for the rest of the weekend."

Jordan put a hand under Abby's armpit, helping her to a seat, just as Delta, Gloria, Nikita, and Erin arrived at the booth.

"What the fuck happened?" Delta's face was stricken.

"My heel broke and I fell." Abby leaned over and felt her ankle. She massaged it, then winced again. "It's not broken, but I might head back."

"Nooooo!" Delta said "We were just getting started. Plus, we've put in a whole load of requests for you."

Abby glanced up. "For music or men to snog?"

Delta grinned. "A bit of both."

"Just because I'm going home doesn't mean you all have to. You can dance to all my records and you can share the men out among you. You'll probably appreciate them more."

"Nonsense!" Gloria said. "It's your hen weekend. If you're going, we all go."

"And as your hen, I insist you stay put. Dance a little." Abby nodded towards the bottle of booze. "If nothing else, we have vodka to drink and champagne ordered. So finish that, dance, then come home." Abby glanced at Jordan. "You can take me home, then send the driver back for the rest, right?"

Jordan nodded. "Of course. Whatever you want."

Abby gave a firm nod. "That's settled then. Now, who's going to help me up?"

# Chapter Eighteen

Abby winced as she hobbled out of the cab and up the path to the villa's front door. In all honesty, she wasn't in quite as much pain as she'd made out, but it had seemed like a good ruse to escape having to kiss any more men. Particularly when Delta had deemed kissing them on the cheek "not really kissing". Abby was glad to be back at the villa. She was especially glad to be here with Jordan, who was the polar opposite of the rest of her hens: calm, considered, and sober.

As they walked onto the terrace, Abby glanced at Jordan. "You know you said you'd do anything for me this weekend?"

Jordan nodded slowly.

"I'd love it if you'd have a glass of wine with me and relax. It would definitely aid my ankle's recovery."

Jordan paused, then tilted her head. "I don't normally drink on the job. But I'll have a glass with you. Just keep it a secret, okay?"

Abby mimed zipping up her lips and throwing away the key.

"Sit down and wait there."

She gave Jordan a salute. "Yes, Ma'am."

When Jordan reappeared, she was carrying two glasses of white. "How's your ankle?"

Abby rotated it right, then left. "Feels much better."

Jordan put down the drinks, before moving a chair and placing Abby's foot on it. "Keep it elevated. That should take the swelling down." She frowned. "Should I get you some ice?"

Abby shook her head, taking her foot off the chair. "I know that's what I should do, but you know what I really want to do?" She had no idea where this daring was coming from.

Jordan stilled. "You've already got me drinking."

Abby hesitated. Her pulse raced. "How about we take those drinks into the hot tub? Seems a shame to waste such a gorgeous warm evening sitting here when the view's just as good down there." Abby assessed Jordan's face. Getting seminaked in water again with Jordan was a risk.

She knew that.

And yet, she couldn't seem to stop herself suggesting it.

"If you don't, I won't write you such a glowing review for your website."

Jordan flicked her gaze to Abby's face, a ghost of a smile crossing her own. "We can't have that, can we?"

Ten minutes later, Jordan held out a hand and Abby stepped into the hot tub, treading carefully to avoid more injuries to her body. She still wasn't sure about her heart.

Jordan was wearing a one-piece black number, a far cry from her red bikini of earlier. She still managed to look stunning, though, causing Abby's throat to thicken with want.

She was trying to get her mind back in the game as Jordan passed her wine, which she'd decanted into plastic glasses for the tub. She really did think of everything. Abby leaned over and pressed a large white button. In seconds, the water began to bubble all around them.

"Eight days until the big day." Jordan sipped her wine, before resting the glass on the lip of the tub. "You think this is going to be you and Marcus on your honeymoon in the Maldives?"

Abby nodded, ignoring the sinking feeling in her stomach. She focused on the gentle stream of bubbles currently massaging the small of her back instead. "I guess so."

"I've always fancied going to the Maldives, but it's very much a honeymooner destination. I have a friend who went on her own but she said it was tricky travelling solo and being surrounded by couples. She had to invent a husband with food poisoning to ward off couples inviting her to their tables." Jordan turned up her smile. "But you'll pass the honeymooner test first time. Handsome man plus gorgeous woman."

Abby's stomach flipped. Jordan thought she was a gorgeous woman? "Thanks, I think."

She recalled a conversation she and Marcus had recently about names for their first-born. Marcus had wanted what Gloria would refer to as "up yourself" names. Abby hadn't wanted to argue, but she knew once they were married, they'd have to work this stuff out. But would they? Would she end up with children called Penelope and Jasper, rather than Harper and Luke? She couldn't imagine it. But maybe it all started by having a honeymoon somewhere she didn't want to go in the first place.

Small decisions with big implications.

"You don't look very happy about going on honeymoon, if you don't mind me saying."

Abby reached for her wine before replying. "I am, it's just the Maldives isn't where I wanted to go. I suggested Paris, but Marcus and Marjorie both said that wasn't grand enough. The Maldives is where everyone goes, like you said. But it's also far away and requires a plane. The less air travel I have to do, the better for my nerves and my life."

"Have you told Marcus how you feel?" Jordan frowned as she spoke.

Abby nodded. "I did, but he didn't listen. He's excited, and thinks this is what all women want. The funny thing is, he always told me he fell in love with me because I wasn't like any other girl he'd been out with. But as soon as I agreed to marry him, all of that flew out the window. Now he's doing everything by the book: wedding venue, cake, massive hens and stags. He's got caught up in the whole thing, and it's not what I ever imagined. When I think about the ceremony, which I have a lot over the past few months, I guess I would have liked something in St Albans, where my parents are. Or perhaps in Scotland, where it all started. Maybe even in a castle on a loch."

"But it's actually happening in a manor house in Surrey."

Abby's shoulder slumped. "It is. Ceremony in the nearby church where Marcus's family go. Then back to the manor house for the reception. All because of Marjorie and Marcus joining forces and being persuasive."

Jordan's gaze was intense as she stared at Abby. "You never had a box under your bed where you kept clippings of the dress you wanted, and all of that?"

Abby's stomach flexed. "Fuck, no. For one, my mother would have thrown it out, demanding I have bigger ambitions than getting married."

Jordan's deep, joyous laugh split the warm evening air.

"Have I told you I love your mum?"

"Most people do." Abby was grateful to have her, too. "She's walking me down the aisle, did I tell you that? My biological dad's not interested. I asked Martin as I call him Dad, but he said Mum brought me up for six years before they met, so it should be her. But no, I never dreamed of a big wedding. It's not really me. Yet, here I am having one." All the while, she was sitting in a hot tub with a woman she was growing increasingly attracted to. Abby swallowed down, glancing up to the night sky, now a midnight blue. There weren't many stars visible. When she glanced back at Jordan, however, her eyes were sparkling in the evening air like diamonds.

"It seems like I've forgotten a lot in my life. The wedding I wanted. The job I wanted." Abby breathed out. "Once you start down a track like project management, it's not easy to change to something else. You get sucked into the culture, the money, the people. And the longer you stay on the track, the harder it is to get out. I always wanted to do something that gave back. I thought project management was helping people, sort of. But now I remember it wasn't my dream. Am I selling out on both counts?" When she said it out loud, she was pretty sure she was.

Jordan shook her head. "Of course not. You can change your job if you want to. For your wedding, you fell in love and went along with what your partner wants. Most people do. Although it's usually the man going along with the woman."

Jordan moved in the water, her hand coming into contact with Abby's elevated foot. She shot a look at Abby that kept her in her place, before taking Abby's ankle in her hands. "This is your bad one, right?"

Abby nodded. Yep. It definitely was. Although Jordan's touch was making it feel so much better.

"You should elevate it more. If you put it in my lap, you'll get a good angle."

"Sure," she replied.

Jordan's fingers skated across her skin. Abby closed her eyes, imagining those fingers elsewhere. Drawing lazy circles on the inside of her thigh. Walking slowly up her midriff. Tracing a path from her neck to her earlobe.

Abby leaned her neck backwards as her fantasy played out, before snapping herself back to reality.

Her body jolted as she opened her eyes.

Jordan looked at her for a long moment, and the corners of her mouth flickered into a smile.

Something shifted inside Abby. Something that made her feel more uncomfortable than she already was.

Perhaps this hadn't been the wisest move. As soon as Jordan touched her, or looked at her in a certain way, Abby's mind scrambled and she couldn't think of anything else.

Nothing but Jordan's hands on her. Then her tongue on her. Then back to Abby's dream, when she was inside Jordan.

She shifted on the hot tub seat, then looked away. She reached for her drink and took a large gulp. What she'd give to be a little more drunk now. Perhaps it would take the edge off her feelings.

The bubbles stopped. Quiet descended. As silence serenaded them, desire and panic crept up Abby's spine like a slow, rising tide.

She searched her mind for something to say. Something that wasn't incriminating.

"I like the feel of your hands on me." *Oh fuck. It wasn't that.*

All of Abby's normal rules had flown out the window since she met Jordan.

"I'm glad." Jordan didn't meet her gaze.

Abby was desperate to get them back on an even keel. But it wasn't easy while Jordan was still holding her foot. "So tell me, how many times have you seen the 'get the bride to kiss a load of men' game played out?"

"A few times before." Jordan's voice was like honey. She ran her tongue along her bottom lip.

Abby's stare followed it, then flicked her gaze to Jordan's.

Boom! Desire hit her full in the gut.

"But I've never squirmed so much while I was watching the bride. Because you're not just any bride-to-be. Or any woman. Marcus was right on that count. You're special, Abby." Jordan looked away. "And I shouldn't be saying any of this, so I'm going to shut up now." She shook her head. "Ignore me," she said quietly, almost as an afterthought.

Jordan had just called her special. Did that mean she liked her, too? And if it did, what then?

"Would it help to know that I hated the idea of kissing anybody else while you were in the room?"

Jordan stilled, before looking up. "You did?"

Abby's heartbeat quickened as Jordan edged warily across the hot tub seat, closer to her.

The calm water kissed Jordan's pert cleavage as she moved.

Abby sucked in a breath and dragged her gaze away. How she longed to be that water.

"It felt wrong. Like I was cheating. On you." She dropped her head, as her heartbeat roared in her ears.

What the hell was she saying? Why were these words dropping from her lips?

But with Jordan sitting beside her, fixing her in place with her eyes, she couldn't do anything else. It was like she'd been overtaken. As if Jordan had slipped some truth serum into her wine.

Now, sitting with the warm Cannes air caressing her skin, the words ballooned in front of her, floating on the water's surface like giant imaginary inflatables. Abby wanted to sit on them, wrestle them under the water. Submerge them. But inflatables and words uttered in the heat of the moment didn't work like that, did they? Rather, they wouldn't be silenced. If you tried to get rid of them, they'd only pop back up and hit you in the head.

"Cheating?" Jordan looked confused as she raised a finger to her chest. "On me?"

Abby gulped. Her next move was going to be critical, wasn't it? Did she lie, or did she tell the truth?

Sirens blared in Abby's head. She ignored them.

Yes, she was teetering on the edge, but she was certain of one thing. For the past few months while organising this wedding, she'd been sleep-walking to the aisle.

Until she'd met Jordan. Jordan had woken her up in so many ways.

She nodded. "I know that makes no sense," she added. "I'm engaged to Marcus and I'm here on my hen weekend, but this is my reality." Abby shook her head, covering her forehead with her left palm. She fixed her gaze on Jordan.

Shocked, beautiful Jordan.

"I have feelings for you, Jordan. I can't ignore them. Even though I'm engaged to Marcus, who's wonderful." She moved her hand, swirling it in the air between them. "This right here is torture. Because here we are, semi-naked and alone. My ankle isn't even that painful. I just saw that I could use it to be alone with you. When I was being forced to kiss that poor guy, all I could think was, 'I wish this was Jordan'." Abby covered her entire face with her hands, bringing both her feet in front of her.

She'd really blown it now, hadn't she? She should have kept her big mouth shut. Stayed at the club. Drank more vodka.

As if sensing the magnitude of the moment, the hot tub chose this moment to restart its bubbles.

Jordan had been listening, rapt, leaning in. Now she jerked backwards, as the jets sprang to life and the water began to bubble all around them.

Abby grabbed her wine and swigged, just to give her hands something to do.

She eyed Jordan warily. "Say something, please. Even if it's that I'm a stupid bride-to-be and that this happens on every job you do. Just something to stop my thoughts going around and around in my head. Because you don't know the chaos that resides up here." She tapped her skull as she spoke.

Jordan sucked in a deep breath, then edged back towards Abby.

Then she took Abby's hand in hers.

That one action stilled Abby under the bubbles. Below the surface, she was frozen.

"Believe me when I say, this is the first time this has happened. You are the first bride to tell me she wants to kiss me." Jordan's gaze dropped to Abby's lips. "You're also the first bride-to-be I've wanted to kiss. But I've been pushing that away because I have a job to do. And no part of that job description involves kissing you."

Arrows of lust landed all over Abby's body, along with a hallelujah chorus in her brain. However, that was quickly followed by a rolling sensation of what-the-fuck as the reality set in.

Abby wanted to kiss Jordan.

Jordan wanted to kiss Abby.

Did that mean they were going to?

"You want to kiss me too?"

Jordan nodded. "I do. Last night. Today in the sea. When you were trying on your wedding dress." She tilted her head towards the sky. "But you know we can't act on it, right?"

If Abby's body could have deflated right there and then, it would have. "I know."

*But it's so unfair!* That's what she wanted to scream. But she didn't.

Jordan scooted a bit closer, and brought Abby's hand to her mouth. She kissed it, then placed it back in her lap.

"Whatever attraction there is here has to stay just that. An attraction."

Abby nodded, dumbstruck by Jordan kissing her hand. Her skin tingled. "Of course." She'd never been so insincere in her life.

"I'm employed by your fiancé and by you. My job is to get you to the altar in one piece. Happy. Content."

"You've already screwed up on that one just by being here."

Now it was Jordan's turn to shake her head.

The bubbles stopped again.

The water calmed.

The silence this time was even louder.

"We can't do this," Jordan began, but she edged a little closer to Abby.

"I know." Abby slid along the seat until she was right beside Jordan.

"You're getting married. To somebody else."

Abby nodded ever so slowly. Like she was on shutter-speed in some old movie.

"I know." She put a hand up to Jordan's face as their legs touched. "But why is it then, that ever since we met, when I go to bed and when I wake up, all I think about is you? I dream about you, Jordan. I did last night."

She had no idea where the courage had come from. Or how she was going to store it up in her future, because she was going to need it if she went through with this.

"Abby," Jordan began.

Her tone said one thing. Her hungry eyes said quite something else.

"Don't say anything else." Abby's words came out as a whisper as she leaned forward. She was about to make her dreams a reality. She was about to kiss Jordan, the woman who'd made her finally wake up.

"Abby! Jordan!"

Or maybe she wasn't.

Because that voice was her mum.

Which meant their party was about to be crashed.

Abby jerked with such ferocity that she went forward before moving backwards.

The crack as her head collided with Jordan's reverberated around her brain. Abby clutched her head, dazed in more ways than one.

"Argh, fuck!" Jordan said.

When Abby peered through her hands, Jordan had moved backwards on the hot tub seat, clutching her head. Abby moved, too, staring at her hands as she pulled them from her head.

No blood.

But now, she had to get her mind back in the game, because she could already hear chatter and laughter coming from the upper terrace.

"I thought you were a cripple!" Delta shouted, hanging over the glass wall. "And here you are, drinking wine in the hot tub." She wagged a finger in their direction. "I should have known you'd do all you could to get out of dancing." She eyed the pair of them, waving the bottle of Grey Goose in the air. "We decided we couldn't leave you, so we brought the booze with us. Are you two catching up on old times?"

Tendrils of a cracking headache began sprouting in Abby's brain. Had Delta's final words had a knowing tone to them? She was too flummoxed to worry.

"Stay where you are. I'm getting changed and coming in!" Delta shouted.

"Okay!" Abby replied, glancing at Jordan.

She was sitting, head flipped towards the stars.
They'd started, but they hadn't finished.
Which was probably for the best.
But clearly, nobody had told Abby's heart.

# Chapter Nineteen

Jordan woke up wondering where she was. Her brain took a little while to put it all into place. She was in purgatory, that's where.

Otherwise known as Cannes, French city of dreams.

Currently her city of what-the-fuck.

She rolled over, cracking open a single eyelid. At least she wasn't rolling over and into Abby. Now that would have been a monumental fuck-up.

Perhaps her habit of not forcing things was a good one. Or perhaps Delta, Gloria et al turning up when they did last night had saved her and Abby the trouble of making one of the biggest mistakes of her life. The one that would cost her job.

And then possibly steal her sanity. Because she might not have been in this situation before, but it was plain as day where it would end. She'd seen it before in books, in movies, and in real life.

Rule number one: don't be someone's final fling.

Rule number two: when one of the party is engaged to be married, things don't normally turn out well.

However, it didn't make her feelings any less real.

Plus, when Abby had looked into her eyes and told her

she couldn't stop thinking about her, that had seemed pretty real, too.

She closed her eyes, regret and relief bubbling in her like an internal hot tub.

Regret at not kissing Abby. Relief she hadn't.

A beep on her phone.

Jordan rolled over and grabbed it. It was a text from Karen.

*How's it going in Cannes? I hope you've put that killer red bikini to good use.'*

Karen had no idea.

*It's going well. Interesting. I nearly kissed the bride last night.*

Her finger hovered over the send button. Should she press it? She did, before she could second-guess herself.

An instant reply. *Whaaaaaat!? How? Why?*

Jordan would love to answer those questions in a clear, honest manner. She couldn't.

*She told me she has feelings for me. It's a mess. We were alone in a hot tub. But we didn't kiss. I have to put things right today. Wish me luck.*

A few seconds went by before she got a reply.

*Good luck. Just remember, she's not who you should be with. Go to a bar, snog a random. Get it out of your system. Just don't snog her.*

Jordan's cheeks flushed as she thought about how close she'd come to doing exactly that. How far the barriers came down in the heat of the night, with nobody around.

Millimetres is how close they'd come. She could still feel the touch of Abby's breath on her lips.

*I won't. Gotta go.* Jordan flung her phone on the bed, then swung her legs onto the parquet floor. Thank god for air conditioning. Between the Cannes heat and her own issues, she'd have been toast by now.

Operation Damage Limitation would start in half an hour. She glanced out at the pool. There was nobody there. Being an early riser had its plus points.

She grabbed her red bikini from the drying rack in her bathroom, and pulled it on. Half an hour in the pool and then she'd be ready to face the day.

As ready as she'd ever be.

\* \* \*

Jordan's muscles ached as she strolled into the kitchen and got the fruit platter George the chef had left before leaving yesterday. The large ticking clock on the spotless kitchen wall told her it was an hour until their big breakfast was going to turn up, enough time to let the fruit come to room temperature, and for her to have a shower, and put the coffee on. She set ten white mugs out on the counter by the coffee machine, placed the cutlery and hen party napkins in neat lines, then stacked the bone china white plates beside that. Satisfied she'd done as much as she could, Jordan gave a nod and walked out of the kitchen.

And straight into an oncoming Abby. She was wearing cut-off denim shorts and a white T-shirt that left little to the imagination. Was she even wearing a bra?

Jordan needed to stop staring. She brought her gaze up to Abby's face.

Being so early, she had no make-up on yet. Jordan liked it.

"Hey." Jordan had been practising her first line to Abby the whole time she was swimming. But now she was in front of her, all her preparation had flown out the window. Abby had that effect on her.

"Hey." But Abby's words weren't what Jordan was following. Instead, she focused on Abby's eyes, which were scanning her body.

Shit. Jordan had thought she'd make it to her room before anyone got up. This hen party liked to sleep late. She was wearing her red bikini again. She might as well have been naked.

Abby seemed to have temporarily lost the gift of speech.

Jordan angled her head towards the door. "I was just going to get changed. Before breakfast turns up."

She curled her toes as time dragged.

Abby stood up taller.

"So I should just…" Jordan edged past Abby. She kept walking before Abby could stop her. Down the corridor. Up the grand, polished stairs. Footsteps followed her. When she turned, Abby was right behind her.

"Keep going." Abby bundled Jordan into her room, then closed the door. Abby pressed her back and palms into its solid wood. She took a deep breath, looking like this was the last place in the world she wanted to be. "I just wanted to chat about last night. We went to bed with everything left a little unsaid and I didn't want it to be awkward today."

Jordan's heart thumped in her chest. Standing in this bikini with Abby wasn't a good start. She walked around the other side of the bed to put some distance between them. "It's good it's out in the open. But like you said, we got carried away. Nothing's changed. We can still work together just like we have been."

Abby nodded. Like this was a solid plan. Not just some words to paper over the cracks. Like they were both master plasterers, and this plan was foolproof. Abby rubbed her hands together in front of her stomach, sucking on the inside of her cheek. "So we're good? Back to being friends?"

Jordan nodded, gritting her teeth. "Of course. Friends and colleagues. I'm your professional bridesmaid."

Abby looked like Jordan had just punched her in the gut.

Jordan hadn't meant to upset her. But perhaps it was the best thing to say. Present Abby with the bare facts, so they stayed in their lanes.

Outside, a door slammed, making them both start.

"You should go." Jordan folded her arms across her chest. "Before your mum or Delta crash in here and think the worst."

"The truth." Abby looked like she wanted to stuff the words back into her mouth. "God, what a mess." She shook her head.

Jordan walked around the bed. "Abby." She took one of Abby's hands in hers. "It's not a mess yet, and it doesn't have to be. A few weeks from now, you'll look back and laugh. For now, you have to let me get showered so I can take charge of today. We've got breakfast to eat, then a wine tour to enjoy. It's going to be fun. The last thing I want to do is spoil your hen weekend. You only get one of these, so please try to enjoy it. For yourself, and for everyone here who wants to celebrate with you." Jordan squeezed her hand. "Will you try?"

Abby nodded. "I'll try."

Jordan dropped her hand. Then immediately wanted to take Abby in her arms and tumble onto the bed.

But that wasn't in the itinerary for today. Falling for the bride wasn't on the spreadsheet. And Jordan was a slave to her spreadsheet.

"I'm going to have a shower. You're going to go out and make coffee. Then at ten, men will arrive on motorbikes to deliver our breakfast. There are worse days to live through, whatever it seems like right now."

* * *

It was the last stop on the wine tour and everybody was a little wasted.

Including Abby.

Okay, especially Abby.

She kept looking at Jordan with sad, doleful eyes.

Every time she did, Jordan shifted a little more uncomfortably in her seat at the front of their minibus. Any minute now, she was sure Abby was going to say something inappropriate. Sometimes, Jordan really hated alcohol and its tongue-loosening affect.

Gloria perched on the front seat, modelling the hen T-shirt wonderfully. Everyone was wearing the same: a white T-shirt with the words *Bride Squad* written in gold swirly letters on the front. Behind them, as the radio strode towards the end of Bruno Mars' song *Marry You*, the group belted out the final chorus. It had been one of the songs of the weekend, and now it was on the minibus radio. Jordan was already sick of it. However, she was smiling through like a dutiful host.

"How many more wine stops have we got, Jordan?" Gloria asked.

"One more before we head back for the final night's dinner on the terrace under the stars."

"Sounds so romantic." Abby was slurring. She whipped her head around and fixed Jordan with her stare. "I want to sit beside Jordan, my best old friend."

Every one of Jordan's muscles tensed. The hot tub flashed through her mind. How they'd so nearly kissed. Now Abby was saying this? Was anyone else clocking it? Jordan looked around the group. She didn't think so.

"You've done such a good job." Gloria beamed at Jordan.

Jordan's cheeks flushed. If only she knew.

"The breakfast this morning was amazing. This wine tour has been out of this world, with a private bus and our own guide. That lunch was spectacular, too."

It had been, exceeding even Jordan's expectations. They'd lunched in the third vineyard, overlooking the vines, and the food had been Mediterranean and glorious. Just like the wine. Jordan had sat as far away from Abby as possible, and got to know her university friends a little more. She'd almost relaxed, but there had still been a couple of moments when she'd looked up and caught Abby's gaze. Both times, her blood had stilled, and the volume turned down.

She wasn't surprised. They'd opened something here, hadn't they? Much as it pained Jordan to admit, whatever *it* was, it was still going. Still rolling down the hill, and she had no idea how to stop its momentum. Not with a week to go before the wedding. A week of working with Abby and Marcus every day.

Still, she was trying not to think about that, lest she give herself a stress ulcer. She'd got one when her parents divorced. It wasn't something she wanted to repeat.

"You should do this professionally, you're that good," Delta added, giving Jordan a wink. She always had to get a dig in.

Still, Delta was the least of Jordan's worries today. Plus, there was always one whose nose Jordan pushed out of joint. If she wasn't careful, it was going to be the whole group.

The radio DJ said something in French, then put the next track on.

Jordan stilled. *Drops Of Jupiter*. The song she'd told Abby she loved. Hopefully she wouldn't remember. With luck…

"Jordan!" Abby's voice was high-pitched.

Too late.

"This song reminds Jordan of her first love. She told me the other day, didn't you Jordan? She was in love once. Just like me and Marcus!" Her tone was sing-song.

Jordan closed her eyes, trying to block this out. It wasn't working.

Abby was trying to sing along even though she didn't know the words. She was just about to launch into the chorus, when the bus pulled up at the final vineyard.

Jordan leaned over and snapped off the radio, giving Abby a stern look. She was pretty sure it sailed right over her head.

They all clambered off the bus, spirits high. Ahead of her, Taran was leaning on the bus, a big beam on her face, phone glued to her ear. On the phone to Ryan again, no doubt. Nikita, Frankie, Delta, and Erin were reminiscing with Abby about a time at university when she drank too much red wine and spilt a glass all over someone else.

"Red wine?" Arielle asked, screwing up her face. "I hope they weren't wearing a white shirt."

Nikita nodded her head. "They were."

Abby grinned as they took their seats at the tasting counter, five stools down one side, five stools down another. "That wasn't even the worst of it. I was very sorry about messing up this woman's top, and I'd read that white wine was a great thing to remove red wine stains. So with my booze-addled brain, I took this woman to the toilet and poured a glass of white wine down her."

Now Gloria had her head in her hands. "Did she scream at you?"

Abby frowned. "I don't recall exactly what she said, but I know I might have shouted if it had been me."

"Again, there are some things mothers never need to know."

"We definitely shouldn't start talking about all of Abby's university conquests, then." Delta was stirring again.

Jordan sat up at that.

Abby threw a glance Delta's way, before shaking her head. "We should not. It's my hen weekend, and I say we drink more wine." She put a hand in the air. "Who's for more wine?"

Cheers all around as the bartender lined up ten shiny glasses, before pouring a generous amount into each glass. Jordan leaned over and put her hand over the top of the final glass, shaking her head.

"Last vineyard, Jordan. You can have a drink, now." That was Abby, giving Jordan the side-eye.

But Jordan wasn't to be swayed. It was still only 4pm. The day was young. "I'll skip this round."

"Who's the bride?" Abby fixed her with a knowing smile. "You were never this goody-two-shoes when we were in primary school." She tapped the base of Jordan's glass. The bartender still hovered, bottle poised. "A sip. For me."

Annoyance fizzed up Jordan, but she was cornered. "Okay. A dash. For you."

The bartender poured a small amount into her glass, before pushing it to Jordan.

Abby turned on her stool, and grabbed the seat with her right hand just in time to stop her from falling. "Oops!" she said. "Wobbly me!"

Jordan put a hand on Abby's arm to steady her. "Okay?"

Abby raised her gaze, nodding as she took her glass.

Jordan sighed. The sooner this was over and they were back at the villa, the better.

"Everyone!" Abby waved her glass in the air.

Jordan winced, taking a step back.

"I just wanted to say, thank you all for coming to one of my last weekends as a single woman." She pulled on her top. "Plus, I love my T-shirts. Cheers!"

Whoops from the group, then clinking all around.

When she reached Jordan, Abby paused, then tapped her glass to hers. Then Abby went to drink, missed her mouth, and poured most of the red wine down her white T-shirt that simply said *Bride*.

She jumped up, distress etched on her face. However, her sudden movement sloshed more wine over the edge of the glass, down her forearms and onto her front. If her face had been contorted before, now she looked like she might cry.

Jordan took the glass out of her hand, as the bartender offered serviettes to wipe herself.

"You want me to throw some white wine on you, Abs?" Delta shouted from her stool.

Abby gave her a steely look, followed by a glimmer of a smile. "A hard no." Then she slumped. "Look at my *Bride* T-shirt!"

Jordan dabbed her arms and her top with the serviette, until Abby glanced up at her as she connected with her breast.

Jordan sucked in a breath. "Shall we go to the bathroom?"

Abby nodded. "I think that's best."

"You want my arm?" Jordan offered it.

Abby frowned. "I'm not that drunk."

It took all Jordan's efforts not to disagree.

Gloria jumped off her stool. "You want me to help?"

Jordan shook her head. "Stay and enjoy your wine. We'll only be a minute."

The bathrooms were large and plush, with plump white hand towels, lit candles, and huge mirrors so they could assess the damage.

As soon as she was in front of a mirror, Abby pouted. "At least it's only my hen T-shirt."

Jordan pulled up a chair and sat Abby down, wetting the end of one of the hand towels right away. "Exactly. For now, it's damage limitation time. You can get the red wine out easier if we soak it up now."

She leaned over Abby and began dabbing at her top, while also trying not to touch her at all. It was an impossible task. Meanwhile, Abby began touching Jordan's hair.

"So blond, so gorgeous." Abby twirled Jordan's hair around

her fingers. "Such a beautiful woman to have come into my life at just the wrong time."

Jordan froze. What should she do? This was unchartered territory.

"Abby." Jordan's tone held a warning she hoped Abby heeded. "Now's not the time. I'm trying to clean you up."

Abby gave her a smirk. "You're not going to do it if you don't touch me, though, are you?" She took Jordan's hand in hers and pressed the towel onto her breast. "That's how you clean me up, Jordan." She pressed harder again. "I need a firm hand."

Jordan gritted her teeth as desire shot down her, landing right at her centre.

She had to shelve her desire and do her job. Especially now Abby was back to pawing her face, her fingertips on the tip of Jordan's nose.

"So perfect, just like a model," Abby said, her voice a lullaby. "But not for me, because off limits." She pouted.

Jordan grabbed both Abby's hands and placed them by her side, before bringing her face level with Abby's. "Listen to me. I'm really going to clean you up now. I need you to stop touching me so I can do that, okay? People are not far away, and I've got a job to do today."

Abby nodded, a smile spreading across her face as she lifted both hands in the air, palms out. "I promise no more touching. Not allowed. Even though you're so pretty. And your hair." She raised a hand to it again.

"Abby!" Jordan was almost shouting.

Abby sat up straighter, putting one hand by her side, the other giving Jordan a swift salute. "Yes, sir!"

Jordan shook her head, suppressing a smile. She wet the towel again and this time, she didn't mess around. She mopped Abby up as best she could. All the while Abby looked at her like she was hanging the moon. Another time, another place, Jordan might have entertained it. But not here, in this bathroom.

"So strict," Abby said.

Jordan ignored her, running her gaze over her front. No, she wasn't going to focus on her breasts.

But Abby obviously had other ideas, as she placed a hand on Jordan's left cheek. "I wonder if you'd be so strict in bed? But I guess I'm never going to know because that would make me a bad person." She gazed into Jordan's eyes.

This time, Jordan let her.

"I'm not a bad person, Jordan."

Jordan's heart boomed. "I know," she replied.

"I just want to kiss you. Is that so bad?" Abby tilted her head, her eyes sad, her lips inviting.

Jordan's body flushed with want.

She stepped back and held out a hand to Abby, who took it, staring at their connection.

Jordan wasn't going to let her dwell. She pulled Abby up.

"Come on. Let's get you back on your wine stool before they send out a search party."

# Chapter Twenty

Abby woke with a start and squeezed her eyes tight shut. Dammit, her head hurt. She put her palm to her forehead, and pressed down, as if that would make it feel better.

It didn't. Abby let out a sigh and grabbed her phone from where she'd abandoned it on the covers beside her. It was 2.30am. She'd drunk far too much yesterday. Day drinking was never a good idea. You could dress it up as a wine tour, a cultural activity, but it was still what it was. An excuse to get a little tipsy. Not that she'd been complaining at the time. It was just now, hours later when she'd woken up gagging for water, that she was questioning her choices.

She rolled off the bed, wobbled, then grabbed a T-shirt and denim shorts. Her wine-stained T-shirt was draped across a chair.

Oh god. Wine stain. The toilets with Jordan. She vaguely recalled it, but she couldn't quite remember what she'd said. She just remembered there had been a lot of touching from her. Of Jordan's face, Jordan's hair.

*Fuck.*

She closed her eyes as nausea rose in her.

A glass of water would make her feel better. Perhaps two.

Abby slipped on her flip-flops and walked to the kitchen in the dark, trying to make as little noise as possible. She wasn't sure she succeeded as she felt her way along the walls. She hit the kitchen spotlights over the dining table, and decided that was enough to illuminate the kitchen. She didn't want too much light, and she was only getting a glass of water.

The detritus of their night was still covering the surfaces: glasses, empty wine bottles, some crisps and nuts still left in bowls. Abby's stomach growled. They'd had a big dinner cooked for them by a visiting chef, but she could still eat. She opened the fridge and spied some fancy potatoes — were they called hasselbacks? Or was that the bloke who used to be in Baywatch? No, that was Hasselhoff. Were they Hasselhoff potatoes?

She shook her head, smiling at herself, and shoved a potato in her mouth. While she chomped, she opened a few cupboards, locating the glasses on the third try. She didn't know where anything was in here. Princess Abby. She'd been waited on hand and foot all weekend. By her whole crew, ably led by Captain Jordan.

Those two words conjured up an image of Jordan in a sailor suit, all tight belts and pressed white fabric. Abby gulped. She focused on glugging the water. If she wasn't so taken with Jordan, she might not have got so drunk. Then again, this was what a bride-to-be was meant to do on her hen weekend, wasn't it? She was just following protocol. Just as she would have done if Jordan was in front of her in uniform and doling out the orders.

When she looked up, her heart caught in her chest and she almost stopped breathing. Jordan was standing in the kitchen doorway, although thankfully, not in a sailor suit. That would have been a little too much to handle. Instead, an orange singlet top and navy shorts adorned her sleepy form.

"What are you doing up?" Abby glanced at the clock. "It's the middle of the night." If anything, she looked even more appealing in the semi-darkness. As Abby walked towards her, she spied a sleep crease indented on Jordan's cheek. Her skin was probably still hot to the touch.

"I'm aware." Jordan went straight to the right cupboard. "Water," she said, filling a glass. She drank some, before settling herself on the other side of the large white kitchen island.

A safe distance away.

"How's your head?" Jordan squinted at Abby.

"It's been better. Good thing I drank a lot of water when we got home, or I'd be way worse."

"Like Delta and Nikita?" Jordan offered. She found a cloth and wiped something from the island.

Abby smiled. "Yes, like them." She paused. "Did they go to their separate rooms?" They'd always been each other's fallback at university, although they hadn't slept together for a couple of years as far as Abby could remember.

"I'd be surprised if they did."

Abby smiled. At least someone had got lucky on her hen weekend. Good for them. "Meanwhile, I woke up thinking what a fool I made of myself in the toilet with you at the vineyard. After I spilt the wine." Her stomach flipped as her gaze connected with Jordan's. Abby stilled as everything at the edges of her vision went into soft focus. Now, all she could hear was the tick of the kitchen clock, along with the thud of her heart in her stomach.

Jordan shook her head, her blond hair brushing her collarbone. What would it feel like to lick along...

*Stop it.*

"You didn't make an idiot of yourself. You were just a little drunk." Jordan paused. "And a little cute, if I'm honest." Jordan winced. "Which I'm trying really hard not to be."

Abby licked her lips. Jordan had thought she was cute. Sexy cute or annoying cute? "We're both too honest, that's our problem. Most British people would have just avoided this altogether, wouldn't they?"

Jordan gave her a half-smile. "Undoubtedly. It's not in our nature, is it? I wonder what the French would do?"

Abby patted the kitchen island. "Have sex on here, then smoke a fag?"

Jordan's laugh was like a bullet, piercing Abby's defences. "You're probably right. They're a bit more carpe diem as a nation, aren't they? Whereas we sweep it under the carpet, hoping it'll all go away."

Abby nodded. It all sounded terribly familiar. "The trouble is, I've been doing that most of my life." It was only when she uttered the words, she realised their truth.

She swigged some more water. Her head was still full of cotton wool.

"I'm going to miss you when we get home."

Jordan smiled. "You won't. I'm still working for you until the wedding."

"I know. But it's not the same as having morning swims with you. Late night drinks. Hot tub chats."

Jordan raised an eyebrow. "Not forgetting middle-of-the-night hydration sessions." She eyed Abby. "Probably for the best."

Abby *should* think the same.

But she didn't.

Jordan refilled her water, then walked towards Abby, stopping when she drew up alongside her. "You coming?"

Abby raised her eyes to Jordan's. As she did, an explosion of want rippled through her. In the dim light, Jordan's eyes were no longer an invitation to dive into the sea. But they were still vibrantly alive, and speaking to Abby. As was Jordan's whole body. She could feel its warmth, the electricity jumping between them.

Abby snaked out a hand. She was acting on impulse. She couldn't let this go. She had to know. What Jordan tasted like. How she felt in her arms. Her hand gripped Jordan by the waist and pulled her close.

Carpe diem.

Jordan's face spelled surprise. She didn't say a word.

Abby stared into her eyes, then dropped her gaze to Jordan's lips. And then, before she could talk herself out of it, she leaned forward and pressed her lips to Jordan.

The effect was like thunder inside her. As her lips slid across Jordan's and drank her in, Abby's whole body shook as a rumble rolled through her.

Abby had dreamed of this. The reality was ten times better.

Jordan gripped her waist, pulling her closer.

Their breasts melded to each other.

Abby groaned as desire slid to her core. When Jordan's tongue snaked into her mouth, she wilted more.

She hadn't been sure what she'd wanted to achieve. In her mind, she'd just wanted to finish what they started in the hot tub. A kiss. Just one. Just to know. To put her mind at rest.

But she knew now that was a complete lie. Because where the fuse had been smouldering, it was now well and truly lit.

Abby's heart gave a kick, and her body flushed with total, overwhelming hunger. This kiss was pure dynamite. Pure lust. Pure her. Sliding her tongue into Jordan's mouth was *everything*.

Abby's fingers clawed at Jordan's breasts, teasing her nipples through the skimpy cotton fabric. She breathed in Jordan's warm, sleepy smell. She never wanted her to leave.

The kiss might have lasted two minutes or a day. Abby had no idea. All sense of time and space left her once their lips connected.

The primal intensity gave way to slow, sensual kissing. Abby was a wreck. The sound of their lips, the beat of her heart, the slow, sure intensity of it all. It was almost too much.

Jordan must have sensed it too, because she pulled back.

They stood like that, mouths open, panting at each other for what seemed like another eternity.

Until Jordan blinked and pulled back a fraction. Just like that, the spell was broken. They were back in the room. The kitchen island. The bowls of snacks. Their abandoned water glasses.

Abby cast her gaze down as they untangled themselves from each other. Her feet were suddenly so interesting. She gulped, her heart still slamming against her ribcage, the torrent of butterflies in her stomach swirling around and around, with nowhere to go. When she eventually looked up, Jordan's face was flushed, her sleep crease intensified.

What was she thinking? Abby wanted to know, but then again, she didn't. Abby stared into her eyes for a few seconds, before it became too much. If she carried on staring at Jordan, she'd step closer. If she stepped closer... yeah, that couldn't happen again.

She'd done it now.

It was out of her system.

That's what she had to keep telling herself.

"I'm not sure what to say." She ground her flip-flop into the floor.

Jordan's feet were bare. Her feet were really pretty. Just like her.

Abby internally rolled her eyes.

"We should go to bed." Jordan bit her lip. "I don't think talking is going to help tonight. Do you?"

Abby shook her head. They were beyond talking now. They'd entered a totally new realm.

Jordan began to walk, but Abby placed a hand on Jordan's arm. Her whole body tingled anew at the touch.

"I'm sorry. That was completely my fault. We'll sort it out when we get home."

The look Jordan gave her was so hot, it left a mark on her skin. Then she left the room.

Abby clutched the island. This was a crossroads. Either a beginning, or a full stop. Static noise began to fill her brain. She pushed herself towards the door and snapped off the light.

Had that really just happened?

She walked up the stairs, glancing at Jordan's door as she passed it.

She touched her fingertips to her still-hot lips.

Yes, it really had.

# Chapter Twenty-One

Breakfast had been one of the most awkward meals she'd ever endured. Jordan had focused on making sure everyone was fed and watered, on talking to the staff and giving them a tip, on finding Gloria's stories fascinating. Luckily, she and Abby had flown under the radar with ease. First, because nobody suspected a thing. Second, because Delta and Nikita disappearing and spending the night together had proved the hot topic of conversation. Delta was Jordan's new favourite person.

She'd been friendly but professional with Abby. Even though, inside she'd been a bundle of frayed nerve endings and conflicted emotions.

Jordan knew what she wanted.

She was also well aware it was something she couldn't possibly have.

Now they were heading back home. As Jordan walked up the short flight of steps to the jet that would take them back to London, she juggled the pieces of the weekend in her head. However, when she tried to lay them out and piece them together, she drew a blank.

In her mind, they fitted. But only there.

She'd got to know Abby a whole lot better.

She'd shared her hopes and dreams with her.

Then she'd kissed the bride. It wasn't an extra she should ever include on her website.

Jordan clutched the handrail, following Gloria's pert bum. Like mother, like daughter.

*Really not helpful.*

"Good afternoon, ladies!" Captain Michelle gave them a wide smile. "I hope you've had a fantastic time in Cannes, and that you were given a hen weekend to remember?" She aimed the final part at Abby, who was at the top of the stairs, in front of her mum.

Abby nodded. "It was incredible," she said, glancing behind. "Mum, Delta, Jordan, everyone." Abby's gaze landed on Jordan and her cheeks coloured pink. "It's been a weekend to remember." Abby walked onto the plane.

Jordan wouldn't argue with that summation. Now they just had to get through the final trip home, before they could finally spend some time apart and try to work out how to handle this situation on their own. There was no handbook. They were going to have to write it themselves.

Jordan nodded at Michelle as she passed her, taking in her starched uniform and shiny shoes. Had she been in the army before becoming a regular pilot? Or did they teach similar skills at pilot school, too? It was nice to have her mind focus on a different issue to the one that had overwhelmed her all weekend. However, once she was in the plane and breathing in Abby's floral perfume that was lingering in the air, that all came crashing down.

She came to a halt near the front of the plane, hovering in the aisle between Abby and Gloria.

"Feel free to sit with your mum on the way back if you like." Jordan smiled at Gloria, then glanced back down the plane to where Delta was sitting next to Nikita. They looked every inch the couple they proclaimed they were not. "Looks like she's been dumped by her travel buddy."

Gloria smiled, reaching down to plump up her travel pillow. "I wouldn't sit next to me." She held up her pillow. "I have my trusty friend here, and I plan to pull up my arm rest and lie down for the flight." She tapped Jordan's arm. "You sit with Abby. You know what she's like on take-off. You can hold her hand." She gave her a wink and turned her attention to getting comfortable.

Okay. She was going to have to call on all her professional qualities for this one. She glanced at Abby, who was busying herself putting her hand luggage in the overhead lockers, studiously ignoring Jordan.

Maybe this could work out. If they just agreed to ignore each other the whole flight, they could get through it no problem.

"You want the window, or the aisle?" Even talking to Abby was strained. As if they were speaking a different language. As if they had nothing in common at all.

Abby stilled at Jordan's words. "I'll take the aisle." She sat, and stared straight ahead.

Jordan stowed her hand luggage, then sat beside her. She fiddled with her phone, ignoring the texts from Karen asking how it was going with her 'hot bride'. Jordan wanted to respond with a scream emoji, but then she'd have to explain it to Karen. Better to leave it until she got home and could unravel the full extent to her best friend then.

That she'd done the wrong thing. That she wasn't sure how to fix it. That she wasn't sure she wanted to fix it.

Jordan put her phone on flight mode, then put it in the pocket on the wall in front of her. She stretched out her legs, wriggling her toes. The silence between her and Abby was deafening. After all the chats they'd had. All the laughs.

Then one kiss.

Now, there was nothing.

Emotion swelled inside Jordan, taking her by surprise. She already missed what they'd had. What they'd built between them this weekend, however brief it had been. Because it had been something. Even before the kiss, they'd had a rapport, a frisson. A connection. After the kiss, that had only increased. Except it couldn't.

Jordan's heart was in pieces. There was no lotion or potion she could use to make herself feel better. That was the thing with heartbreak, whatever size. You had to feel it. There was no cure.

Sitting beside the person who'd just wrecked you was definitely not the thing to do. But Jordan didn't have a choice.

Michelle made the announcement they were ready to leave, and the plane began to taxi along the runway.

Jordan glanced Abby's way. Her face was pale, her gaze glued straight ahead. She was clutching her armrest so hard, her knuckles were white. When they'd flown over, Jordan had taken Abby's hand at this point. But now there was an invisible barrier between them, it wasn't so easy.

However, Jordan was still on the clock. She was still getting paid to make Abby's weekend as good as it could possibly be. She'd already overstepped the mark on that one. Perhaps she should overstep their invisible barrier now and make Abby's flight that little bit more bearable. They might not be talking to each other, but they could still communicate.

Jordan took a deep breath, and wrapped her fingers around Abby's.

Abby's head jerked, and she went to pull her hand away.

Jordan let go. She wasn't going to force her if she didn't want to.

However, seconds later, Abby glanced at Jordan and their eyes locked.

Desire and despair flowed down Jordan. She gave Abby a sad smile.

Abby returned it, before she wrapped her fingers around Jordan's and squeezed tight. She held on until the plane had taken off, gripping until Jordan felt the blood supply might soon be cut off. She didn't say a word. Once they were airborne, Abby stopped squeezing so tight, but still held on.

There was far less chatter on the way back, everyone tired after a packed weekend. When Jordan turned around, everyone had their eyes closed, lulled by the engine's gentle rhythms. Gavin came up to Jordan, tapping her on the arm.

"I just wanted to ask, do you want me to do trolley service? Everyone's either asleep or resting their eyes, and I don't want to disturb them."

Jordan shook her head. "Don't bother. If they want something, they can press their call button."

Gavin nodded. "Do you want anything while I'm here?"

Jordan glanced at Abby, who shook her head. "We're good, thanks."

Jordan pressed her head into the back of her seat, just as

Abby began stroking the pad of her thumb up and over the back of Jordan's right hand.

The desire that had been like a car idling at the side of the road revved up. As Abby moved her thumb left and right, a tingle spread through Jordan, starting at her clit and booming out through her body. Damn, she was in trouble.

She glanced at Abby, holding her gaze. She dropped down to Abby's lips, and then back up, shaking her head.

She shouldn't wind herself up like this. But Abby had started it, hadn't she? Or had Jordan?

It didn't matter in the end. From the heated stare Abby was giving her, she knew she felt it too. Whatever it was. This thing between them was growing bigger by the second.

Heat swirled in Jordan, and suddenly, it was too much.

The fasten seatbelt sign went off.

Jordan unclipped her seatbelt and stood, throwing Abby a pained look. She had to calm down and get away. It was all too much.

She took a deep breath, walking unsteadily down the aisle, passing the rest of the oblivious hens.

When Jordan looked back, Abby was standing and staring.

Then she strode towards her.

* * *

What the hell was she doing?

Abby had no idea. It was as if her legs were propelling her to an action she had no control over, and her conscience was absent without leave.

Something bigger than her was at work. Some greater power. Something that knew far more than she did.

Jordan opened the toilet door, and when she turned, did a double-take. "What are you…" she began.

However, as Abby followed her into the toilet and shut the door, the words died on Jordan's lips.

Desire thrummed through Abby as she slid the lock on the door across with a definite clunk. The noise was deafening. It was also decisive. That one lock sealing their fate.

Their mouths hadn't touched, but Abby was excruciatingly aware of Jordan. Those crystal-blue eyes watching her. The air dripped with delicious tension. Was this a mistake? She didn't know. All she knew was she was sick of feeling bad. Especially when being with Jordan felt so good.

Abby locked her gaze with Jordan and like two magnets drawn together, they moved as one, their mouths fusing in a beautiful, forceful way.

Jordan's kiss was bruising, exactly what Abby wanted.

She was done pussyfooting around. If she didn't act now, she never would. This was her hen weekend. The last chance to dream. The final chance to push her limits, before she settled down.

She was going out in a blaze of glory.

"Abby."

The way Jordan said her name sent tingles up and down her spine.

Abby silenced her with a bruising, burning kiss. "I want you," she replied. "Do you want me, too?"

Jordan nodded.

This was what they both wanted.

She pushed up Jordan's top, and snapped open the back of her bra. Her breasts were right there in front of her. Just as they had been in the hot tub. But this time, she was going to act on it.

Abby sucked Jordan's nipple into her mouth. Desire flooded her.

She pressed her feet into the ground, to stop herself from lifting off. Because that's what this felt like. Like her passion was rocket-fuelled, on another level. She swirled her tongue around Jordan's breast.

Jordan sucked in a breath.

Abby lifted her head and their gazes met.

Her hands moved swiftly then, undoing Jordan's beige shorts and pushing them down her legs. Jordan was wearing a pair of black lacy knickers. Somehow, Abby hadn't expected that. But it only added a little more fuel to the fire.

She slid a single finger inside them, and ran it though Jordan's hot core.

Another growl.

Abby kissed her again, before she shed those too, and spread Jordan's legs with her thigh. She was just going on instinct, and pure animal attraction. She wanted to know Jordan intimately. Inside and out. There was only one way to do that.

Abby pulled her lips temporarily away and locked their gaze.

Then she slid two fingers inside Jordan. Just as she had in her dream.

Nothing could have prepared her for this moment. Jordan was so ready, so wet. Just like Abby. They'd been fighting their attraction all weekend, and for good reason. But right now, in this moment, nothing could have felt more right. As Abby sank deeper into Jordan and their mouths found each other again, Abby abandoned any sense that she might have control over this.

She had none.

With her fingers inside Jordan and Jordan's tongue inside her, this moment felt like the pinnacle of her life so far. What she'd been driving towards all along, even though she'd been totally unaware of it. As Jordan clung to her, shifting her right leg up and around Abby, they rocked together as one. Abby sliding in and out. Jordan moving her hips, arching her back, crying out, then stopping, realising where she was.

Their eyes locked.

A fleeting thought of stopping before they were found out skated across Abby's mind. But then she looked at them in the large toilet mirror. She couldn't stop. She was in too deep. Literally and metaphorically.

Jordan grabbed Abby's shoulders, and pulled her close to rest her head on Abby's shoulder.

"You feel so good," she said. She reached down and placed Abby's thumb onto her clit. Jordan moved Abby's thumb in small circles. She closed her eyes as she did, and let out an almost inaudible gasp. "Just like that," she said, before removing her hand.

Abby didn't need telling twice. As she fucked Jordan, she marvelled at the effect she had on her. Also, at her utter beauty in this moment. Abby had never felt so alive. So in the moment. So herself. She circled Jordan's clit as instructed, picking up speed and pressure to Jordan's movements. Jordan was perfection in her hands.

Moments later Abby curled her fingers into Jordan and watched as she toppled over the edge.

Jordan clutched Abby's fingers inside her.

Perfection was rewritten.

Jordan panted, her cheeks flushed, her blond hair framing her face exquisitely. This was the Jordan-face she'd been dreaming about. She couldn't believe her dreams had come true. Or that she'd joined the mile-high club in the process.

Abby pressed her lips to Jordan's once more. Electricity flared inside her. This is what her life had been missing. She eased her fingers out, never dropping Jordan's gaze. She had no idea what Jordan's stare was saying, but it was loaded — with desire, with want, with questions. Abby didn't have any answers. All she knew was that she wanted Jordan to strip off her clothes and take her right now.

Jordan pulled back after a few moments, eyeing Abby. She was still mostly naked, her hands clutching the sink. She let her head drop backwards. "Fucking hell, Abby. What are you doing to me?"

Abby had no words.

She had no idea anymore.

She ran a hand up the back of Jordan's thigh, over her pert bum, then up her back, before kissing her breasts.

Jordan brought her gaze back to her.

"I've no idea," Abby said. "But that was incredible. I want to do it again and again."

A knock on the door interrupted their conversation.

Jordan jolted.

Abby froze. A siren went off in her head. She glanced at Jordan, and saw her own horrified expression reflected back in the bathroom mirror.

"Abby? Are you in there?" It was Mum.

Jordan reached down and pulled up her knickers and shorts, cracking her head on the sink in the process.

That would have hurt, but Jordan didn't utter a word. She was probably holding her breath.

Abby knew she was. "Just coming!"

Abby's voice was breezy. In utter contrast to her world, which was crashing down before her. From being the best decision, now she was wondering if it was the absolute worst of her life. She'd just fucked her bridesmaid on her hen weekend. With everyone she knew and loved in earshot. Who the hell was she? What the hell was she doing? And how was she going to explain this to her mum when they walked out?

"Everything okay?" Gloria asked, concern etched in her voice. "You've been gone a while."

Hadn't she been going to sleep? "It's fine. I wasn't feeling well. Jordan came to give me something to settle my stomach." The lie fell from her lips so easily, even she was shocked.

When she glanced up, Jordan gave her a nod. It was almost like she was too scared to speak, for fear of what might come out.

"We'll be out in a minute. You go back to your seat."

A few seconds of silence. "If you're sure?"

"Positive, Mum." *Oh god, oh god, oh god, oh god.*

What had she done? And was it bad that despite it all, she just wanted to do it again? Abby turned, flattening herself against the door. Had they got away with it? Abby would have no idea until she looked into her mum's eyes.

"You think she believed us?"

Jordan nodded. She turned to the mirror and fluffed her

hair. "She has no reason not to. Unless you're in the habit of fucking women when you're 30,000 feet in the air?"

"I'm not." Abby let out a long sigh. "You okay?"

Jordan turned, taking her hand. "I'm…" She paused. "I don't know what I am. Horny. Confused. Overwhelmed. This was exactly what we've been trying to avoid all weekend, wasn't it?"

"It was." She couldn't deny it. They'd come so close, but then the thought of losing Jordan had been too much.

It was her fault. Now she had to work out a way to fix it. Abby reached around Jordan, pumping some handwash and washing her hands. It felt crude to do it so soon. It brought her back to reality.

"But now what? Can we carry on working together?" Jordan's face clouded over.

"I hope so?" But Abby had no idea. This wasn't anything she'd bargained for. She grabbed some hand towels. "I don't know. We have to get back out there now. Let's talk tomorrow. Are you coming to London?"

Jordan nodded. "That was the plan."

"Okay. Well let's have lunch." She leaned forward and kissed her. Lightly. Then more forcefully. Until Abby's hands were tangled in Jordan's hair, and she had to force herself to let go.

"I don't want to let you go. I can't let you go."

Jordan closed her eyes. "You need to go."

Abby nodded. "I know. But I want you to know this isn't over."

"It has to be, Abby. It can't go anywhere."

Abby shook her head. She refused to believe that. Her

feelings were just too strong. "I'm falling for you. We can't just sweep this aside. I know you feel it, too."

Jordan stared at her. "I do," she whispered.

"Only, when I'm just about to get married, that's a problem, isn't it?"

Jordan didn't reply.

She didn't need to.

# Chapter Twenty-Two

Abby walked through the door of her first-floor flat, then shut it hard. The only sound was her breathing, along with her neighbour's TV below. They were an old couple whose TV was always blaring. She was so used to it now, she tuned it out. However, she wasn't going to miss it when she moved in with Marcus after they got married.

Her heart stuttered at the thought.

*Not now.*

Her flat had that not-lived-in smell about it, even though she'd only been gone four days. Her empty coffee cups from before she left were still on the side, as were two small plates. She walked over to her grey couch and grabbed the cushions, plumping them up. Then she arranged her three remote controls on the coffee table, and tidied her copies of *BBC Good Food* into a pile next to them. Abby had taken out a subscription in the hope of following some of the recipes. That hadn't quite happened yet, but the magazine made for great aspirational reading.

She strolled over to her kitchen at one end of the all-in-one room, wiping up a couple of stray crumbs from the side. She put the kettle on, then checked the fridge. No milk.

She'd have to have a black coffee. Pretend she was from Italy. She could do that.

Ten minutes later, she was slumped on her sofa, her coffee going cold. She didn't want it. She didn't want anything. Well, apart from one particular thing. She put her head in her hands, then rubbed her face.

She could still smell Jordan faintly on her fingers. Still remembered what it felt like to be inside her.

Exciting. Sexy. Glorious.

She shook her head.

All the way home in the cab, she'd been wondering what to do next. She'd got her phone out a few times, stared at Jordan's number, then put it away. What was she going to write? 'Fantastic to fuck you on the plane. Now, about those flowers for my wedding…' It didn't really work, did it?

Nothing did, that was the problem.

Her mind kept shying away from calling Marcus and asking him to come round for a chat. Even the thought of calling him felt weird. They were *so* not Taran and Ryan.

Perhaps they could postpone the wedding, give her some time to think. But he'd be hurt. He'd want to know why. She couldn't possibly tell him. "Because I'm falling for my professional bridesmaid, the one you hired?"

No, it would kill him. It would kill her, too. Then she'd have to deal with Marjorie. And everyone else.

She blew out a long breath. What a mess. She was supposed to be meeting Jordan tomorrow about her speech. But could she? If they met, it'd have to be about business. But would that happen? Could she trust herself? She'd never considered herself an untrustworthy person. Somebody who couldn't control her actions. But that's what had happened.

It's what Jordan did to her.

She'd made her see the world differently. This weekend, they'd bonded. She'd spoken about stuff she hadn't spoken about in years. Things she'd forgotten she'd wanted in her busy life. Like working for a charity. Like making a difference. Like not being caught up in the corporate world. When had her life run away from her?

She picked up her work phone and checked her emails. She had 152. Not bad for four days away. One at the top in particular caught her notice. It was from her boss. When she clicked on it, she saw he was asking for a meeting about 'something important' tomorrow lunchtime. Maybe it was about the project she was hoping to take the lead on.

She sat up straight. Tomorrow? When she was meant to be meeting Jordan?

*Damn it.*

Before Jordan, Abby would have been so excited to get this email. Now, not so much. She'd have to see if Jordan could meet her in the evening instead. She missed her so much already.

A knock on her door made her jump.

When she opened it, her heart dropped. She was well aware that wasn't meant to be her reaction to seeing her fiancé. Marcus's head was barely visible behind the bouquet of red roses he held in one hand. He clutched a gift bag in the other. Abby's heart slumped a little more. Shit, had he brought her a gift from his stag do? She'd brought him nothing apart from a truckload of guilt.

She was a terrible person.

Marcus stepped forward and hugged her, giving her

the flowers with a kiss on the cheek. "Hello future Mrs Montgomery." He grinned, walked past her and grabbed a vase from the kitchen counter. He filled it with water, then took the flowers from her to arrange. Marcus was the better flower arranger in the relationship. This had been established very early on. Hence Delta's jibes about Marcus's sexuality. He wasn't gay, though. Just creative.

Abby, on the other hand...

"How was it? Isn't the villa spectacular?"

Abby nodded, slapping on a fake smile. Flashes of kissing Jordan kept popping into her head, but she pushed them aside. She had to if she was going to survive. "It was amazing. Everyone had a great time, and Jordan made sure it went off without a hitch." Very nearly true. She placed a hand on his arm as he began trimming the rose leaves and snipping the bottom of the stems.

Precise. That was Marcus.

"How about you? How was your weekend?"

Marcus shrugged, not quite looking her in the eye. "You know, the usual. Too much booze, and bawdy behaviour. And..." He paused, eyeing her, before dropping the flowers on the kitchen bench and taking a deep breath. "They got me a stripper, too. I told them not to, but you know what Philip's like when he gets something in his head. Johnny, too. There were pictures taken, so just in case they surface, I wanted you to know. I feel terrible about it." He stopped, and held out the gift bag. "I bought you a gift. It's not a guilt offering. I was going to buy you one anyway."

Abby swallowed, rooted to the spot. Marcus was worried about having a stripper?

She opened the gift box. Inside was a gorgeous silver bracelet with what looked like diamonds studded in the band. She didn't deserve it, but she couldn't let him see that.

She glanced up at his face. "It's gorgeous, but you didn't need to." She was a very bad person.

"I know, but I wanted to. Even though I was on my stag do, I missed you. Is that corny?" He threw up his hands, and gave her a grin "I don't care if it's corny, it's how I feel. Plus, if you can't be corny when you're just about to get married to your best friend, when can you be?"

Abby grinned despite the sinking feeling in her stomach. It was no easy task. Like rubbing your stomach and patting your head at the same time.

"The other reason I bought it, as well as to say I love you, was because I have a favour to ask. My parents want to have us over for dinner tomorrow night. No agenda, just a dinner to spend some time together, to get to know their future daughter-in-law. I've said yes already, because I assumed that a Tuesday would be okay for you. Is it okay?"

Her spirits dropped to a new low for the day. "Tomorrow night?" She'd hoped to see Jordan, but now she wasn't free at lunch or in the evening.

She couldn't say no to this, could she? Not when Marcus was looking at her like a puppydog. She sucked her top lip between her teeth. "Sure, tomorrow is fine."

Marcus studied her face. "Good acting. You're getting better at this." He grinned. "Thank you."

Her phone beeped, and she walked over to the couch, as Marcus resumed his flower arranging. It was a message from Jordan.

Abby gulped. Should she cover it with her hand, or take it in the bedroom?

She was being stupid. She clicked on it.

*Hope you got home okay. We still on for lunch tomorrow? To talk about your speech and everything else?*

She ground her teeth together. Jordan was going to think she was fobbing her off, but there was nothing she could do.

*Really sorry, but something's come up. I'll text you in the week to rearrange.* She studied the message. Did it sound cold? She deleted what she'd written, looked up at Marcus, then wrote it again. She didn't have time to worry. She'd explain it to Jordan when she saw her. She clicked *send*, a feeling of foreboding settling in her stomach. She'd just postponed seeing her, and now she was going to have to sit through a dinner with Marcus and his parents.

"Everything okay?" Marcus asked. He walked over and kissed her lips.

It took everything Abby had to hold it together in that moment. "Fine."

But now she knew.

She didn't want to be kissed by anyone but Jordan.

# Chapter Twenty-Three

Jordan didn't ever recall running so hard or so fast, but today she needed it. Karen was lagging behind as Jordan ripped up Brighton seafront. Even the circling seagulls avoided her, knowing she meant business. The June weather was hitting the late 20s, but the seafront still held a pleasant breeze for running. However, even the sun on her face couldn't change her mood. She was running to forget.

It was only when she stopped that her body remembered she wasn't a natural runner, and she began wheezing for Britain. That was how Karen found her moments later: doubled over and gasping for breath. Her flatmate guided her to one of the weathered benches overlooking the sea. They sat, until Jordan got her breath back.

Only then did Karen speak. "What's going on? I don't see you for five days. Then when I do, you demand we go for a run and then you take off like you're Paula Radcliffe. Which we both know you are not. So what gives? Why have you come back from your weekend away trying to break world speed records?" Karen shaded her eyes with her hand. "I take it this has something to do with a certain hot bride-to-be."

Jordan frowned. "Don't call her that."

"What should I call her?"

Jordan thought for a moment. "Trouble."

"Oh dear." Karen sat forward and fixed Jordan with her stare. "Tell me."

"We kissed." Jordan's tone was matter-of-fact. As if this was nothing at all.

It was the opposite of that. Before Karen could reply, Jordan continued.

"Then she fucked me in the plane toilet." Her body reacted as she'd known it would. As if Abby was right there, her fingers inside her all over again. It was too recent. Too exciting. Too much. "And now she's cancelling arrangements and I don't know if I have a job or a business anymore because I might just have buggered it all up. And for what?" Jordan sat forward, and put her head in her hands.

She'd spent last night alone, trying to convince herself the situation wasn't as bad as she thought it was. But when she said it out loud, it sounded a whole lot worse.

"Holy shit," Karen replied. "If I clamber over the whole 'you kissed the bride' vibe, the thing I'm stuck on is she fucked you in the toilet? She fucked *you*?" Karen couldn't sound any more surprised if she tried. "Is Little Miss Sunshine not so straight?"

It had taken Jordan by surprise, too. "It seems like she's not." She sighed. "But that's beside the point. The upshot is, I now have a bride who's getting married in," she held up her right hand and splayed her fingers, "five days. Someone I'm contracted to work for. Plus, I've added to my tally of one-night stands. With someone I really didn't want to have a one-night stand with. It's not ideal."

Karen shook her head. "It's not. I know we joked about this before you went, but I didn't expect anything to happen. What's different about her?"

Jordan had been asking herself that constantly since she'd left Abby at the airport. All the way home. All night long, lying in her bed, willing sleep. Why had she kissed her in the kitchen? And yes, Abby had been the aggressor on the plane, but she could have said no. She could have stopped her. But she hadn't wanted to.

She'd wanted Abby just as much as Abby had wanted her. *She still wanted Abby.*

But she had to stop thinking that.

"I don't know. We had such a great time together over the weekend, really getting to know each other. She got under my skin. There was an attraction there. I could feel it, but I didn't know if it was reciprocated. Until we were in the hot tub together. We nearly kissed then. I thought we'd managed to avoid it. To stay professional. Until the night we left when we kissed. And then the plane... I can't explain it. It just happened."

She sounded like a cliché. She didn't need to see Karen's face to know that. Jordan had heard enough 'I just landed in her vagina' defences to know exactly what they sounded like. Made up. But it really had just spiralled out of control right at the end, and she had no idea how.

"But now we're back and we have business to attend to. Wedding business. But she says something's come up, and we can't meet up. So I don't know what's going on." She shook her head, squinting as she looked up at the sky. "It's a mess. That's what I know for sure."

"Wow." Karen stretched her arms above her head, giving Jordan a look. "I mean, you've really buggered this up good and proper."

She could always count on Karen to be blunt.

"Kissing the bride is one thing. Not a *good* thing. Joining the mile-high club with her is quite another."

Jordan got up. Sitting and talking about this was turning up the noise in her head. She liked it better when she'd been running. Then, she'd just focused on the sun on her skin, and the wind in her hair. Nature could be comforting at times.

"Let's walk and talk. Or maybe run and talk."

Karen nodded, as they both began pumping their arms, taking long strides along the promenade. In front of them, a woman was struggling to contain a husky. To their right, a small boy in a red T-shirt was elated with his ice cream, which he proceeded to face plant into.

"Look on the bright side. At least you got laid."

That made Jordan smile. "You'd think I would be feeling a bit more positive about that, wouldn't you? I can normally cope with one-night stands. I'm prepared. I control them. Not this one. Plus, when my business and reputation are hanging in the balance, getting a shag isn't top priority." She picked up the pace and began to run. There was too much thinking going on. She needed distraction.

"How did you leave it with Abby?" Karen kept up with Jordan this time around.

It was a good question. Images flashed through Jordan's mind. Stroking Abby in the hot tub. Her own orgasm on the plane, head falling back as she came hard. Abby's lips pressed to hers.

The electricity sparked inside her. It was still there. Abby was still there. Jordan could feel it. Or had the near desperation of the plane been Abby's version of a last hurrah before she signed on the dotted line with Marcus? Had she been using Jordan to get something out of her system? It hadn't felt like that at the time, but looking back, the truth was staring her in the face.

She stopped running abruptly, hands on her thighs, trying to catch her breath. Her heart was beating so fast, it almost caught in her throat.

How could she have been so stupid?

She glanced up at Karen. It was hopeless, wasn't it?

"I don't know how we left it. She said we'd meet for lunch. Carry on working together. But now she's pulling back, changing things around."

Karen stroked her back. It was soothing. Jordan needed it. The world didn't make sense right now. It was swirling around her, and it was out of control.

Jordan was out of control. She hated that feeling.

"Can I do anything to help?"

Jordan shook her head. This was her mess, and she had to work out how to get out of it.

"Then here's my advice before I race you home. You ready?"

Jordan brought herself up to standing. "I'm all ears."

"You need to see her and talk to her. You need to find out what she's thinking, and work out a proper plan of action. Whether you carry on working with her or not. If you carry on, you figure out some boundaries and an exit strategy. If you decide to stop working with her, you agree on an excuse —

a family emergency or something. It happens. But the main thing is that you need clarity. So does she, come to that. She's the one getting married."

"I know."

"Let's run home and then you can call her and arrange to see her. If she doesn't answer, go to London anyway. She's not calling the shots here. You've got a lot on the line, too. So take control. Okay?"

Karen was right.

Jordan needed to get this back on track.

She needed to start project managing her bride once again, rather than the other way around.

# Chapter Twenty-Four

Abby sat in her firm's green meeting room, opposite her boss, Neil. He was smiling at her in a strange manner she couldn't quite pin down. He was wearing too much aftershave again, along with a cerise-pink tie that should be illegal. What did Neil do for fun? She'd love to know.

There was nothing wrong with him. He wasn't nasty. He didn't talk over her or steal her credit for work. However, the past year or so, Abby had resented him just for asking her to come into work every day and do the job she was paid to do. She thought back to her chats with Jordan, where Jordan had told her not to forget her dreams. To go after what she'd wanted to do when she was eight and they were friends. In their fake childhood.

Their childhood might have been fake, but their present was very much real. In fact, for the first time in a long time, Abby had been positively glad to come to work and be distracted by it.

It'd been a whole day since they'd got back, and she'd been avoiding Jordan's calls and texts. Avoiding thinking about her or processing anything that had happened.

Neil was talking, but she wasn't listening. Did he really think that tie was okay? Had he looked at himself in the mirror this morning and thought, "looking good!" She glanced at his ring finger. Neil wasn't married. He wasn't dating. He needed to date someone to get a second opinion on his clothing choices. Although him not getting married was the smart choice from where she was sitting. You needed to be sure you wanted to marry the person you were marrying. You needed to be sure he didn't then hire a bridesmaid who you were attracted to. And you needed to be doubly sure that you didn't accidentally have sex with the bridesmaid on the plane home.

Abby closed her eyes.

When she refocused on Neil, he was smiling at her. "So, what do you think?"

Abby sat up. About what? Shit, she was going to have to try to feel her way back into this conversation. "I think it sounds great. Could you just run over the finer points again?"

Neil looked pleased at her answer. That was a good start. "That is terrific!" He sat forward, clasping his hands together on the oval table that could easily seat eight. "So you're up for heading up the project?"

Abby blinked. Heading up the project? She really needed to listen to Neil. "The Asset Management project?"

Neil frowned. "Of course. Is there another one you've been preparing for?"

Wow. She was getting the project. Neil was promoting her. Maybe she could overlook his tie choice, just this once.

"No!" she replied. "That's great! I mean, amazing, of course I'd love to."

"And you're fine with the amount of travel it might involve? Of late-night conference calls? You'd be the lead on this, Abby.

The project would be totally yours. The buck would stop with you."

Abby chewed on the side of her cheek. She waited for the euphoria of her work win to register.

But there was nothing.

Instead, all she had was a feeling like she was drowning. Like this wasn't her beautiful life anymore.

Two months ago, she'd have been dancing through her office at this news. She'd have been revelling in the responsibility, excited for the challenge.

But now? Now all she saw ahead were late-night conference calls when she should be sleeping. Unnecessary stress. More commitment to a job she'd never truly wanted in the first place.

Plus, more plane travel, with nobody to hold her hand.

Not like Jordan had.

That's what all this came back to, didn't it? Jordan.

Neil was still waiting for an answer.

Abby didn't care about Neil. But she nodded anyway. "Of course. Totally. Buck stops with me."

Now Neil was getting up. Was he going to hug her? He was. *Oh god.* Neil was so *nice.* She let him hug her. His aftershave really was overpowering.

He opened the office door, and motioned for her to go first.

She was greeted by a bang, then another, as streamers burst into the air.

Abby screamed, clutching her chest. She hated surprises.

Her whole office was staring at her, though, so she had to change her face into a smile. It took a few moments, but she made it happen.

It wasn't easy.

Because there on her desk sat a large flat cake covered in white icing and sparkles, with the words 'Congratulations!' iced in pink on the top. Someone had also stuck a photo of her and Marcus to her monitor. The one of them taken at New Year last year. She had red eyes from drinking too much. Her chair was covered in shiny red love hearts, and next to the cake was a card. A wedding card. No doubt signed by everyone. With perhaps a voucher for John Lewis or Selfridges inside.

She bit the inside of her cheek. Emotion bubbled up inside her.

When did her life turn into this? The same week she was getting married, she also got a promotion.

The trouble was, she didn't want either of them.

Abby sniffed, then wiped her face with the back of her hand. Her cheeks were wet.

Oh shit. She was crying in her office.

What the actual fuck?

"Oh Abby! I hope those are tears of joy!" That was her office manager, Maisy.

Abby nodded. "Of course!" she replied. "Cake always makes me cry!"

Neil's arm came back around her shoulder and he squeezed. "We thought this was the perfect moment. You're heading up our big project and you're getting married. This is a perfect time in your life. So congratulations seemed apt." He looked around the team who were all beaming. "Let's give Abby a round of applause for being fantastic!"

The applause was deafening.

Abby was still crying.

# Chapter Twenty-Five

Neil insisted Abby leave a couple of hours before the end of the day, so she got home early. In his mind, he was probably preparing her for the future long days and nights to come by giving her a few hours off. Whatever his motive, Abby was grateful. But it truly couldn't have been more absurd to walk through the door to her flat carrying a huge cake that said *Congratulations!* on it. Well, half a cake after the office had a go at it. It now said *Congratu.* But still.

Nothing felt worth celebrating at the moment.

Abby put her cake down on the kitchen counter, then walked over to her sofa and sank into it.

This wasn't the big-day countdown she'd read about in bridal magazines. Then again, she was pretty sure none of them had the bride sleeping with the bridesmaid either. She leaned forward and picked up *Perfect Bride* magazine from the stack on the coffee table. She'd bought it just after Marcus had proposed, determined to have the perfect wedding. However, she'd lost interest after a while, and Marcus had taken over. He was the perfect groom. He deserved the perfect bride. Could Abby be that still?

Her phone buzzed beside her with a text. Jordan.

The familiar tremor hit her body. She was almost used to it by now.

*We need to talk. I'm on your street. What number are you?*

Abby's heart leapt up her body and into her throat as she vaulted off the sofa. She went straight to the huge bay window and stared down. Across the street, Jordan was looking around, then staring at her phone, shifting from one foot to another. Abby couldn't avoid her if she was standing right outside.

Then Jordan looked up, and their gazes connected.

Abby's heart exploded in a rush of joy. It was such a traitor.

This wasn't who she was marrying. She had to keep a lid on this, accept her promotion, become Mrs Montgomery. Everything was organised. She owed it to herself and all her future dreams to go through with her plans. Besides, marrying Marcus was hardly a bad plan. For everyone else in the whole wide world, it would be the best plan in the world.

Abby needed to put all of this into perspective.

However, Jordan was right. Maybe talking would help get her head straight.

Abby pointed towards her front door, then took a deep breath. She plumped up a few cushions even though she was pretty sure Jordan wouldn't be worrying about those. Then she ran to the mirror, and smoothed down her hair. She still had her work gear on. Was a red dress a good suit of armour? She had her doubts. Her eyes were still puffy, but she'd fixed her make-up at work. She'd have to do.

When she answered the door, all rationale and sense left Abby. How could she think about anything when Jordan was so breathtakingly beautiful? Her hair like summer painted onto her head. Her kissable lips. Abby remembered doing just that. She wanted to lean forward and do it again.

*It was all she wanted to do.*

But instead, she stood back.

Jordan's lips were pursed.

"Come in," Abby said. "Straight up the stairs." Not that there was anywhere else to go, but she always pointed it out.

Jordan standing in her flat was odd. She didn't quite fit. This was Abby's lair. It wasn't to do with her and Marcus. Her and anyone else. The flat was Abby's sanctuary. But Jordan did not make Abby feel calm. Not when her blue jeans were cupping her round arse so deliciously.

"Please, sit."

Jordan did, perching on the edge of the sofa.

"How did you find me?"

"You told me you lived on Charity Street, so I looked it up."

Abby gulped. "You remembered."

Jordan met her gaze. "It was pretty recent. I remember it all."

Abby squirmed under her stare. She remembered it all, too. "Cup of tea?" Abby had no idea what she was saying. She was on auto-pilot.

A shake of her head. "I think we need to talk. So when you're finished being polite, come and sit on the sofa with me, please."

Jordan was being firm. Pushy. That wasn't doing anything to quell Abby's desire for her. If she'd turned up crying, that might have repelled her.

But not this.

Abby did as she was told.

Jordan stared at her. It wasn't a warm stare. Or one filled with want. It was a hard stare. Jordan meant business.

Abby sat up straighter, trying to get her head into the same game.

"You've been ignoring my calls and my texts."

"I texted you back to cancel lunch." Jordan couldn't deny that.

"Once," Jordan said. "But this isn't just about us, Abby, or about what went on over the weekend. This is about our work, too. My professional reputation. I can't drop the ball on your wedding so close to the finish line. People talk. So even if you want nothing more to do with me personally, we still have to decide what we're doing professionally. Either we carry on and get this done, or we agree to sever ties and make up a lie."

Abby nodded. Everything Jordan was saying made perfect sense. But it didn't stop her feeling like she was being ripped in two from the inside out.

However, she had to do the right thing.

But what was the right thing?

Everyone told her Marcus was the real deal.

Everyone couldn't be wrong, could they?

"I know. I've just been so busy since we got back. Then Marcus stayed last night." *Why had she said that?* They hadn't had sex, after all.

Too late.

Jordan's lip wobbled, but the rest of her face hardened. Clouds gathered in her eyes. Once they were sky-blue, now they were icy.

Abby's stomach rolled. She never wanted to be the cause of pain for Jordan, but she didn't see how she could avoid it. "Then I went to work and got that promotion. The one I told you about?"

Jordan nodded. "Congratulations."

"Thanks." Abby felt hollow. "Then my team gave me a congratulations cake. Marcus is picking me up at six to go for dinner at his parents." She threw up her hands. "I haven't been avoiding you, Jordan, but I can't change the path my life is on. It's too late. Everything's on track, and I can't stop it rolling." She went to take Jordan's hand, then thought better of it. Better if they didn't touch each other.

Her throat had gone dry. Did she believe the words she was saying? It didn't matter. She had to say them. She had no choice.

"The weekend was a mistake." She gulped hard. "I'm marrying Marcus. I'm sorry you got hurt in this. I really am. But I can't just turn my back on the life that I've built over the past few years. The man I'm due to marry. The job I've worked hard for."

Jordan was still staring. Then she took a deep breath, stood, and walked over to the bay window. Standing just where Abby had stood a few minutes earlier. Where her heart had exploded when she'd seen Jordan. She wasn't going to dwell on that.

"What about everything we spoke about in Cannes?" Jordan turned.

Her stare rooted Abby to the spot.

"About you getting a new career? Saying you'd fallen for me? Are you forgetting all that? Are you able to forget what happened between us?"

Abby stood, too. "I can't overthrow everything in my life because of one shag." As soon as those words were out of her mouth, she wished she could put them back. Lock them up and leave them on a high shelf, where nobody ever had to hear them or see them. But she couldn't. They were out there and they'd sliced through Jordan's soul. Abby could see that in the way her face dropped.

"I'm sorry." Abby winced. "That came out wrong."

Jordan shook her head. "You're right. It was only a shag. A one-night stand. My speciality, as you well know. Who would change their life for that? Not me."

Abby's hand wanted to shoot up in the air, but she kept it firmly planted by her side. She couldn't risk it.

Jordan folded her arms across her chest. "But that still leaves the problem of what to do about the wedding. I'm the wedding planner now, too. I can't bail totally. Maybe I could take a step back? I'll give you a list of what needs finishing. Maybe Delta can step up to the plate."

The thought of Jordan not being there was torture. But Abby knew she was being unfair. "Is there any chance you could stay on? If it's about money, I can pay you more."

A look of disgust crossed Jordan's face. "Really? It's not about the money, Abby. It never was. At least, not with me."

Abby looked at the floor, biting her lip. She couldn't say anything right today. That wasn't what she'd meant to say.

"Nothing I say can persuade you? I know Marcus would appreciate it. And Marjorie. Everyone. We all loved you on the hen weekend, Jordan."

"I know. Some more than others."

Abby was empty. "I'm sorry this is how it's worked out,

but please, will you think about it? If you leave, I understand. I'll make sure Marcus pays you until the end as agreed. But please can you stay to do the last few days? If not for me, for Marcus? I'm not sure how I'd explain it away otherwise. I promise he'll big you up to everyone he comes across."

\* \* \*

Jordan wanted to step forward and shout in Abby's face. *"This is not about business or about money. This is about feelings. About us. About not walking away from us!"*

But she was still on a job, and she was always professional. *Always.*

Could she finish this? Get Abby to the altar as she'd promised Marcus? Despite everything, she still liked him. Plus, she still wanted to do a good job. It was in her genes.

Abby's doorbell rang. She twisted on one foot, then twisted back, panic etched on her face. She checked her watch and swore lightly under her breath. "This might be Marcus." She winced again. "He's early. I better get it."

Jordan nodded. Of course it was Marcus. Could this day get any worse?

Marcus was still in his office gear, just like Abby. Jordan had to admit, they looked like the perfect corporate couple. They always had. That wasn't the issue.

The issue was that Abby had told her she was falling for her. Yet now she was sticking with the original plan and marrying Marcus.

Feelings didn't change that quickly. Jordan was well aware of that.

She gulped, painting on a smile she hoped would fool

most. Her outside looked normal. Inside, her heart was slowly breaking.

"Jordan! How are you?" Marcus approached her, offering his hand.

She shook it. "Good. How was your weekend?"

Marcus gave her a grin. "You know. Booze, women, wine. How about yours?"

"Remarkably similar," she replied, snagging Abby's gaze. Abby looked away.

"But that's out the way now, we can concentrate on the final week. Only five days to the big day." He rubbed his hands together. "You're helping Abby with her speech, aren't you?"

Abby shook her head, butting in. "Jordan's done more than enough already. I'm sure I can write my speech on my own."

"But she's a pro!" Marcus pointed at Jordan. "You've got a load of jokes that are guaranteed laughter points, right?"

Jordan nodded. "I do." She ground her teeth together, still smiling.

Marcus nudged Abby with his elbow. "Get some pointers. If you don't, I will."

Abby's eyes widened. "She's my bridesmaid not yours. I'll take some hints." She stared at Jordan, then looked away.

Jordan held her face steady. What kind of tips was Abby planning on taking, exactly?

"And you're coming to the rehearsal dinner on Friday?"

Jordan screwed up her face. She'd forgotten about the rehearsal dinner. She had it on her spreadsheet, of course. However, since they'd landed yesterday, she'd forgotten everything she was meant to be doing for this wedding.

On the most important week.

She couldn't abandon it now, could she? It would seem weird. She'd promised Marjorie she'd be at the rehearsal dinner. She'd promised everyone. Could she do it? Her body tensed with the weight of expectation in Marcus's stare.

"I'm not sure. I was just telling Abby something's come up." She hated lying to him.

Marcus's face fell. "I'm so sorry. Is there anything we can do to help? Of course, we both want you to be there, but you have to make sure you're okay first."

He really was the nicest man in the world, wasn't he? His niceness made Jordan feel terrible.

She could do the final few days. Abby wanted her to. Marcus wanted her to. And if she wanted her business to go well in the future, she should.

"Forget I said that, I'll be there. I'll make it work." Jordan rolled her shoulders. "Got to make sure we get this one to the altar, haven't we? It's in my remit."

Marcus grinned. "Fabulous. Although I'm hoping she comes of her own accord, not just because you're making her!"

Jordan glanced at Abby, whose face had frozen into a mask she couldn't quite decipher. It was going to be torture, but it was only for the next five days. After that, Marcus and Abby would be married, and Jordan could bank her pay cheque and lick her wounds. At least she'd learned something from this whole debacle. To never get too close to the bride again. To never let her guard down.

"It'll be a pleasure to ensure that everything is just as you want it to be for your big day."

Abby turned away.

Marcus looked from Abby, to Jordan, then back. He

frowned. "Everything okay? I'm getting some weird vibes from you two. Did something happen on the weekend I should know about?"

Jordan's blood stilled, but she kept her mouth tight shut.

Abby went to speak, but Marcus held up his hand. "You know what, whatever it was, I don't need to know. More to the point, I don't want to know." He smiled at Abby, such love held in his expression that Jordan's stomach turned. "If you had a stripper, even if you snogged another man, it's all part of it. So long as you're ready to marry me now, that's all that matters."

Jordan didn't even look at Abby. Because it didn't really matter what her face said or what she was thinking.

Abby was choosing Marcus.

Jordan just had to finish the job and move on.

# Chapter Twenty-Six

Jordan walked into Turnbull House, the manor house hotel hosting the wedding reception. She didn't need to ask the reception staff where the restaurant was, because she'd been here a few times already over the past couple of weeks, co-ordinating last-minute details with florists, caterers, the band and MCs. At least taking over the wedding planning had meant her duties weren't solely focused on Abby. She was pretty sure Abby had been wholly in favour of it, too.

What meetings they had been in together had been short and sweet, with Abby preferring to do a lot of it via email and text, with minimal personal contact.

But when they had been in a room together, it'd been charged. How could it not be? It had only been four days ago that Abby had been inside Jordan.

Now, they had to pretend they were just professionally tied, nothing more.

Jordan had managed to keep her composure. Even earlier, when they'd run through the ceremony. She'd been the Jordan everyone expected her to be. A consummate pro.

However, tonight was different. Jordan couldn't keep still. Couldn't relax. It made sense, though. Because tonight's rehearsal dinner was in front of everyone. The first celebration of Marcus and Abby as the happy couple. How was Jordan going to react? She was about to find out. She smoothed down her pink cocktail dress, centred her silver brooch, and took a deep breath.

The first person she encountered was Marjorie. The woman never looked anything less than glamorous. Did she go to sleep in her make-up and pearls? Jordan wouldn't be surprised. Marjorie greeted Jordan with a measured smile and an approving nod.

"You, my dear, know how to wear a dress. Perhaps you could give Abby some tips in that department? She always tends to wear the wrong colour, or the wrong cut, don't you think?"

Jordan did not think. Any time she'd seen Abby, she'd looked nothing short of stunning. "I think she does just fine," she replied.

But Marjorie wasn't to be deterred. "It's her pale Scottish skin, you see. It doesn't suit much. I did offer her the use of my tanning lady, but she fobbed me off. I was just trying to help, particularly as she'll be wearing white on the big day, which isn't going to be her natural bliss point."

Jordan smiled. Ah, the mother-in-law rant. It was good to know that Marjorie was converting to type. It set Jordan back on track and gave her more of a gauge on where she was in the wedding.

It wasn't until she looked over Marjorie's shoulder and spotted Abby and Marcus walking towards her that her muscles locked.

Because Jordan's gauge of Abby was far more accurate than Marjorie's had been.

When their eyes met, something passed between them. Something that made Jordan ache.

Nobody she'd met had impacted her like this in a long time. She had something with Abby. She made her laugh, which went a long way. Plus, they shared a similar life view. If only Abby would let herself believe her first instincts.

But she hadn't. And now she was marrying Marcus.

Jordan had to let it go.

"Here they are, the couple of the moment!" Marjorie greeted the pair with air kisses and not-quite-hugs, the way rich people did. "Ready to do your practice wedding?"

Abby nodded, focusing on her future mother-in-law. "The ceremony went well. Now let's do the dinner and speeches."

"Not too much wine, that's the key," Marjorie replied.

Marcus shook his head. "Nonsense. You can never have too much wine. Isn't that right, Jordan?" He gave her a smile. "By the way, you look stunning. Hot pink is definitely your colour." He put an arm around his mother and they walked away, leaving Abby staring at Jordan.

"He's right," she said, as she drew level with Jordan, her gaze dropping to Jordan's lips. "You do look stunning."

Jordan stared right back. "So do you."

Abby touched her arm, before walking after Marcus. But she turned back, and the look she gave Jordan was scorched with want.

Jordan closed her eyes and took a deep breath.

Two more days and this would all be over.

\* \* \*

Two hours later, and they were onto their main course of the rehearsal dinner.

Jordan's stomach growled, but she wasn't listening. She'd lost her appetite. Down the long table she could hear Delta laughing at something, Taran and Gloria flanking her. Jordan had insisted she was sat on the end, so she could be on hand to iron out any issues.

However, it had meant that when she turned to her right, she kept glimpsing Abby chatting and looking for all the world like someone who was excited to be getting married this weekend. So Jordan had to surmise she was. Jordan wished she could accept it for what it was, but as the evening wore on, she just wanted to leave.

Marcus's best man, Philip, tapped his glass, and all eyes turned to him.

"I just wanted to say, I couldn't think of a better fit for Marcus than Abby. She's kind, caring, and has done the right thing by keeping him hanging on and not moving in with him until after the big day. I asked if she was waiting to consummate the marriage, too, but she wouldn't answer."

Jordan took another swig of her wine. She should stop. She had to drive home tonight. Carrie the Capri was waiting outside, much to the consternation of the hotel staff who would rather it wasn't. Jordan had always thought posh people appreciated antiques. Apparently it didn't extend to cars.

Marcus was on his feet now, waving at Philip. "Whatever Abby stipulated, I'd have gone along with. Just so long as she agreed to marry me. And she did." He took her hand in his, looking at her with adoration.

Jordan looked away.

However, she could still hear him.

"Abby, I can't wait to reveal my vows to you on Sunday. To tell you how much I love you. To promise you I'm ready to be yours for the rest of our lives. There's nobody I'd rather go on my life journey with than you, and I'm the luckiest man alive to know that you feel the same way, too."

Jordan's stomach turned. She pushed away her food. This was a little too much, even for her. She needed some air. She got to her feet, wooziness seeping through her. A mixture of half a glass of wine, minimal food, and a broken heart.

"I also just wanted to say a huge thank you to Abby's bridesmaids who've made this journey epic. Obviously I'll do a proper toast at the wedding with gifts for you all."

Jordan sat with a thud.

"But I especially wanted to say a huge thank you to Abby's best friend Delta, and her oldest friend, Jordan. Particularly to Jordan, who's stepped in and really made the run-up a breeze. So much so, she's selflessly sitting at the end in hot pink, dealing with any issues and making them disappear. Here's to you!" Marcus raised a glass in her direction.

The whole table turned to clap Jordan. She raised a weary smile.

Then she caught Abby's gaze.

*She was so beautiful.*

Jordan was so over tonight.

When the clapping died down and Marcus was saying something else, she grabbed her bag and squeezed out the side door of the dining room as silently as she could. Then she walked back through the reception and out onto the main steps of the manor house. Its neatly manicured lawns stretched out under the imminent sunset. It really was a gorgeous setting for a gorgeous couple. This was how the world worked. Jordan had seen it enough to understand. If she ever got married, it would never happen in a place like this. She wouldn't want it to, either. This venue wasn't for the likes of her.

She was just about to walk down the steps to the car park and garden, when the main door opened.

It was Abby, with her beautiful shoulders on show. The same ones Jordan had gripped on the plane.

Jordan stilled, staring. "Are you lost?"

Abby shook her head. "I saw you slip out. I wanted to check you were okay."

Jordan turned, and walked down the steps in a bid to get away. "I'm fine."

Footsteps on the stairs signalled Abby was following. "Jordan," she said, touching her arm. Abby had quick feet when she needed to.

Jordan shrugged her off, turning. "Go back to your rehearsal dinner, Abby. You heard Marcus. He's the luckiest man in the world. You wouldn't want to do anything to spoil that."

Abby stared at her. "I'm sorry, okay? For it all. For kissing you. For having sex with you. It's all my fault, and you're the one who got caught up in it."

"Not as sorry as I am." Jordan's heart hammered as her anger rose. "This is easy for you." Jordan swept an arm out from her side. "You've got this whole cosy world to fall back on. A tall, rich man to run to. I don't have any of that. And you made me feel things. *Want things.*" Her chest heaved. "And you just brush it off like it was nothing."

"It wasn't nothing! It was the opposite of nothing!" Abby's voice was raised, her tone staining the air. She seemed shocked by her volume, glancing around before turning herself down.

"You know it wasn't nothing," she whispered. "It was a whole lot of something. But it was wrong time, wrong place. I can't change my mind now. No matter how much I might want to." Her shoulders slumped, defeated. "You've no idea. My life is not as easy as you think. I haven't slept all week, my job is getting bigger, and I haven't been able to think about much else but you."

Jordan scoffed. "Save it, Abby. You could change it if you wanted to. But you don't want to." Jordan squared up to her, unsure what she'd prefer to do. Shake Abby, or kiss her. Neither would do any good, though. Abby might harbour dreams of them being together, but if she was going to do anything about it, she'd have done it by now, wouldn't she?

"I do want to, it's just not that easy." Now it was Abby's turn to sweep her arm. "You might think this is something to fall back on. But it can also be a prison, too. One that stops me from doing what I want."

"But you're not from this rich and rarified world! What would your mum say?"

Abby dipped her head, obviously not wanting to answer that.

Jordan threw her hands in the air and began to pace. "I'm not sure I can take much more of this. I thought I could style it out, but the lying keeps sticking in my throat."

"It's not me, either!" Abby told her. "This, my job, none of it is."

Jordan sighed. "It looks like it is, from where I'm standing."

She paused. "But I'll finish the job as promised. Just don't expect me to stick around on the day, toasting the happy couple."

Abby nodded, her shoulders rising and falling. "Of course. Just know, I wish things could have been different. That we'd met under different circumstances." She touched Jordan's arm with her fingertips.

Even that light brush caused a frisson of desire to course through Jordan. She flicked her eyes to Abby.

"I never meant to hurt you, please know that. That I did absolutely crushes me."

Jordan gulped, emotion rising in her. She couldn't go back in now. She couldn't shake Marjorie's hand, pretend to Marcus that everything was fine.

She had to go.

She shook her bag from her shoulder and fished inside, locating her car keys. She bit her lip, fighting back tears. She wasn't going to let Abby see them. She swallowed hard, breathing in the evening air. She had to stay strong.

"I can't stay now," Jordan began, waving her keys in the air. "Will you tell them I had an emergency I had to deal with?"

Abby's gaze was kind. Too much so. It nearly sent Jordan over the edge.

"Of course." Abby's nose twitched.

Jordan gave her a nod, confusion swirling inside her. What did Abby do to her? One minute she wanted to shake her, the next she wanted to hold her in her arms and never let her go.

She cast those thoughts from her mind as she stumbled across the gravel, thankful her car wasn't far away. She got in, and slammed the rusty door with finality. The quiet inside was eerie and deafening.

Jordan gripped the steering wheel, taking deep breaths. She had to get going. Get away from here, from this weird life she'd carved out for herself that was now slowly tearing her apart. She had to get another job. One that didn't open her up to this madness.

She turned the key. The engine turned over, then died. She tried again. Same thing. She tried one more time.

Nothing.

She slammed the wheel, tears now right behind her eyes. She'd been loyal to Carrie. Why was she failing her now?

Why was her whole life failing her now?

*Why did she never get the girl?*

Tears fell, and she could do nothing to stop them. Soon, she was full-on crying. She didn't care.

Despair tumbled down her, as the normally staid and put-together Jordan, professional bridesmaid extraordinaire, slowly crumbled. The irony that she was sat in the driver's seat wasn't lost on her. Jordan was normally the driver in her life. The one who had full control. However, since she'd met Abby, control had been taken from her. Now, she didn't know what to do.

Abby was marrying Marcus.

Jordan had fallen for Abby.

A noise to her right made her sit up. Someone was knocking on her window. Jordan clenched her eyes tight shut, then reopened them. Another knock. She turned her head right.

It was Abby.

She couldn't let Abby see her like this. Abby couldn't know that Jordan was falling apart.

More knocking, then a gust of warm air as the door opened.

Then Abby was kneeling next to her, holding her hand.

It was too much. They shouldn't be doing this. Abby was like a class A drug to Jordan. One hit was never enough.

"Jordan, let me help you." Abby's voice was warm, inviting.

Jordan shook her head. "Go back to your party, Abby."

"Not when you're like this. Especially not when your car won't start."

Jordan reached over, got a tissue and blew her nose. All thoughts of how she looked were long gone. Jordan was in survival mode. "I'm fine. I might just have to call a cab and leave my car here."

Abby stood up, holding out a hand.

Jordan stared at it for a while, then grasped it, the gravel crunching beneath her feet. When her head drew level with Abby, she wobbled.

In response, Abby took Jordan in her arms and held her tight.

Jordan didn't have enough strength left to resist. Instead, she sank into the embrace. Every part of her body rejoiced. She let it. She couldn't do anything else today.

A few moments of bliss went by, when Jordan could almost believe that everything was okay. That she and Abby were together. But they weren't. When that realisation hit, she pulled back, their faces still inches apart.

"I'm sorry I'm such a mess. This doesn't normally happen. I don't normally sleep with my brides." Jordan forced a smile.

"I'm glad." Abby gave her a sad smile. "Just know, my heart's breaking, too." She paused. "I love… your car. It's gorgeous. One of a kind. Just like you."

Jordan gripped Abby's arms. She was shaking. That made it somehow even worse. She stared at her lips. She was moving closer to them, as was Abby to hers.

What was wrong with her? She had to stop. There was no way she was going to be the other woman.

Their lips touched. Just for a moment, the world righted itself. With Abby's lips on hers, anything was possible.

Until it wasn't.

"What the fuck is going on?" Delta had materialised out of thin air.

Jordan jumped back, as did Abby.

She had no idea where to look. Not at Delta. Certainly not at Abby.

"It's not what it looks like," Abby began, holding up a hand.

Delta put a hand on her hip. "Explain to me what it is, then? Because it looks to me like you were just kissing each other. And it didn't look like it was the first time, either." She looked from Jordan to Abby.

They both looked away.

Delta stilled, realisation dawning. "Oh. My. God. It's not the first time, is it? I knew there was something odd in Cannes, but I didn't realise this. How long has this been—"

"There you all are! I was wondering where my bride and two key bridesmaids had disappeared to!" Marcus walked up, all smiles. Until he saw the faces all around him.

"What's happened? Are you all okay?" He looked from

Jordan to Abby to Delta, before settling on Abby. "What's happened? Jordan's crying and you both look freaked."

Jordan shook her head. "I just had some sad news, so I'm afraid I've got to go. I should be fine for Sunday. I just need to head home now, but my car won't start. My flatmate would say that was my fault for having such an ancient car." She tried a smile, but it didn't work.

Marcus studied her, before pulling his phone from his inside pocket. "Let me help you out. I'll call a car to take you home. I'll have our mechanic come and see to Carrie in the morning."

Did Marcus come out of the womb gallant?

"You don't have to," Jordan said.

"I know, but I want to. You're upset, and you love your car." Marcus stroked the roof. "Let me sort this out for you. You've been sorting us out for the past few weeks, and doing it with style."

"You can say that again." Delta's words were spiked.

"Exactly," Marcus agreed, giving Delta a smile. "She's been attending to Abby's every need." He switched his gaze to Jordan. "Let me fix something for you, too. Okay?"

Guilt cascaded down Jordan. "That would be lovely, thanks."

# Chapter Twenty-Seven

It was the night before the wedding. Abby was staying at Turnbull House. Marjorie had made a five-minute stop in to say good luck, which had unnerved Abby. The way she had looked at her, it was as if she knew Abby needed all the luck she could get.

Which was ridiculous. Marjorie knew nothing.

Up until yesterday, *nobody* had known anything.

But now Delta did. Her best friend was pretty pissed off Abby hadn't said anything before. Delta had tried to get Abby to talk the night before, but she'd stuck to Marcus like glue, then avoided her phone until this afternoon. However, now it was less than 24 hours until she got married, there was no getting away from Delta or Taran. This was what brides and bridesmaids did the night before the wedding. Drank wine and gossiped. Only, Abby's gossip was off the scale.

Delta poured them another glass of fizz, then settled on the golden sofa at the end of the bed. With Taran in the room, Abby had given Delta pointed looks that told her no discussion of Jordan. Delta had given her a tacit nod of agreement.

Instead, she'd applied spot cream to Abby's face — another delightful side effect of being so stressed was Abby had broken out in zits on her chin. After that, Delta had filled Abby and Taran in on how things were going with Nikita. The answer: well. In a week, they'd even progressed to talking about being a proper couple. This was a big thing for Delta. It had certainly snapped her out of her doldrums for being dumped.

"Because we just click, you know? I know I was upset about Nora and I put her first. Sorry about that. But just one week with Nikita has made me see my whole six months with Nora was nothing. Isn't it strange how you can be with someone for a long time, put so much time and energy into them, and then wonder what you've been doing?" Delta gave her a sharp look.

Abby closed her eyes.

"Nikita's come fully into my life and it's like the clouds have cleared."

Delta's words struck home. Was that what Abby had been doing with Marcus? Going along and pretending? Even just having a conversation with Jordan, or touching her hand made Abby light up more than Marcus had ever managed. A warmth swept through her as she remembered kissing Jordan in the kitchen. Yes, she'd made an impression. When she'd run off after the rehearsal dinner, Abby had wanted to follow her, but she'd been rooted to the spot.

Taran's phone went off. She looked at it with a smile. "That's Ryan." She got up. "Be right back."

"Sure you will," Delta shouted as she left the room. When the door shut, she turned to Abby. "Now it's just the two of us, I believe we have some things to discuss." Delta raised an eyebrow. "Did anything I just said ring true? Because I don't know what the fuck's going on Abby, but you need to face it."

Abby drew in a long breath, nodding. "I know."

"Has something happened with Marcus to cause this?"

Abby shook her head. "No, he doesn't suspect anything. At least I hope he doesn't. He thinks everything's fine. Normal."

"It doesn't look that way from where I'm standing." Delta paused. "Are you going to tell me exactly what happened? I mean, I caught you in a lip-lock last night, but that's all I know."

There was no easy way to say this, so Abby was just going to come out with it. "I kissed Jordan in Cannes. Then I had sex with her. And now I'm ignoring her because I have no idea what to do."

Delta stopped mid-sip of her bubbles. She stared at Abby like she'd gone mad. "What?" She frowned. "You shagged Jordan? When the hell did you shag Jordan?"

Abby dipped her head. "On the plane."

"On the plane!?" Delta's voice had gone up a few octaves.

Abby put down her drink, and flapped a hand in front of her. "Keep it down. I don't want everyone to know about it."

"I can imagine you don't." Delta shook her head. "And there was me thinking I was the only one who got lucky that weekend." Then she frowned. "But this isn't good news, right?"

Abby let her head flop back. "Not when I'm about to get married, no."

"But you and Jordan." Abby didn't think Delta could have sounded more perplexed. "This is the real reason she's too busy to be here tonight?"

Abby nodded. "I texted her and told her to just come tomorrow."

Delta's raised eyebrow told Abby what she thought of that plan. "But how? I mean, I know you slept with a woman at uni, but you've been very much into men since then."

She had. Until Jordan. "It just happened. I mean, we chatted a lot over the weekend. I like her. And then somehow, we kissed. And then the plane."

"I can't believe you joined the mile-high club. How did you manage that with nobody knowing?"

"Everyone was knackered on the way back. But now, I'm knackered. I'm not sleeping. I just got given a massive project at work. I'm getting married tomorrow and I should be deliriously happy about it. And all I can think about is my fake bridesmaid who I'm avoiding. How did my life get so messy?"

"Honestly, I have no idea." Delta sat back, shaking her head. "What does this mean, though? I thought you loved Marcus?" She prodded her chest with her thumb. "I love Marcus. *Everyone* loves Marcus."

Abby didn't need that spelt out. "I know everyone loves bloody Marcus. Because Marcus is bloody lovely. Believe me, I *did* love Marcus." Dread slid down her. No, that wasn't right. "I *do* love Marcus." She raised her shoulders up, then down. "I don't know what I think anymore."

Delta leaned forward. "You're getting married, Abs. If you've got doubts, you need to say so." She paused. "Are you gay now? Bi?"

"I don't know. I like Jordan. But I love Marcus."

Delta stared at her. "Do you like Jordan or love her?"

Abby put her head in her hands. She wasn't going to cry. But that was the question she'd been avoiding at all costs.

"I don't know. It's like, I was happy, going along, doing my thing. Then I met Jordan, and something changed. She flipped a switch in me, and now I can't unflip it."

Delta sat forward, shaking her head. "You know, I'm all for experimenting. I'm all for people realising who they really are. But this is serious. You're getting married in less than 24 hours."

"You don't need to keep pointing that out."

"It kinda seems like I do because you've let this drift. This is so unlike you. You normally know what you want and go after it. You wanted marriage, kids. That's what you've always said to me."

"That hasn't changed."

"But do you want them with Marcus? Because if you don't, it's not fair to put him through a wedding where the marriage is already doomed."

"I can't call it off now."

Delta took Abby's hand in hers. "Do you still love Marcus and think you can make it work?"

Abby stilled. "Yes." Her stomach flipped. "No." She threw up her hands. "I don't know."

Delta shook her head, flopping back on the sofa herself. "Abs, what would you tell me to do if the roles were reversed?"

That comment got through. "I'd tell you exactly what you just told me. That it's not fair to do this to either Marcus or me unless I'm totally sure."

A knock on the door interrupted them. "Abs?" It was Marcus.

Abby shot to her feet. "Do you think he heard anything?" Dread screamed through her. She felt like she was tripping.

Delta shook her head. "He didn't. Thick walls."

Abby hoped she was right. She walked towards the door, still not opening it. "I can't see you," she said. "It's bad luck."

"I know," he replied. "It's just, Jordan's here to pick up her car now that it's fixed. I messaged her today, and she wanted to come and get it tonight. Only, you've got the keys. She's downstairs in reception. Can you let her have them?"

Jordan was here? Abby wobbled. Her legs felt like they might give way at any minute. "Of course."

"Great." A pause. "See you tomorrow, nearly wife!"

Abby waited for a few moments, before turning to Delta. She was pretty sure her face was saying exactly what her insides were feeling. Luckily, Delta articulated it before she could.

"You can't go down there."

"I know."

"Let me go."

Abby nodded. "Okay." She walked to her overnight bag, every nerve ending in her body on high alert. Delta could deal with Jordan. She'd see her briefly tomorrow. Then get married and put this episode down to pre-wedding jitters.

Then again, maybe she should cut Jordan off right now. She grabbed the keys, turning to Delta. "Second thoughts, I'm going to take them. Sort this out now."

Delta sprang up, taking the keys from where they were dangling from Abby's fingers. "Because that turned out so well last time." She gave her a look. "Let me do this. For your own good."

Abby swallowed down.

Delta left the room.

Abby stared at the door as if it held the key to her future.

Which it sort of did. She hopped from foot to foot. Maybe she should just see Jordan. See how she reacted? Wouldn't it be better to do it now than tomorrow?

Before she could second guess herself, she yanked open the door and ran down the thick carpeted corridor, until she reached the top of the grand wooden staircase, and clattered down it.

She made it to the bottom, where Delta was standing with Jordan. They both stared at her. It was only then she remembered she still had spot cream on her face. She shook her head. It was incidental tonight.

"Hi," Abby said. She searched Jordan's face for a sign, but she was giving nothing away.

"Hi," Jordan replied. "Just came to get my car. That way, I can be in and out tomorrow with minimum fuss."

Abby nodded. "Good thinking." You could cut the tension with a knife.

"Is it wise for you to come tomorrow at all?" Delta asked Jordan. "With everything that's happened?"

Jordan dipped her head. She took a breath before she replied. "That's up to Abby. She's paid for a service."

"And you've over-delivered, I understand," Delta replied.

Abby gulped, but said nothing.

"If she doesn't want me to come, Abby just has to say the word. I'm here to help the bride, not hinder. But unless I hear otherwise, I'll turn up and fulfil my duties as planned. Even if it kills me."

Jordan's chest heaved as she gave Abby a searing look.

Then she turned on her heel and left.

# Chapter Twenty-Eight

Jordan cut the engine and sat inside her car outside her flat. She gripped the steering wheel.

*Fuck. Fuck. Fuck.*

What the hell was she going to do? She was in too deep. Abby knew it. She knew it. They'd been trying to contain it all week, but it was impossible. The genie was out of the bottle.

Her passenger door creaking open startled Jordan. Moments later, Karen sat down beside her and slammed the door.

"You really should lock your door, you know. Any kind of knife-wielding freak could open it and get you at any time."

"Or worse still, you." Jordan gave her a smile despite herself.

Karen flicked on the interior light and twisted in her seat, assessing Jordan. "So did you see her?"

A nod.

"And? All sorted?"

Jordan gave her a look. "Yep. We had a farewell shag, and now it's done."

Karen snorted. "Pub, then?"

Jordan sighed. "I wish."

Karen banged on the dashboard. "What actually happened?"

"I picked up my keys, saw Marcus, then Delta came down, then Abby, and it was all sorts of awkward." She sighed. "There's just… every time we're in proximity of each other, there's a tension in the air, you know? Something I can't quite pin down. But when Abby's anywhere near me, I can hardly breathe."

"It's called desire, Jordan. It's called kissing someone, having illicit sex with them once, and now not being able to think of anything else until it happens again."

"It's bloody draining, that's what it is. How does anybody get any work done when this is happening? I can't concentrate on anything. All I'm thinking about is her. Abby, 24/7."

Karen put a hand on her knee. "I believe it's known as falling for someone."

Jordan threw up her hands. "I don't have time to fall for someone. Especially when that someone is the one I'm meant to be getting down the aisle. She's saying 'I do' tomorrow, and I'm sitting in my car, wondering if she might change her mind. Honestly, who am I kidding? I'm the wedding expert, aren't I? I've done nearly 30 weddings. How many of them have resulted in a bride or groom not going through with it?"

Karen twisted her mouth one way, then the other. "None?"

"Precisely. Not one. These brides never run, even when they don't love the groom. Even when they've slept with someone else. Even when she's told me she's fallen for me."

A few moments passed when nobody spoke. Outside, a couple walked by on the pavement, laughing as they walked.

What Jordan would give to be that carefree. Right now, her life was balanced on a knife edge, and either way she jumped, she was going to get hurt.

"Do you have to go to the wedding tomorrow? If she's not going to follow through with you, it seems unnecessarily cruel for you to have to watch her get married."

"It's my job. The one she employed me to do."

"But the circumstances have changed. Surely there's some leeway if you end up falling in love with the bride, and her with you?"

Jordan quaked at Karen's words. "Nobody said anything about love."

"What do you think this is, then? Infatuation? Because it doesn't look like it from where I'm sitting. You've been a basket case since you got back on Monday. From what you've said, so has she."

"It doesn't matter, does it? Nothing's going to change before tomorrow."

"Unless something or somebody makes it change."

Jordan turned to Karen. "What are you suggesting?"

"That you don't fall for people willy-nilly. Abby's got under your skin, and you can't ignore how you feel. If she feels the same way, maybe you should ask her before she walks down the aisle. Straight up, ask her."

"Are you crazy? I know my feelings are real. I think hers are, too. But what if I'm wrong? Or worse still, I'm right, but she's not prepared to blow up her wedding day?" Because that was what had happened up until now.

"Then at least you'll know, and you won't spend the next year wondering what if."

"No, but I will spend the next year looking for another profession, seeing as nobody will employ me as a professional bridesmaid anymore."

Karen waved a hand. "You said yourself you can't stay in this game forever. Besides, you could work again, just maybe not in these precise social circles."

"I think word of a bridesmaid shagging a bride might get around."

"I don't think you should focus on that. Instead, turn your attention to how you're feeling about Abby." Karen put a hand over Jordan's chest. "What happens in here when I say her name?"

Jordan gulped. "My heart starts to race."

"How does it feel when I tell you she's going to marry Marcus?"

"Devastating." Jordan sat back, and removed Karen's hand. That answer came in a flash. "If she goes through with it, I don't think I'll ever do this job again, anyway. It'll always remind me of her."

"Wow." Karen tapped the dashboard again. "So if she gets married, you're changing careers. If she doesn't get married, you'll have to change careers, too. With the job out of the equation, what have you got to lose? You're her bridesmaid. You're going to see her in the morning before the church. Just tell her how you feel. And if she still goes through with it, she was never worth it in the first place. Because you deserve someone who wants you and only you."

Jordan stared at her best friend.

Karen was right. This was a matter of the heart. As such, she couldn't ignore it.

Her phone lit up with a text message. Jordan glanced down at it.

It was from Abby.

Jordan began to shake. Was she thinking the same thing and taking action? Jordan's heartbeat vaulted upwards as she grabbed her phone and pressed the text button.

*Hi Jordan. I've been thinking about what Delta said, and maybe she's right. You shouldn't come tomorrow. It's going to make it too hard for both of us. Thanks for everything. A x*

Jordan stared at the text message. All the stars in the universe burst. The sun drained of heat. Her heart shattered into a million tiny pieces.

Abby had made her decision.

She put her forehead on the steering wheel, a gentle sob escaping her throat as her face crumpled.

She'd known it would go this way.

But when it actually happened, the truth was so much harder to take.

# Chapter Twenty-Nine

Abby took a step up into the vintage white Jaguar, helped by her mum. Gloria was looking incredible, dressed in monochrome, with a black-and-white fascinator placed perfectly on her freshly cut red hair. The car door shut, and then it was just the two of them. The bonnet of the car was adorned with festive cream ribbons. Her bridesmaids had already gone ahead in a different car. Sitting up front was the driver, replete with peaked cap. It reminded her of Michelle.

Of the plane.

Jordan.

*Stop.*

They drove down the main road in the village. Past the HSBC bank. Past the park with its trees in full bloom.

The sun was a bright yellow button stitched into the sky, yet everywhere Abby looked seemed to have a gloom filter applied. She had perfect hair, perfect make-up, perfect dress. However, underneath her dress, it felt like her bones and flesh weren't attached to her anymore. That she was sitting in someone else's body. "You're sure Dad was okay with not coming in the car?"

Gloria nodded. "He was fine. Someone needs to be with

his mum anyway, so it worked out." She paused. "Smile, love. You're getting married, remember? It's meant to be a happy occasion?"

Abby gave her a tight grin. "People say that, but is this bit ever something people look forward to? I mean the whole getting ready, the nerves about being in front of everyone and saying your vows? Is that anyone's idea of fun?"

Gloria took her hand and squeezed. "It's nervy, sure. But it's exciting, too. This is the day you're declaring to everyone that you love Marcus. That you've chosen him to be your life partner. It's nerve-wracking, but it's also the start of your new life." She squeezed again.

Abby gulped. She didn't dare look at Mum for fear of giving away what she was feeling. That she wasn't sure she wanted this particular new life.

So she kept quiet and stared at a motorbike that drew up alongside their car. The woman on the back was dressed in full leather. When she turned her head left and saw Abby in her white dress and veil, the woman gave Abby a thumbs-up.

Abby returned the gesture. It wasn't the most absurd thing she was doing today.

Gloria stroked her hand.

Abby blinked, then turned, catching her mum's gaze. When she saw concern in her mum's eyes, Abby turned away.

"I know everyone says it's the best day of your life, and they're right, it should be," Gloria said. "But sometimes, it's far from it."

Abby took a deep breath. Could Mum read her mind?

"And if it's not the best day, not even a semi-good day, you can still change your mind. It's not too late, Abby."

Abby's stomach tensed. Nausea rose up in her. What was Mum saying?

"On the contrary, it's the perfect time to change your mind. Better than after you get married. Remember, you're speaking to someone who knows. My first marriage looked good on paper, but the reality wasn't the same."

Abby turned. This wasn't the first time she'd heard this story. But somehow, here, it had so much more poignancy.

"I remember going to my first wedding, even though I try to block it out. I was so scared in the wedding car. It was pouring with rain. Like the weather knew. I had a nagging feeling I shouldn't do it, but I didn't listen." She waved a hand at Abby. "Look at you. You're gorgeous, your dress is perfect, just like you, but I'm not sure this is ever going to be the happiest day of your life. I certainly don't want it to go down as one of the worst. Right now, I'm scared it will."

Abby couldn't believe what she was hearing.

"I saw the way you were looking at Jordan on the hen weekend. I saw the way she was looking at you. I don't know if anything went on. That's between you two. I also know she wasn't there this morning, and she conveniently isn't coming to your wedding. Are those two things connected?"

Abby took a deep breath and turned to her mum. She couldn't lie.

She gave her a nod, and covered her mouth. She wasn't going to cry. It would ruin her make-up.

"I've stepped back and let this play out, but I can't sit back and watch you make the worst mistake of your life. And believe me, this is nothing to do with Marcus. I love Marcus. Everybody loves Marcus. But that's not a reason to marry him. You have to follow your heart, Abby. Always follow your heart. I don't know whether or not you love Jordan. Or whether what's between you could become something else. Only you know that.

"But this is about you and Marcus. If you don't love him, don't marry him. Whatever you decide, you have my full support." Gloria paused. "Does he suspect anything at all?"

Abby's chest heaved. "I don't think so."

Gloria let a few moments go by. "Did something happen between you?"

Abby's breathing quickened, then she nodded. "Yes." It came out in a whisper. Underlined with shame and longing.

"Could it be something more?"

Abby sighed. "I don't know. Yes. Maybe. If she'll have anything to do with me after I treated her so badly." If she could turn back time, Abby would. Did she have the guts to make a change now, though?

"Just say the word, Abby." Mum took her hand again. "Today can be whatever you want it to be. The start of a new life. Whether that's being married to Marcus or not. Your dad and I love you, and will stand by you whatever you decide."

# Chapter Thirty

" I still can't quite believe we're doing this. It's like we're in a Richard Curtis movie. Or a revival of *Carry On Wedding*. Was that even a film?"

Jordan gripped her knees as Karen's car screeched to a halt at the traffic lights. She checked her watch. It was nearly 1.40pm. The wedding was due to take place at 2pm. They were cutting it fine.

"If it wasn't, it should have been. If Barbara Windsor shows up, then we'll know it definitely was."

Jordan had woken up this morning with a tight stomach and an ache in her heart. She'd pushed some toast around her plate, stared at her coffee, and then Karen had forced her to face up to what she may or may not want. Did she want Abby? Because if she did, she really didn't have a choice. Sure, this wasn't Jordan's normal way of doing things, of taking life by the scruff of the neck and declaring her feelings. However, her past dealings with women hadn't come to much success, so maybe a change of tactics was due.

Karen had offered to drive, and Jordan had agreed. She was going after what she wanted. She needed to know beyond doubt they were done. She didn't want any what-ifs. However, what she was going to find when she saw Abby, she had no idea. Would she listen? Or would she slap her across the face? Either would prove there was something between them.

The traffic lights turned green. Something fluttered inside Jordan's chest. She swallowed down, staring at her phone. According to the sat nav, they were two minutes away from the church. St Christopher's. The patron saint of travellers. Would Abby take the road less travelled?

"You ready? We're getting pretty close."

Jordan nodded, her denim-clad knee jigging up and down. She'd considered wearing her bridesmaid dress, to finish the job no matter what. But then Karen had reminded her she wasn't a masochist and there were no prizes for being so. So clean jeans, brogues, a white shirt and a navy blazer had won the day. Because she had to look like an option Abby wanted to ditch her wedding for.

Jordan flipped down the car's visor mirror. Her make-up still looked good. Her hair was held in place. Now, she just needed the happy ending she so craved. Or at least the possibility of a happy ending, at least. Was she doing the right thing? She had no idea. But she couldn't ignore the thump of her heart every time she thought about Abby.

This wasn't just her doing. Abby had played her part, too. Now it was time to find out if she wanted to take up her leading role for good.

"Do you know what wedding car she's got?" Karen glanced in her rear-view mirror. "It's not a white Jaguar, is it?"

Jordan nodded. "Yep, vintage. I booked it."

Karen indicated with her thumb. "Like the one behind us?"

Jordan twisted, then her heart burst.

Instinctively, she sank down in her seat. "Shit. I think it's them."

Karen glanced left, then she indicated and pulled up in front of the church, where the last stragglers were milling about outside.

She cut the engine, then turned, gripping Jordan's hand in hers. "Showtime. You ready?"

Jordan gave a definite nod that belied the butterflies in her stomach. "Let's do it." As she looked up, Delta and Taran were walking down the church path towards her. She had to ignore them and concentrate on what she had to do.

Jordan jumped out of the car, just as the Jaguar pulled up behind them. In her head, their wheels screeched. Warm June air caressed her face. Church bells rang. Across the street, a small boy kicked a football on a green with his mum. It was just a normal day for them. Not for Jordan. This was the most important day of her life.

The driver of the wedding car walked around the car and opened the passenger door.

Gloria stepped down first, a pensive look on her face.

Then the driver held out a hand and Abby climbed out, her elegant wedding dress embracing her with some style.

Jordan gulped.

Abby was beyond beautiful. Also about to marry someone else. Maybe she still would. It didn't mean Jordan shouldn't do this. She strode over to Abby, just as the photographer, Heidi, appeared beside her, directing Abby to pose in front of the car. Jordan recognised Heidi from previous weddings she'd been a part of.

"Abby," Jordan said.

Abby turned, emitting an audible gasp as she saw her. "Jordan," she began.

She could listen to Abby say her name all day long.

"Before you start having photos taken, can I say something?"

Abby gave her a confused look, before nodding. "Okay." Her tone was quizzical. She turned to Heidi. "Can you give us two minutes?"

Heidi checked her watch. "We really need to get these shots done."

"It wasn't a question," Abby replied, steel to her tone.

Heidi stepped back, nodding.

"Abby." Delta appeared beside her. "You don't have to do this."

Abby's eyes hardened. "Yes, I do." She glared at her maid of honour. "This isn't your decision, Delta."

Jordan held her breath.

Delta held out her hand. "At least give me your flowers."

Abby handed them over.

Now it really was show time.

Jordan took a deep breath, shoulders back, just as she'd practised. Only, being on this pavement with an audience close by was putting more pressure on her. She tried to keep her body still even though every inch of her was shaking. Could she get her words out?

She had to. There was no other choice.

"I'm sorry to do this so late in the proceedings." That wasn't what she'd practised. She scanned her mind for the script she'd rehearsed. It was there, she just had to focus and reach for it. "But I can't let you marry Marcus without saying something." Jordan gazed into Abby's eyes, taking in her stunning cheekbones, her just-so hair. She was heart-stoppingly beautiful.

If this didn't go Jordan's way, her heart might well stop.

"Over the past few weeks, it's been equal parts amazing and excruciating working with you. Amazing because I got to know you and the gorgeous person you are. Excruciating because you were marrying someone else."

Abby blinked. She was listening. She hadn't run.

"Because of that, I consigned us to the box marked *wrong time, wrong place*. I resolved to be the best professional bridesmaid I could be. To smile through the pain. To get you to the altar as I promised, and then get over you. I was doing well until we went away. Until we kissed. Until my feelings demanded to be let out of the box." Jordan closed her eyes as a nervous warmth spread through her. When she reopened them, Abby was staring at her lips.

"After that, all bets were off. As I told you, I don't do this." She circled the space in front of them with her right hand. "I don't get involved with people, full stop, but certainly not my clients. But from the moment we met, there was something there. The more I got to know you, the more I wanted to know you. You're special, Abby. You've taken up room in my heart. So I couldn't let you do this today without seeing if you felt the same."

Jordan stepped forward, and took Abby's hand.

Just that small action felt so daring.

Daring, but also, *so right*.

Desire slid down her like warm honey.

Abby's hand shook. Jordan couldn't remember a word of her speech now. She was going to have to do this from the heart.

"I know this isn't the optimal time to be saying this. But I had to give it a go. Because saying it after you got married would be worse." Jordan took both of Abby's hands in hers, then looked her in the eye.

"I started this journey as your professional bridesmaid. But I ended up falling for you." Jordan's chest rose as she breathed in. "I love you, Abby." Sensation overwhelmed her, but she carried on. "I never expected that to happen, and I'm sorry if this messes with your plans for today. If you feel the same in any small way, maybe we can build on that. Maybe we could make it work in the real world. In a world where you're not marrying someone else."

Jordan didn't break their gaze as she waited for what seemed like an eternity. Eventually, Abby began to shake her head.

Jordan's stomach hit the floor.

This wasn't how this was supposed to go.

Abby was supposed to fall into her arms.

"I never expected this to happen, either." Abby's words came out as a whisper. "But I made the car drive around the block three times, because I knew if it stopped, I was going to have to go through with it. Either that, or break Marcus's heart. Neither of those options were appealing. I didn't want to get out of the car. I'd just decided I wouldn't go through with the wedding. Then you appeared, and my heart boomed. I've tried to ignore my feelings too, but I can't anymore."

It was all Jordan could do not to collapse on the spot.

A trickle of hope slid down her spine, but she wasn't going to embrace it just yet.

Abby dropped her hands. "I'm sorry for telling you not to come. I couldn't face you, without the truth about how I felt leaking out. But you're right. I shouldn't marry someone else if my heart tells me not to." She glanced over at Gloria, who was dabbing her eyes with a tissue. "My mum was just telling me the same thing. That I should be with someone I truly love, not someone I think I should love."

Jordan held her breath.

"I'm so glad you came back and took a chance. You were brave. You've made me brave in return." Abby fixed Jordan with her gaze. She took a deep breath before she continued. "I love you, too. I'm sorry I never told you before. I'm sorry we got this far before I said anything." Abby glanced down at herself, before bringing her face back level with Jordan. "But here I am, standing in a wedding dress, declaring love for someone I'm not going to marry." She shook her head, before lifting her gaze, staring directly into Jordan's eyes. "Not yet, anyway."

Jordan's heart soared.

For a few brief moments, everything was perfect.

"Abby!" Marcus's voice rang out through the air.

They both stepped back, turning to where Marcus was running down the path of the church towards where the mini congregation were stood: Gloria, Karen, the driver, Heidi, Delta, Taran, Abby and Jordan. His best man, Philip, was right behind.

Marcus was dressed in a sharp blue suit and pink tie.

He looked from Abby to Jordan and back. "What's going on? Why is Jordan not wearing her dress?" He couldn't seem to make sense of the picture, no matter how hard he tried.

"What are you doing here? It's bad luck to see each other before the wedding!" Even Abby looked confused by her own statement.

"I decided I'd chance it when one of my groomsmen told me there appeared to be some sort of hold-up." He paused. "Is someone going to fill me in?"

Abby glanced at Jordan, shaking her head. "I will," she said, her voice cracking. "This is up to me." She took Marcus by the hand and steered him away from the others, but still in earshot of Jordan.

"Marcus, I need you to know that I never meant for any of this to happen. Hold on to that thought, even when it's really hard." She paused, taking a breath. "Also, that I really do love you. A part of me always will. You are a wonderful man, and I've no doubt you're going to make someone a wonderful husband."

Marcus's shoulders slumped, and his face crumpled. "Someone?"

Jordan hoped he didn't cry. This must be his worst nightmare. It certainly would be hers.

Abby nodded. "Just not me. I'm so sorry." She paused and gripped his arm, clearly just about holding it together. "I know this is a terrible time to do this, and I hope one day you can forgive me. But I really do believe this is the best decision for both of us." She took his hand. "But I can't marry you when I have feelings for someone else." Abby dipped her head. "Feelings for Jordan."

Marcus looked like he'd just been punched. He dropped Abby's hands, and tangled his fingers in his dark hair. "Jordan? But she's your bridesmaid."

He looked at Jordan, disbelief staining his face.

Abby took a deep breath. "She was. But now, she's something more. I can't ignore how I feel, and I can't marry you knowing that. You and I have been friends for so long. I truly never meant to hurt you."

Marcus shook his head, his face full of disbelief. "You and Jordan? But you're not gay?"

Abby ignored his comment. Now was not the time for explanations. "I was happy with you. Please believe that. But I was having doubts over the past few months. I should have told you. I know that now."

Marcus turned to Jordan. "I knew you were too good to be true."

Jordan gulped. This was so hard. She moved closer to them. "I'm really sorry, Marcus. I never meant for this to happen either."

Still he stared. "I knew something wasn't right, but this? You were meant to sort everything out. Make Abby's worries disappear. If you were a man, I'd punch you." He clenched and unclenched his fist.

Jordan didn't move. "And you'd be within your rights."

"Please don't," Abby said, her voice high-pitched.

"Nobody's hitting anybody." Delta pushed in between them. "Marcus, get in the wedding car and let the driver take you home. Or to a pub. Wherever you need to go. Take your best man with you. I'll go and tell everyone the wedding is cancelled."

Delta was finally stepping up to the plate. Jordan could have kissed her.

"Thanks, Delta," Abby said.

"That's it? Just like that we're over?" Marcus turned his volume higher.

Jordan winced.

Gloria jumped in and squeezed his arm. "I'm sorry Marcus. This isn't fair on you. But please, get in the car and get away like Delta suggested. It'll be easier on you."

"Please, Marcus," Delta said.

Marcus's face turned red. Then he shook off Gloria's arm, walked over to the wedding car, got in and slammed the door.

Jordan's heart went out to him.

Delta turned to Karen. "You're driving the other car?"

Karen nodded.

"Okay. You take Gloria, Abby and Jordan. I think we need to split this party up."

"Will do," Karen said, already heading for the car.

Gloria put an arm around Abby's shoulders, just as Marjorie appeared.

"What's going on? Why are you all standing around out here?" She looked around one more time, then frowned. "Where's my son?"

Gloria went over, took Marjorie's arm and steered her away, just as Abby had done to Marcus minutes before. This time, Jordan couldn't hear the words, but she could read the body language.

Marjorie glared at Abby, anger oozing from her face. She went to walk in Abby's direction, but Gloria stopped her, saying something else. Then she pointed towards the wedding car, with Marcus in the back.

"I knew you weren't right for him," Marjorie told Abby, before storming over to the wedding car and getting in.

Gloria clapped her hands, grabbing everyone's attention. "Alright everyone. Show's over. Time to disperse." She looked at Delta. "You're good to do the honours inside?"

Delta nodded. "Of course."

Gloria steered Abby towards Karen's car. She put Abby in the back seat, then got in the front.

Jordan glanced at Delta and Taran, then at the church. "I'm so sorry," she said, to nobody in particular.

Then she sprinted for the back seat and slammed the door.

The whole car was silent for a few moments. Shock reverberated around the interior.

Jordan pressed her head into the back seat, taking Abby's hand in hers. It was limp. She kissed her fingers. They were going to recover from this, but it might take a while. Especially for Abby.

Karen started the car, then turned to the back seat. "Are we going home?"

Jordan looked at Abby, then back to Karen. She nodded. "I think some distance from Surrey would be a good idea. And can you put the radio on? I don't know about everyone else, but I need something to drown out the thud of my heartbeat."

Karen did as she was told, and the sound of a DJ floated into their ears. It was weird to have someone else in the car with them at this auspicious moment.

"And now, a request from Gary and Heather, on their way back from a Sunday trip to Ikea. This one is called *Drops of Jupiter.*"

Jordan's heart almost stopped beating, as she sucked in a deep breath and turned to Abby, tears brimming in her eyes. She had no idea how this was going to turn out. Ambushing a bride and running off with her was all new territory. However, with her favourite song on the radio, and Abby's hand in hers, it was as if the world was giving her a sign. That they'd done the right thing. That everything was going to work out just fine. She had to believe that.

Right now, looking into Abby's eyes, she could believe in anything.

She pulled Abby close.

Everything from this point on was forward.

No looking back.

Because Jordan had got her girl.

Finally.

# Chapter Thirty-One

Abby stepped into Jordan's flat in a daze. She let herself be led through to the kitchen, where the digital dial on the microwave told her it was 15:22.

She was meant to be married by now. Mrs Marcus Montgomery.

Instead, Jordan was making her a cup of tea for the first time in her flat. Jordan's flat. Were they a couple now? She couldn't quite get her head around the speed of change.

However, her overriding emotion, apart from disbelief and hope that Marcus was okay, was relief.

She hadn't married him. Abby had changed the direction of her day. It hadn't been in her original plan, but it was definitely her best move yet.

For the first time in quite a while, the knot in her stomach was beginning to unfurl. She hadn't even realised the knot was there. But now, she felt lighter.

Freer.

Herself.

But also, overwhelmed. She was in completely new territory here. Metaphorically but also, practically.

She glanced around, taking in the flat decor. Could she and Jordan work as a couple? Would she have chosen that golden rug? Those striped cushions? Were they Jordan's choice, or Karen's?

She shook herself, as Jordan led her into the lounge. She sat on the cream sofa, and hitched up her dress. Her mind was still reeling. The look on Marcus's face when she'd told him. Perhaps in time he'd be able to forgive her for hurting him. Especially when her heart told her it was the right thing to do. Maybe she'd forgive herself soon, too.

She sat back, trying to regulate her breathing. It was no easy task.

"You know, the first thing I want to do is get out of this dress. Lovely as it is, I'm not getting married."

Jordan fixed her with her sapphire gaze. "You're most definitely not." She leaned forward and pressed her lips to Abby's.

Abby had always dreamed of being kissed the way Jordan kissed her. Jordan made her feel it in her bones, in every beat of her heart, in every atom of her being.

She could never walk away from this. She knew that now.

Abby could build a life around Jordan's kisses. Build a future. Build a world for the two of them.

That thought made her smile as she pulled back.

Jordan stared at her, her face a question mark. "What's funny? Because that wasn't the reaction I was looking for from that kiss."

Abby shook her head. "Nothing's funny. I was just thinking that I've been craving your kisses. Now, I can have them all the time. That made me smile."

"Any time you like." Jordan placed another gentler kiss

on Abby's lips. "I'd also like to get you out of your dress, but for other reasons." She gave her a knowing smile. "You want to see if any of my clothes might fit you? Then you'd at least have something, until we can make it back to your place?"

Abby nodded. "That's an added benefit of being with a woman I hadn't considered: double the wardrobe."

"One of many." Jordan stood, holding out a hand to help Abby up.

Abby took it, just as Gloria walked into the room.

"Okay, you two. I'd say you've got some things to talk about and maybe you need a little space of your own. So I took the liberty of booking you into a hotel on the seafront. Get changed, get a cab or walk if you fancy the fresh air. Just have tonight to yourself, to chat and be together. You can work the rest out tomorrow. I've paid for the room, consider it my gift to you both."

Abby stepped forward and hugged her, before holding her mum at arm's length. "What about you?"

"Karen has already offered to drive me back to the venue. I've been in touch with Delta and Martin, and help is needed there, so that's where I'm going. Don't worry about anything that end. Delta, Taran, Martin and I can help on your behalf, and Marcus's family can pitch in, too.

"I'm aware that tonight was meant to be the start of your new life, and there's no reason it still can't be. It's just a different start to what you expected. Go to the hotel, have tonight, and when you wake up in the morning, it'll all feel more clear. The good thing is, you didn't move in with Marcus before the wedding, so there's no mess there." She raised a single eyebrow. "Although, I always thought that said a lot.

When you fall in love, you want to be with that person all the time."

Abby glanced Jordan's way, before taking her hand.

She knew that now she'd found Jordan.

Now she had her, she never wanted to let her go.

# Chapter Thirty-Two

"Wow." Jordan walked over to the window, and stared out at the sea beyond. "Your mum didn't skimp on the room. A suite, no less." She glanced around at the sofa, the bottle of champagne on ice in a shiny silver bucket on the coffee table. Through a large open doorway, a king-size bed with crisp white linen awaited. "It's almost like she's congratulating us. Like it's our big day."

Abby walked up behind her, and put a hand on Jordan's shoulder. Heat crept up her back. "It sort of is." Abby still couldn't quite come to terms with what had happened. Should she be more contrite? More sorry for everything? In part, she was. But by lying about how she truly felt, the person she'd hurt the most was herself.

Standing here with Jordan, she wasn't hurting anymore. She might have begun the day pressed down with fear. But now, she was awash with fresh bliss.

Like from here on in, nothing could go wrong.

Jordan turned and caught Abby's gaze.

"I'm exactly where I want to be, so no complaints."

Jordan twisted right around, putting her arms around Abby's waist. "Are you sure? I know it's a lot." She laughed at her own joke. "Is that the understatement of the year?"

Abby snorted. "Let's see. My wedding dress is currently lying on your bed. I'm standing in your jeans and T-shirt. And right now, I should be having my first dance with my husband."

Jordan pulled her closer. "You look gorgeous in my jeans, if that helps at all?"

"Do I?" Abby looked down. "They're a little short."

"It's how all the kids are wearing them. On trend," Jordan replied.

Abby leaned in. So close, she could almost taste her. "Do you prefer me with your clothes on or off, though?" Desire coursed through her.

"Follow your heart," Mum had said. Today was her day for doing that. She closed the gap between them and pressed her lips to Jordan's.

The effect was like a starburst in her heart. From a day stained with harm, something so much better was springing up. Something akin to a hug from the universe.

Jordan slid her tongue into Abby's mouth, and she welcomed it.

She wanted all of Jordan. She wanted her now. But they had time. There was no need to rush.

She had to keep telling herself that. They didn't have to hide anymore.

They were out in the open, which meant they could open themselves up together. No more kisses in darkness. No more sex in confined spaces. Today was about luxuriating in each other. Touching every part of Jordan. Kissing every part of Jordan.

Abby pulled back, her brain scrambled by Jordan's kisses.

She stared into her blue eyes, seeing for the first time some green flecks. She'd never relaxed enough this close to Jordan to notice. She could now. Abby kissed Jordan's eyelids. "I can't believe we're here," she said. "I can't believe you did what you did." She shook her head. "I almost got married today. To someone whose kisses never made my head spin."

Jordan planted another on her lips. She glanced over at the champagne. "You want to pop the cork on the champagne?"

Abby stared at her, desire blazing through her core. "I'd rather pop the cork on you."

Jordan gave her a grin. "Now you're talking." She placed a hand under Abby's shirt and touched her back.

Abby's skin tingled. She pressed her lips back to Jordan's, and this time, she was going to let her body do the talking.

Today had been hard. It was time to make it all better.

Abby's kisses grew more urgent. It had only been five days since the plane, but it might as well have been a lifetime.

They staggered through the lounge, Jordan shedding her top, Abby flinging hers off.

Jordan made short work of Abby's bra. It dropped to the floor, leaving her breasts exposed. When Jordan saw them fully, she stilled.

She ran a reverent hand over them both, before bringing her tongue to Abby's nipple and circling first one, then the other.

Every muscle inside Abby contracted. She drew in a breath as Jordan sucked her into her mouth.

Abby ran a hand through Jordan's golden hair, leaning on her so she wouldn't collapse. If this was what happened when Jordan kissed her breasts, she couldn't imagine the rest.

Jordan brought her head level with Abby again, a sly grin on her face. "Shall we find the bed and get naked?"

Abby nodded. "Fuck, yes."

Jordan guided them there, before shucking her jeans, then sliding off Abby's jeans and pants. She stood back to admire her naked form.

"I said you'd look better with no clothes on." Jordan leaned in. "I was right."

Abby shook her head, waving a hand up and down. "I'm naked, and you're standing there in black lace looking like a Victoria's Secret model."

Jordan looked down at herself. "You don't like?"

"Oh no, I very much like." Abby pulled her closer. She ran a finger inside the top of Jordan's pants.

Jordan sucked in a long breath. "I gambled on getting lucky today. Karen's a lingerie buyer for M&S. It pays to have connections."

Abby slipped her hand further down. "Tell her I'd like some crotchless pants for you next, okay?"

Jordan's eyelids fluttered shut. "What are you doing to me?" She opened her eyes. "But you're going to have to wait. You had your way with me on the plane. Now it's my turn, wouldn't you say?"

Abby wasn't putting up a fight. "Whatever you say. So long as you keep your underwear on to fuck me."

"Your wish is my command." Jordan moved Abby up the bed, before working her way down her body, covering every inch of her skin with hot, urgent kisses.

Abby closed her eyes and gave in to the moment. The attention Jordan was giving her, the look in her eyes when their gazes connected, was pure lust. Jordan was making her feel like the most desirable woman in the world.

That hadn't happened in a very long time.

When Jordan licked her way up her thighs, Abby sighed. When she teased her nipples again, Abby saw stars. When she kissed her way up her neck, she purred. And then, when Jordan's hand hovered over her pussy, Abby's whole body roared to life. All the lovers that had gone before were wiped away. All the feelings she could never work out, all the indifference she'd felt in past relationships.

Gone.

Vanished.

Abby was a clean slate.

Jordan slipped a finger into her hot centre. Abby was pulled under. She went willingly. When Jordan slipped in another finger, Abby's insides pulsed. When Jordan connected with Abby's clit and got into a perfect rhythm, Abby wondered if she'd ever come down from this. And when she did, what would life be like afterwards?

Abby hadn't known she needed a change. She hadn't known what life had in store, until Jordan walked into that café six weeks ago. If she had, would she have agreed to Jordan becoming her professional bridesmaid?

A thousand times, yes.

Because Jordan had lit up her life. She'd shone a light and made Abby reconsider key areas of her life. Her job. Her relationships. Herself. Jordan had made her look at the world differently.

She was certainly experiencing it differently now. Particularly when Jordan climbed on top of her and pressed a thigh behind her hand. Applied some gentle thrusts that made Abby cry out. Jordan's skilled fingers made the fire inside her roar. With Jordan's urging in her ears, and her own heartbeat thumping in her chest, Abby let out a guttural moan as she fell over the edge, everything inside her shaking, a kaleidoscope of desire flexing under her eyelids.

As her body shook and Jordan's fingers directed her to the summit once more, Abby knew life would never be the same again. Jordan had changed it forever. She came apart in a rush of delicious spasms. They rode it out together, mouths fused, bodies locked, every movement deepening the intimacy.

She opened her eyes and focused on Jordan, giving her a sizzling smile.

Her decisions over the past couple of years hadn't always been the best.

But choosing Jordan? That decision was solid gold.

\* \* \*

Jordan eased her fingers out of Abby, kissed her lips, then rolled off her. When she refocused, Abby's eyes were closed, her breathing ragged.

You never knew how things were going to go when you first got together with someone. But with Abby, Jordan hadn't had a single doubt. If you counted the plane, this was their second time. More than one night. New territory for Jordan. She kissed Abby's shoulder and stroked her hair. She ached to be touched. Their chemistry was off the scale. If this was the start, Jordan couldn't wait to see what happened next.

Abby opened her eyes.

"Hey."

"Hey yourself." She gave her a grin. "I think you might have just killed me. Death by orgasm. That's a thing, right?"

"It would make a great story in the local paper. 'Bride runs out of wedding, then dies of lesbian orgasm'."

Abby laughed, covering her face with her hand. "*That's Life* magazine would pay you at least £250 for that story."

"Well worth it," Jordan replied.

Abby rolled on top of her, silencing her. "But enough talk of selling our story to the papers."

Jordan smiled. "I'm all for that."

"I only got to touch you very briefly first time around. I'm hoping we can remedy that." Abby crushed her mouth to hers, her thigh finding Jordan's hot, wet core and pressing down.

Jordan was so ready. She had been for weeks. However, she'd never given herself permission to dream anything might happen. Until now.

Now the green light was flashing in her mind. She spread her legs to convey her feelings to Abby.

Abby smiled down at her. "Remember, I'm new at this. Let me know if I need to change direction at any point, okay? Just like I did with you at the driving range. If you need to change the position of my fingers, feel free."

Jordan grinned. She couldn't imagine not liking anything Abby did. "I will. You're doing brilliantly so far."

"You make it easy."

As soon as Abby began to make her way down Jordan's body, her fingers deft, her lips light, Jordan let herself focus only on what Abby was doing. Kissing. Stroking. Loving.

Moments later, when Abby's mouth was between her thighs, her hot breath over her centre, Jordan closed her eyes, anticipation throbbing inside her. As soon as Abby stroked her tongue up and through her centre, Jordan's head crashed back into the pillow.

Abby didn't need much direction. She was doing just fine.

Jordan's hands gripped the bed sheets as Abby's tongue slid one way, then the other, slaloming over and around her, as if Abby were a world champion skier. Jordan was the course. She had no doubt she was glistening like virgin snow.

As her orgasm rumbled to life in her feet, then up through her legs and into her very core, Jordan writhed on the bed, her fingers clinging to Abby's hair, driving her on.

"Don't stop," Jordan said, her voice barely audible, her spirit soaring.

In her mind, Jordan glimpsed the past six weeks in a flickering montage. Their meeting, their kiss, their sky-high fuck. But from the despair of the rehearsal dinner, now Abby was thrusting her fingers into Jordan, and sweeping her tongue over her one last time.

As she did, Jordan toppled into her own gorgeous oblivion, clutching Abby inside her. She came so hard, she wasn't sure her vision would ever return to normal. She didn't care. It was all worth it. Because it had all led to this.

To Abby thrusting once more. To Jordan sitting up, Abby's fingers still inside her, their mouths coming together in a tangle of emotion and lust. To Jordan moaning into Abby's mouth as she came again with such a force, she was surprised Abby was still on the bed. But when she stopped shaking and opened her eyes, Abby was still there. Still inside her. They were still one.

When they finally pulled away from each other, Jordan toppled back onto the bed, her laughter coating the air.

Abby flopped down beside her, laughing too.

Jordan was pleasantly, deliciously fucked, the sugar rush of sex still rolling through her. She couldn't wipe the smile from her face.

"You look like the cat who got the cream." Abby kissed her lips once more.

Jordan cupped Abby's cheek with her palm. "Does that make you the cat who ate the cream?"

Abby laughed. "Guilty as charged." She took a deep breath, her gaze never wavering, before her cheeks coloured red and she looked away.

Jordan frowned. "What is it? Did I do something wrong?"

Abby shook her head, alarm creasing her face. "No," she said. "If anything, the absolute opposite." She paused. "I was just thinking this moment is so perfect, and you're so perfect."

Jordan let out a bark of laughter. She was far from perfect. "I'll remind you of this moment when you find out the truth about me."

Abby laughed again. "Keep up the facade as long as you can." She brought her gaze back to Jordan. "But right now, you are. At least, you make me feel so much. It's kinda scary."

Jordan brought Abby's fingers to her mouth and kissed them. "I know this is all new, but we can navigate it together. Rest assured, the next six weeks will not be as fraught as the past six."

"Promise?"

"Cross my heart." Jordan did just that. "You're not scared about being with a woman?"

Abby smiled, shaking her head. "That's the least of my worries. You can't help who you fall in love with."

Jordan's heart boomed. Abby loved her. It would take a while to get used to. "I love that you love me."

Abby squeezed her bum. "You sound like a bad pop song."

"I don't care." Jordan kissed Abby's lips again. "Just to check, one more time. This isn't a one-night stand? This is going to happen again?"

Abby grinned. "Hell, yes. Way sooner than you might imagine."

# Chapter Thirty-Three

Jordan woke up the next morning, her body aching in places she forgot she could ache. Even her calf muscles were sore. She smiled as she recalled the night before. Abby had given her a full-body work out, so she wasn't surprised about the aches. In fact, as she wriggled in the bed, she revelled in them. They'd been a long time coming.

Unlike either of them.

She glanced left, where Abby's eyes were still closed, her breathing regular. Her beauty made Jordan still.

She'd taken a chance yesterday. The biggest chance she'd ever taken in her life. The whole way driving with Karen, she'd questioned herself. Was she doing the right thing? Was her whole life about to unravel before her eyes? But every time she'd asked, she'd come up with the same answer. She had to try. She had to see if Abby felt the same way. If she crashed and burned, so be it.

But she hadn't. She was lying in a posh hotel bed with the woman she loved.

That didn't even feel that scary to say anymore. Go figure. The relationship dodger had only gone and fallen in love. She was never going to hear the end of it from Karen.

As if sensing she was being watched, Abby murmured,

before opening one eye, then another. When she saw Jordan, her face cracked into a smile. She rolled into her.

Jordan gathered her in her arms as Abby's limbs slotted into place with hers.

They fitted perfectly.

"Morning beautiful." Jordan had never meant those words so much in her life. "I dreamed about doing this on the yacht, you know?"

Abby frowned. "Doing what?"

"This. Waking up with you. When your mum said you should cook me square sausage for breakfast — which you still need to do, by the way. But when she said it, a thought flashed through my mind of waking up after a night of sex with you. Now my dreams have come true."

"I'm glad." Abby rolled onto her back, wincing. "I ache deliciously this morning." She turned her head. "All because of you."

Jordan kissed her lips. "What did I do?"

Abby smirked. "What didn't you?" She sighed. "I'm meant to be on a flight to the Maldives right now. I'm so glad I'm not."

"I second that," Jordan replied. "Plus, you don't have me there to hold your hand, so you couldn't possibly be on a flight."

Abby rolled onto her side, fixing Jordan with an intense stare. "I loved that, you know. I knew how much I felt for you even then. You holding my hand on the flight to Cannes made the difference. Marcus didn't listen to me when I said I didn't want to go to the Maldives. He wanted to do what honeymooners do."

Marcus's face outside the church ran through Jordan's

mind. She was sure he hadn't woken up so chipper this morning. "You think he'll still go on honeymoon?"

"Maybe. I don't know." Abby sighed. "I'll message him later. I'll go and see him soon, too. Explain a bit more if he'll let me. I still feel bad."

Jordan reached down and took Abby's hand in hers. "Me, too. But it was the right thing to do." She squeezed. "I'll always be there to hold your hand, okay?" She meant it, too. With every fibre of her being.

Abby nodded. "Okay."

"And I promise never to take you to the Maldives. If we ever get married, how does a honeymoon in Blackpool sound?"

"It sounds like the perfect location," Abby replied. "Plus, I know someone who can give us some great recommendations."

"Can we go on a giant rollercoaster and eat fish and chips on the seafront straight out of the paper?"

Abby's laughter pierced the air. "I had a lucky escape meeting you." She gathered all her breath, then let out a high-pitched scream, before covering her face with her hands.

Jordan sat up. "What was that?"

Abby peaked through her fingers. "Just a reaction to my life right now." She put her weight on one elbow.

Jordan's gaze was drawn to her breasts. She leaned down and kissed them, before rolling back to admire the view.

"I don't think I'll ever tire of waking up with you."

"You've only done it once. Give it five years, then see what you think," Jordan replied.

Abby shook her head. "I won't change my mind. I'm going to really think about my decisions and what I want with my life from now on." She paused. "I nearly married a man who

274

wouldn't eat fish and chips from the paper. He always needed a plate."

"It's not the crime of the century."

"No, but it's a sign. A red flag." She kissed Jordan's lips. "Thanks for making me see things more clearly."

"You're very welcome. I'm just glad you don't hate me for hijacking your wedding."

Abby blew out a breath. "What would you have done if I'd said no?"

"Had a tantrum on the pavement like a toddler?"

Abby laughed. "Very sexy. That would have been sure to win me over." She moved swiftly, climbing on top of Jordan. "But seriously, you saved my life yesterday. And yes, I need to go back and speak to Marcus, and everyone else who put time and effort into the wedding. I owe them all. Money and my apologies. But it was the right thing to do."

Jordan couldn't concentrate on much more than Abby's full weight on top of her, her naked form causing waves of want to pulse through her. But she tried her best to decipher the conversation, too.

"I can come with you." Jordan stroked Abby's arse, as her leg fell between her thighs. More waves crashed through her.

"I'm not sure both of us going would be the best thing. This is my mess. I have to clear it up."

"Whatever I can do to help."

Abby tilted her head. "Do you think you're going to carry on being a professional bridesmaid?"

Jordan couldn't tell if she was asking her not to. She shook her head. "I've got a few jobs booked in, so I'm going to talk to them, and be honest. If they still want me, I'll honour my commitments this year. But after that, I think it's time to look for a new job. I was going to do that anyway. This has just pushed the agenda forward." She squeezed Abby's bum cheek. "You're worth it, though."

Abby stroked a hand up the outside of Jordan's thigh.

Jordan quivered anew.

"You think this relationship can take both of us changing jobs at once?"

Jordan blinked. "You don't need to, do you? Didn't you just get a promotion?"

"I did, but meeting you has made me see things differently. Made me remember what we talked about when we were kids."

"We didn't know each other when we were kids."

"It feels like we did. If feels like we've always known each other. You made me remember my dreams. I still want to do something that makes a difference, that changes the world."

"You've changed my world, if it helps."

"A good start."

"Do you have anything in mind?"

"Not yet. But once I've sorted out my old life, I can look at my new life with fresh eyes. It might need a new job to go along with it. Something I'm passionate about. Something that makes me excited to get out of bed in the morning. Although I might not be so excited to get out of bed if you're in it, but these are all things we can overcome. Together."

"I agree." Jordan paused. "Can I rewind, though? Am I staying in your bed a lot already?"

"I hope so. I didn't just turn my life upside down for nothing."

"Says the woman who wouldn't even move in with her former lover."

"Maybe my mum had a point. That was a sign. Whereas you," Abby said, wriggling on top of Jordan, "I want to move you into my bed, tie you up and make sure you never leave." She kissed her lips with more force.

"That's a plan I can totally get on-board with. Particularly now I might be unemployed."

Abby shook her head, giving Jordan a gentle smile. "I'm sorry I blew up your business."

"I'm sorry I blew up your life."

"I'm not," Abby replied.

"Neither am I." Jordan lifted her head and Abby duly kissed her lips. They stayed like that for a long moment, before they pulled apart, lust ramped up in Jordan's heart.

"I love you, did I tell you that?"

Abby nodded. "You did. And I've never been more pleased to hear those three words. They're my absolute favourite."

"More than fish and chips?"

Abby kissed her lips. "Close call, but yes."

"More than Honeymoon in Blackpool?"

"Just about."

"More than fuck me now?"

Abby leaned down. "I have a strong affection for those words, too," she said, before sliding her wet tongue into Jordan's mouth.

# Epilogue

## One Year Later...

"Jordan! Jordan!" Abby rolled her eyes, walking from the kitchen into the lounge. "I swear, when Wimbledon is on, you go tone-deaf."

Jordan didn't take her gaze from the screen. "Wimbledon is my one sporting love. Plus, the lesbian's winning. I have an excuse." She flicked her gaze up at Abby. "What were you asking?"

"If you wanted square sausage with brunch? Too much or not?"

Jordan got up, and walked over to drop a kiss on Abby's lips. "Of course I want square sausage. I always want square sausage. If I don't, you'll divorce me. Isn't that how it works?"

"I can't divorce you if we're not married yet." A smile graced Abby's lips.

Jordan waved a hand at her. "Details. Ones we're going to talk about over brunch with all our parents, right?" Jordan's insides rolled. "I still can't quite believe we're introducing everyone. Especially when the tennis is on. What sort of planning is that?"

"Yours, I believe." Abby gave her a look. "Will your parents eat square sausage?"

"They'll eat anything you put in front of them. Including each other. So let's keep the conversation going before that happens, okay?"

Abby shook her head. "You make them sound terrible. They're both lovely people."

"Individually, yes. Together, not so much." Jordan pursed her lips. "But they have to meet sometime, so it might as well be today." She pulled Abby close to her. "It's all worth it, though, if I get to marry you at the end of it all."

Abby smiled. The smile she kept just for Jordan. "Whoever thought Mrs One Night Stand would be saying that?"

Jordan pressed a finger to her chest. "Not me." She cocked her head. "You definitely want to marry me?"

Abby slapped her arse. "Stop asking stupid questions."

"You sure this is the wedding of your dreams?"

"I never had a wedding of my dreams. I had a wedding I thought I had to have. But I didn't go through with it." She paused. "Talking of which, I meant to tell you. I saw Arielle last week in London when I was at a meeting about my new job."

Jordan stilled. "Marcus's cousin?"

Abby nodded.

"How was that?" Awkward would be the first word that sprang to mind.

Abby dropped her head. "Okay, surprisingly. Almost normal. We had coffee. She told me my hen weekend was one of the best she'd been on. I wasn't expecting that."

Jordan exhaled a breath. "Did she bring up Marcus?"

Abby nodded. "She did. He's got a new girlfriend. A new

fiancée, in fact." She rubbed her palms up and down her thighs. "So, Marcus has moved on. I'm pleased for him."

Jordan hugged her tight. Abby had agonised over the pain they'd caused him. It was good to know Marcus was going to get the happy ending he deserved, too.

"I'm thrilled for him as well," Jordan replied. "Wedding fever is clearly in the air. But our wedding: St Albans town hall, pizza, beer, a live band. It's not too low-rent for you?"

Abby laughed. "You remember I come from Glasgow, right? We might live in the mean streets of Hove now, but I can take on all-comers." She paused. "Plus, did you see Mum's face when we told her? I think it reminds her of her wedding. Far more casual and DIY. So that's another thing in your favour. Along with the fact that you love her daughter."

"I can't deny it." Jordan stared at Abby. Still gorgeous. Still hers. Some mornings, she woke up and couldn't believe her luck. And now they were going to make it official. Get married, and then try for a baby. A baby Abby sounded adorable.

"What about this week? Ready to start your new job?"

After the wedding that never was, Abby had stayed on at her old job for nearly a year, before handing in her notice. Neil had almost cried. She was renting out her London flat and the pair were renting in Hove, while they looked for something to buy together. However, it might be a while before they had the funds, because Abby had taken a pay cut in her new charity job, and Jordan was still running her own company, although now focusing more on wedding planning and still working ad-hoc as a bridal PA. She'd kicked the professional bridesmaid part of her business into touch. Too much time away from Abby wasn't time well spent, in Jordan's opinion.

"Can't wait," Abby replied. "I'm finally going to be fulfilling my childhood dreams, and it's all because of you, my fake childhood friend."

"You're welcome," Jordan replied. "Of all my fake friendships, I loved ours the most."

"What about the current, real-life version?"

Jordan kissed her lips. "It's right out of my dreams."

THE END

*Want more from me? Sign up to join my VIP Readers' Group and get a FREE lesbian romance,* **It Had To Be You!** *Claim your free book here: www.clarelydon.co.uk/it-had-to-be-you*